DEFENSIVE
TACTICS

DEFENSIVE TACTICS

STEVE WESTOVER

Bonneville Books
Springville, Utah

The views expressed within this work are the sole responsibility of the author and do not necessarily reflect the position of Cedar Fort, Inc., or any other entity.

This is a work of fiction. The characters, names, incidents, places, and dialogue are products of the author's imagination, and are not to be construed as real.

ISBN 13: 978-1-59955-445-7

Published by Bonneville Books, an imprint of Cedar Fort, Inc., 2373 W. 700 S., Springville, UT 84663
Distributed by Cedar Fort, Inc., www.cedarfort.com

LIBRARY OF CONGRESS CATALOGING-IN-PUBLICATION DATA
Westover, Steve, 1974-
 Defensive tactics / Steve Westover.
   p. cm.
 Summary: Three friends are tested emotionally, physically, and spiritually
when they are caught in the middle of an investigation involving public
corruption and organized crime.
 ISBN 978-1-59955-445-7
 1. United States. Federal Bureau of Investigation--Officials and
employees--Fiction. 2. Kansas City (Mo.)--Fiction. 3. Mormons--Fiction.
I. Title.

 PS3623.E876E83 2010
 813'.6--dc22

 2010019540

Cover design by Angela D. Olsen
Cover design © 2010 by Lyle Mortimer
Edited and typeset by Melissa J. Caldwell

Printed in Canada

10 9 8 7 6 5 4 3 2 1

Printed on acid-free paper

To my wife, Mica.
You are my inspiration, motivation, and support.
Thank you for your encouragement.

PROLOGUE

November—Five Years Ago

JIMMY WAS SLUMBERING TRANQUILLY WHEN the ringing phone rattled him into consciousness. Pulling it to his ear, he glanced at the time—it was nearly 8:00 a.m. On the other end, a man spoke frantically, hyperventilating as he sobbed. Unable to calm the man, Jimmy sat and listened, waiting for a clue about the hysterical caller and his purpose. Fear struck as the voice finally registered in Jimmy's awakening mind. Jimmy had never heard his father speak this way. The voice was different. It was older, wounded. Anguish clung to every word.

"Dad, stop! I can't understand you. You have to calm down. What's wrong?" Jimmy shouted into the telephone.

The sobs began to subside, but the pained words did not. Jimmy listened carefully, struggling to interpret, but the weeping phrases seemed to float through the air, unwilling to land in his ears.

"They're gone! They're gone!" his father said. "My beautiful girls are gone."

Jimmy understood in an instant. His face went pale and his expression blank. Closing his eyes, he breathed heavily, attempting to subdue the emotions welling inside. His father was still speaking, but the only sound he heard was the replay in his mind, "They're gone."

The phone fell from his hand and knocked hard onto the floor. There was nothing left but intruding memories, thoughts of guilt, and the tenderness of emotion as Jimmy let loose a muffled howl into his pillow.

* * * * *

At 5:00 a.m. two sisters approached the door to their brother's apartment. Meg, with hands deep in her coat pocket, stood behind the oldest, Shelly, in the doorway. Snowflakes caught in Meg's straight brown hair and on the bright red stocking cap and matching sweater that Shelly wore. With tilted head down and eyes pinched, Shelly looked hopefully at her little brother. The porch light spread its glow onto the women and the teal station wagon that waited only yards away in the parking lot. The car's exhaust steamed through the air as snowflakes the size of quarters collected rapidly on the windshield between intermittent wipes.

Occasionally organizing mini-reunions with outings and activities, Shelly nurtured relationships with each family member. Being the oldest of the three children, she was the instigator, the family glue. Even at this early hour, excitement shone in her eyes as she imagined the happiness she would bring when the three siblings pulled into the driveway of her parents' new home. Her husband had reluctantly agreed to stay home with the children while she took her brother and sister on the three-hour drive to St. Louis. Shelly smiled. Today, on her father's fiftieth birthday, it would be just the three of them and Mom and Dad.

Jimmy was surprised to see his sisters at the door and invited them inside, eager to trap the escaping heat. Awakened by the strident knocking at his front door, he was still barefoot in his flannel pajama pants and a T-shirt. He smiled and rubbed his tired, watering eyes.

Meg followed Shelly into the dimly lit apartment and eased onto the sofa with some difficulty, backing gently into the seat. Her appearance was comical, but Jimmy did his best not to poke fun. They were buddies, but he questioned the wisdom in ever laughing at a pregnant woman. Meg's pink coat no longer fit over her pregnant stomach, exposing her shirt that had its own difficulty providing cover. At only seven months along, the protruding belly on her tiny frame already appeared ready to pop.

Jimmy couldn't resist. Winking subtly at Shelly, he cast wisdom aside. "So, Meg, it's good to see you. *All* of you," he said, eyes wide with exaggerated amazement. "You having triplets or something?"

Meg simply gave her usual sweet smile and then gestured rudely.

Jimmy laughed loudly, but Shelly looked on disapprovingly. Meg's innocent face belied her devilish attitude. Being the baby and the family's wild child, she somewhat relished her ability to shock and displease, particularly when it came to Shelly.

As her older brother and protector, Jimmy was much more subtle than Shelly in his attempts to direct Meg back onto a respectable path, but both Jimmy's subtlety and Shelly's sometimes self-righteous approach seemed to be failing in concert. Meg had continued living raucously during her first semester at college. Her pregnancy was cramping her style a bit, but she was still able to make plenty of mischief.

"Jimmy, why aren't you ready? We need to get moving if we want to catch Mom and Dad before breakfast. Run upstairs and get dressed," Shelly said.

Though Shelly was overbearing at times, Jimmy appreciated the sincerity of her efforts. "Sis, I told you I can't go today. I've got big plans with Ally this afternoon. I can't cancel."

"Come on. You can see Ally when we get back Sunday night. This is going to be fun—I promise. Besides, I was kind of hoping you'd drive a little."

"Yeah, come on, Jimmy. Road trip!" Meg said in agreement.

Jimmy glanced at Meg, then at Shelly, and then out the window. "Am I the only one watching the weather out there?"

"Oh, is wittle Jimmy afwaid of the white, fwuffy snow?" Meg asked in her best baby voice.

Jimmy grinned at his sister's feeble attempt at mockery. "Normally I'd love to come. You know that. But my plans today are . . . well, it's different today. Here, wait just a second."

Speeding to his room, Jimmy returned moments later, holding a burgundy felt box. He positioned the front of the box near his sisters, and then opened it slowly. Inside was a simple but shining one-third carat diamond engagement ring.

"Now, the wedding ring fits around this one, so it'll end up looking bigger, but what do you think?" he asked, great pride showing on his face. "I've arranged everything, and I'm proposing today. By this time tomorrow morning, I'll be engaged."

Shelly's mouth dropped as she let out a high-pitched squeal, and hardly able to control her excitement, she embraced Jimmy, nearly knocking the ring from his hand. Shelly rattled off a sentence or two, speaking quickly. Jimmy couldn't understand a word she said, but her enthusiasm was obvious. He looked to Meg, who was awkwardly attempting to stand. He moved toward Meg, extended both hands, and helped her rise from the sunken seat.

Meg whispered softly into Jimmy's ear with a sarcastic monotone, "Please don't make me ride three hours alone with her."

Jimmy laughed.

Still beaming, Shelly gave a satisfied look of approval. "The ring is beautiful. I'll want to hear all about it—every detail, okay? Good luck, Jimmy! Now we've really got to get going. Come on, Meg."

"I love you, guys. Sorry I can't go, but I'm glad you understand. Tell Mom and Dad hi for me. And Meg, be good. You two have fun, but please be careful out there." Jimmy gave his sisters each another hug, kissed them both on the cheek, and then led them to the door.

Opening to the wintry morning, it appeared the snow was slowing down; at least, the flakes were getting smaller. Still in bare feet, Jimmy extended his arm to Meg, and she grabbed hold. Together, they walked through the numbing snow to the car. Jimmy opened the passenger side door, eased Meg comfortably inside, and then slammed the door shut, clearing the view as most of the snow fell away from the glass. Shelly climbed in the driver's seat, and the car backed away. Shivering, Jimmy stood and waved. He smiled as he saw Meg gently blow a kiss before disappearing into the darkness.

* * * * *

Miles away, somewhere on I-70 between Kansas City and St. Louis, the eastbound lanes of the interstate were being prepared to reopen. The flashing red and blue from the first emergency responders reflected off the snow and, as they left, could be seen for miles, since the highway lowered toward the east. Only a few clouds remained in the blue sky. The snow stopped momentarily, leaving a white blanket surrounding the pathetic vehicle, which lay silent and still, flattened on the side of the road.

There were no signs of life when the snow once again began to fall from the nearly cloudless sky.

ONE

October—Present Day

Jimmy pushed through the front door of the Downtown Sand-wich Shoppe with a sense of freedom he had not felt for . . . well, at least two weeks. No longer would he be burdened with the hassle of waking up before noon or taking orders from a supervisor who had barely graduated from high school.

Standing on the vacant sidewalk with a grin on his face, Jimmy stretched his arms, arched his back, and tilted his head. A single drop of rain hit his face just below the eye. The sky turned instantly black, and the deluge, although only moments long, soaked him from his unbrushed hair down to his flip-flops.

"Outstanding!" Jimmy muttered, the grin at once replaced with a scowl. But his grin quickly returned. "I knew there was a reason I didn't bother showering this morning," he exclaimed loudly enough for everyone to hear—had anyone been present.

Jimmy seldom showered, brushed his hair, shaved, or even looked in a mirror. To look at him, it would be difficult to distinguish him from a vagrant on the street. Jimmy didn't worry about trivial matters such as clean clothes or deodorant. He was grungy to the core, except for his perfectly maintained teeth, which were essential in supporting his winning smile.

Jimmy's appearance had changed dramatically over the past few years. At first, it was because he just stopped caring, but over time, his unkempt appearance became part of a character he played. The flip-flops, the pastel-checkered Bermuda shorts, the Velcro watch, and a T-shirt with bull dogs playing cards were all integral parts of his costume.

Two weeks earlier, when he had interviewed and accepted his job at the Downtown Sandwich Shoppe, Jimmy had cleaned up nicely. He was clean shaven, had worn cologne, and had even worn long pants and dress shoes. Jimmy charmed the interviewer and was hired on the spot.

As he semi-skipped down the street, occasionally drumming in the air, he recalled the recent events of his hiring and even more recent firing. According to his usual plan, he was hired, worked a couple of weeks, garnered a modest paycheck (enough for a little fun), and was once again free from the watchful eye of anyone who could hassle him.

"Life is good when you have no expectations," Jimmy said to no one in particular. He was mostly sincere but was also trying to convince himself. *If you don't expect much, you'll never be disappointed . . .* He stopped mid-step before finishing his thought.

Something suddenly occurred to him. He needed to find a place to stay the night. The only downside of losing his job at the Downtown Sandwich Shoppe was that he also lost his temporary room and board. He had conned his supervisor into letting him stay in a spare bedroom while he "looked for another place." Of course, Jimmy never looked for "another place," but now he needed something quick. Although he looked homeless, he had never spent a night on the street, and he was not about to start now.

"What's my plan? What's my plan?" he asked rapidly, challenging himself for an answer. Jimmy had long since exhausted his family and friends, and even most acquaintances, as useful stooges in giving him free food and lodging. But then came a flash of genius. "Paul!"

* * * * *

Paul leaned casually against the wall outside the office suites on the second floor of the FBI's Kansas City Field Office. It was nearly lunchtime, and the corridor bustled with the usual midday activity. Coworkers passed, but few noticed him.

The frosted glass door swung open, and Paul adjusted his tie, straightened his suit jacket, and improved his posture, standing tall and ready. Emerging from the offices was a small group of coworkers, including Emily Mathews.

Everyone around Emily faded into the background as Paul focused on her confident stride. Emily looked toward Paul and made eye contact. Her exuberant smile caused a nervous thrill to bubble in his stomach.

Paul was unable to keep a silly grin from crossing his face when he met Emily's gaze. Her shoulder-length blonde hair, clear skin, and simple pearl necklace and earrings all accented her usual professional attire. Even her shapely figure was magnified by the gentle sweetness she carried with her. She was a pure, angelic vision.

Emily was a bright contrast from the other female agents who desired to be equal with men in their dress and demeanor. To Emily, this attitude lacked ambition. She was confident and feminine and made no apologies for it, despite the jealous mumblings she overheard from female coworkers.

"Hey, Emmy, you're going to come with us today, aren't you?" Rick called from midway down the hall. "Come on, you can do it. We'll be nice. I promise."

"No, thank you," was all she said before politely turning away.

Emily touched Paul's elbow, and he mentally returned from daydream to reality. It was hard to believe he was having another lunch date with Emily. They had met a month earlier at church and were surprised to find they worked in the same building. It was stunning how much they had in common. An instant friendship was started—a friendship Paul hoped would develop into much more.

"I hope you're hungry. Where do you want to go?" Paul asked.

"I was thinking we could grab something from the hot dog guy down the street and sit at the corner park," Emily said as they started down the corridor.

"All right! Let's do it," Paul said. He pressed the down button at the bank of elevators.

They descended the exterior steps with the sun shining high overhead. The black skies and brief rain that had darkened the street just an hour before had given way to pale blue.

"It feels great to get out of the building. It seems so gloomy in there sometimes," Emily commented. Although it was late October and the leaves on the tree-lined street were prematurely fallen, it felt more like late summer. "Today is absolutely gorgeous!"

Sneaking a quick peek at Emily's smiling lips, Paul agreed. "Absolutely gorgeous is right."

"Hi-dee-ho!" Paul heard someone shout but was unable to see who was calling.

The street was full of people on lunch break, but once again he heard the same loud voice. "Hey there, hold on!"

From fifteen yards away, Paul caught view of the shouting man, and it appeared the man was calling to him. Paul positioned himself between the approaching man and Emily and watched the transient come closer.

"Emily, would you mind excusing me for a moment? I want to see what this guy wants."

"Sure, no problem," she replied and headed toward the street vendor, steeling a quick glance back.

"Thanks, I'll be right over."

* * * * *

"Paul, buddy, how are you doing? Who's the lovely lady?" the man asked.

"Do I know you? Can I help you with something?"

"Paul, come on. It's me, Jimmy."

"Jimmy? From . . . ?" Paul asked. His eyes narrowed and eyebrows rose.

"Jimmy from high school . . . church . . . man, we grew up together. But don't worry, I forgive you. I know I look a little different than the last time you saw me, and it's been a while," Jimmy said, shining his perfect smile.

"James Younger? I'm sorry, Jimmy. I just didn't recognize you . . . not even a little bit," Paul said with an uneasy chuckle.

"No worries, I get that a lot. You know, it's funny. You asked if you could help me and, well, the truth is, yeah, I could use a little help," Jimmy admitted.

"Oh, really?" Paul asked suspiciously. He glanced impatiently to where Emily was waiting. This was not going to be as quick as he had hoped.

"Yeah, nothing big. It's just that, well, times are a little tough right now. I lost my job today and my room for the night. I was hoping I could stay with you, just for a day or two while I look for a new place. Come on, Paul, please. You know it's the right thing to do. The Paul I know could never say no to a friend in need," Jimmy said, his eyes pleading.

Jimmy didn't look like much, but he was still a smooth talker, slathering every word with charm and a pinch of guilt. That's the guy Paul remembered. Eyeing his old friend closely, Paul attempted to determine the level of risk associated with accepting Jimmy into his home. Generally, Paul tried to follow his conscience, usually as a guilt avoidance tactic. But this? Not only was it a hassle, but Paul also didn't want a drifter living in his house. Besides, was Jimmy even the same guy he knew from his youth? He didn't look like it.

"Are you telling me that you had a job today looking like that?" Paul asked with a faint smirk on his face. "Seriously?"

"That's pretty good." Jimmy chuckled. "Yeah, I had a job today. I just had a personality conflict with my supervisor. Nothing big. Come on, Paul, what do you say? A little help, please?"

Paul turned back toward a sidewalk bench where Emily was waiting. He waved in apology for taking so long.

"Jimmy, I've got to be honest. I don't know if I can help you. You don't really look like someone I can trust in my house. When's the last time you showered?"

"As a matter of fact, just an hour ago," Jimmy retorted, thinking of the recent rainstorm.

"Look, I want to do the right thing, but I'm going to need to think about this."

"I got you—the whole pros and cons list, right? I completely understand. You get back to lunch, and think about it this afternoon," Jimmy said. "Honestly, I get it. I know I don't look like much, but you can trust me. I'm the same guy you've always known, just not as nicely dressed. Give me a chance, and I'll prove it to you."

Not saying a word for what felt like minutes, Paul's usually easy eyes burned into Jimmy, evaluating his possible decisions.

"All right, here's what we'll do. I'm done with work at six. I'll meet you right here, and I'll let you know what I can do for you—if anything."

"Paul, you *are* the man! Just think about it, that's all I ask. I'll see you at six o'clock sharp," Jimmy said with exaggerated clarity.

Paul shook his head and started toward Emily. What was he getting himself into? He suddenly felt a great weight upon him—literally. Jimmy had jumped on his back and was hurriedly mussing his hair. "I'll see you at six o'clock sharp," Jimmy repeated.

Climbing off Paul's back, Jimmy gave a distinct salute and walked back in the direction from which he came. Paul straightened his suit, which now had a kind of funky dampness to it. The silly grin Paul had been sporting since seeing Emily at the beginning of lunch was long gone. It was replaced with a somber, contemplative look punctuated by his furrowed eyebrows.

Returning to Emily, Paul said nothing. He didn't make eye contact so he didn't notice Emily struggling to maintain her composure. Her head nodded gently as if to say, *Well, what was that about?*

"I thought I'd make myself useful so I ordered our food. I finished mine so I started eating yours too. You don't mind, do you?" Emily teased, earning a wry smile from Paul. Emily handed Paul his food and set her lunch on the bench. She then reached up to fix the back of his hair. "The homeless man on your back sure did a number on your hair, big guy," Emily said. "You know, if you didn't want to eat with me today, you could have just said so. But paying a homeless man to interrupt lunch? It's unique."

Paul looked at Emily and smiled, unsure how to explain the strange occurrence. "You know, this is shaping up to be an interesting day."

TWO

ALTHOUGH HE HAD NO SUPERVISORY role or any official command authority, Rick Stark fancied himself a power broker at the Kansas City Field Office. Now in his mid-forties, stout, and with an unusually full head of graying red hair, Rick was adept at parlaying success from years ago into current capital in office politics, largely due to his close personal friendship with the Assistant Special Agent in Charge. Rick wielded this power like a club, but with a smile on his face and a pat on the back of the ASAC.

Sitting at her second floor cubical near the back of the office suites, Emily trained her eyes on her monitor, trying to ignore the bustle of colleagues leaving for the day. The office was technically open twenty-four hours a day, seven days a week, but the Field Office unofficially closed each day at 5:00 p.m. During her brief tenure, Emily had quickly learned it was taboo for anyone to leave the office before 5:30, but once 5:30 hit, the office cleared out promptly. Recently transferred from a satellite office in Jefferson City, Emily never left before 5:45 p.m., slightly later than others to show she was a hard worker, but not long enough to be considered a kiss-up.

"Emmy, you missed a great lunch today. A couple of us are going out after work to get a drink. What do you say?" Rick asked in his usual schmaltzy tone, helping himself to a seat on the corner of her desk.

Emily looked up from her work and smiled politely. "No, thank you. I have plans," she said, returning her attention to the computer screen.

Scooting closer, Rick placed a hand on Emily's shoulder and rubbed gently. "Come on. What's the problem? Have a couple of drinks. I promise you'll have a good time."

Emily shrugged off the touch, her shoulders instantly becoming rigid. "Rick, like I told you yesterday, and the day before, and the day before that, I'm not a drinker, and I'm not interested in going with you. If you don't mind, I'm trying to finish some work before I leave."

Rick bristled at Emily's cold honesty. Breathing loudly, he cursed under his breath as he leaned closer toward Emily. "What's your problem? Am I not handsome enough for you? Is my car not fancy enough? Am *I* not good enough?" He moved to the front of her desk while maintaining his usual smile.

Emily glanced around the room, suddenly feeling watchful eyes upon her. Her stomach churned. "Rick, all I'm saying is that I'm not interested. Please, let me finish my work."

"You can at least show me the courtesy and respect I've earned around here."

Her pulse quickened, but she remained calm. Standing, she pushed back her chair, glanced around the room, and leaned toward Rick. She spoke quietly, determined to keep the conversation private. "Listen, you are wasting your time," Emily enunciated with a whisper. "Do you get that? And my name is Emily, not Emmy."

"You really are something," Rick said, leering crudely.

"Rick, you have zero chance here, and your odds are getting worse. Please, move on." Emily sat down, returned her attention to the computer, and tried to ignore him.

Rick was undaunted. Moving around her desk, he stepped behind her and leaned in close. His breath sent chills down her neck.

Emily stopped typing, turned, and met his gaze. "Oh, and to answer your questions, *Rick*," she said with heavy emphasis on the consonants in his name, "I don't know that much about you. I don't know what kind of car you drive, and I don't care. What I do know about you so far is not impressive, and if alcohol is required to make you charming or even bearable, I have just one more reason to politely decline your invitation." Emily smiled and said, adding a slight southern drawl, "Do you have any more questions? If not, good night."

Rick's face turned crimson. He slowly arose and looked methodically around the room, but all eyes were on their monitors. He looked at his watch and announced to his coworkers, "Five-thirty! Quitting time!" Then he returned his attention to Emily. "And, Emmy, you have a nice evening too," he said with an exaggerated friendliness, mimicking her southern drawl. He leaned in closely enough for Emily to smell the Big Red on his breath and then walked away.

Emily tilted her head back, and her cheeks puffed out as she exhaled deeply. *Finally, he's gone.* Spinning from the back credenza toward her monitor, Emily caught the curious stare of a coworker.

"Have a nice evening," Emily offered civilly, again returning to her work.

* * * * *

Jimmy looked at his watch, waiting anxiously for Paul to appear at the building's front steps. As the sun fell lower in the southwestern sky, shadows unfurled over the bench where he waited, and then, just as expected, Paul emerged from the building.

Jimmy looked at his watch again and gave a whistle. "Five-fifty-nine. My friend, you are good. Right on time!"

"Hey, Jimmy. You have a good afternoon?" Paul asked.

"Oh, you bet. Fantastic!" Jimmy said.

"Good. I was thinking we could get something to eat and talk a little. Have you had anything to eat?"

"As a matter of fact, I've been snacking most of the afternoon," Jimmy responded, pulling out a bulging, bloodred plastic sandwich bag from his pocket.

"What is that?"

"Meatballs. You want one?" Jimmy pulled a sloppy meatball from the bag and held it between his fingers.

"Thank you, but *no.*" Paul shook his head, a disgusted look on his face.

"Yeah, I keep meatballs in my pocket. What can I say? It's kind of funny, but I was filling the bag at work today when my boss walked in," Jimmy said, as if anticipating Paul's next question. "He acted pretty mad, but I think he was just jealous." Jimmy shoved the meatball in his mouth.

"Jealous? About meatballs? Maybe he was upset you were stealing food," Paul stated.

"No, I don't think so. Last week I caught him sneaking meatballs into his pocket, but he didn't use a plastic sandwich bag. He was using tin foil, and it got everywhere," Jimmy said, gesturing wildly with his hands. "It was pretty gross. Anyway, when he saw I was using a plastic bag, he blew his top. That's when I got fired."

"So you're saying you got fired because of a personality conflict revolving around the proper storage of meatballs in your pocket?" Paul asked incredulously.

"Look, Paul, not to be nitpicky, but do you really have to repeat everything I say as if it is the dumbest thing you've ever heard?"

"You're right. How rude of me." Paul gave an uncomfortable chuckle. Already, he was exasperated. He put both hands behind his head and turned away from Jimmy and toward the sun, which was setting quickly behind the office buildings.

When Paul turned away, Jimmy grinned, pleased with his manipulation skills. As Paul turned back, Jimmy replaced his grin with wide eyes and a look of desperation.

Paul began to walk slowly "Let's get something to eat anyway. We have a lot to talk about."

Crossing the street and entering the parking garage, Paul clicked the chirp button on his car's keyless entry. The brief horn burst echoed throughout the garage, the doors unlocked, and the headlights flashed as the engine started.

The running boards descended from the undercarriage when the doors opened, and the two climbed into the black late model SUV.

"Paul, this is nice," Jimmy said, investigating the additional features and pushing every visible button. "This is *really* nice! In fact, if you don't have room at your place, I'll sleep in this thing."

"Thanks, but I've got plenty of room. Besides, I don't really want your drool on the leather," Paul quipped to Jimmy's amusement. "Jimmy, here's the thing. We were never close growing up. We just didn't run in the same circles. I always liked you fine, but I'm curious, why did you come to me? And how did you know I was here?"

"Last Christmas I was home visiting my mom. You couldn't believe how much she bragged about you. Your mom must have said something to her at church—you know, that you were working downtown for the FBI. I swear, my mom wouldn't stop talking about how great you were doing, how responsible you are—you know, the stuff parents get excited about. When I was walking on the street this morning after getting fired, I really had no idea what I was going to do tonight and then I thought of you. I knew the FBI building was only blocks away, so I thought I'd give it a shot. And the timing was unbelievable. I mean, seriously, I saw you coming down the steps just as I walked up to the building. I couldn't believe it worked out so easily. Someone upstairs is looking out for me," Jimmy said with a smile.

Paul pulled the SUV into a parking spot at the front of one of the ubiquitous downtown fast food joints. "Does this work for you?" Paul asked with a smirk. "They don't have meatballs, but you know, it's still pretty good."

"This is great, Paul. Meatballs are getting a little old anyway."

Inside, Paul sat with his back to the wall, allowing the entire restaurant to be in view. "Jimmy, I have my concerns about this, but I've decided I'm willing to take a chance. I wouldn't be able to sleep wondering what you were doing tonight. I did the pros and cons list like you suggested, and frankly, the cons list was much longer." Paul paused. "But the pros were more meaningful. I've decided you can stay for a few days while you get back on your feet."

"Thank you, brother! I was getting a little worried. I thought you were going to buy me a burger and call it good."

"You're welcome, but I have some requirements," Paul said in a dry monotone.

"Okay, I wasn't exactly expecting a list of stipulations, but hey, that's fine," Jimmy said. Already his mind was searching for options and hoping for loopholes.

"I know you're not a child, and it's not my intention to treat you like one, but there are certain things I expect from someone staying in my home. Some of the things you may think are fair and some you won't. You're going to have to make a decision, basically, whether you want to accept my conditions or not."

"Lay it on me, friend," Jimmy said nervously.

From his right breast pocket, Paul pulled an envelope with two tri-folded pieces of paper inside. Unfolding the papers and holding them up, Paul said, "This is the contract. We'll read it together. You can ask me any questions you have, because I don't want there to be any misunderstandings. Then, if you choose to accept it, you will sign both copies, one for you to keep, and one for me."

Jimmy gazed out the window. The night had come on fast. Heavy cloud cover had moved in at dusk, threatening rain and blocking any light from what would have been a nearly full moon.

Jimmy turned from the window, reengaging Paul, and looked him square in the eyes, "Come on, Paul. This is a little much, don't you think? At lunch I said you should think about it, not write up a contract. Do I need to get this notarized? Or maybe I could find a couple of people in the next booth to act as witness," Jimmy said.

"Should I start reading, or have you already made up your mind?" Paul asked.

"Go ahead. I'm going to jot down a couple of my own expectations while we're at it."

"That's fine, but if your expectations include anything other than having a clean, warm place to sleep, and some food to eat, all while abiding by my house rules, you might as well forget it. I'm serious, Jimmy. I'm not messing around. You make me nervous, but I'm willing to trust you—within limits. Now, let's talk about my expectations, and then you can tell me if I can trust you to meet them.

"*Rule #1*—You will get a haircut—tonight.

"*Rule #2*—You will shower, shave, and wear deodorant and clean clothes daily.

"*Rule #3*—You will trash your current wardrobe.

"*Rule #4*—You will be up and out of the house by 10 a.m. daily to look for work and a new place to stay, and spend at least six hours out of the house daily.

"*Rule #5*—You will keep your living space clean.

"*Rule #6*—You will respect my property. You will not use or borrow anything in my home without express permission.

"*Rule #7*—You will . . ."

Was Paul still talking? These weren't just "some requirements," Jimmy thought. *This is a complete infringement on my lifestyle. My mom didn't even hassle me like this.* Finally Paul stopped reading as he noted Jimmy's glazed look.

"Well, Jimmy, do you accept?

Jimmy did not respond.

"Jimmy?" Paul asked more forcefully.

Taking another quick look outside into the blackness, a slight scowl formed on Jimmy's lips, but he quickly reacquired the proper perspective. This was temporary. He would make sure of it.

A grin returned to Jimmy's face. "My friend, thank you. I will gladly accept. Where do I sign?"

The next two hours were spent at the barber shop, the drug store for some personal hygiene items, and a discount store to pick up a couple of inexpensive outfits and a pair of shoes. Sometime after nine o'clock, the men lumbered into Paul's apartment. Jimmy hopped into the shower while Paul made up the bed in the spare bedroom.

Emerging from his room after the shower, Jimmy was already looking better. He was clean, and his hair was respectable. Paul offered him two plastic shopping bags from under the kitchen sink to double wrap his old clothes before tossing them in the trash. All that remained of the man Paul met on the street earlier that day was the Velcro watch and an unshaven face.

"You'll take care of that in the morning?" Paul asked, pointing at Jimmy before gently rubbing his own face.

"Yes, boss."

"Thank you. You know where your room is. Now I'm going to bed," Paul said wearily, punching the keypad buttons next to the door and setting the security system.

"Hey, don't I need that code too?" Jimmy asked.

"Not tonight you don't. We'll talk in the morning. Good night."

Paul entered his bedroom and closed the door, leaving Jimmy standing near the kitchen counter. Choosing an apple from a bowl on the table, Jimmy slowly surveyed the room, taking in the red brick walls, the high ceiling, and the oversized fan hanging in the middle of the room above the coffee table. The leather sofa and chair faced an expansive entertainment center in the corner, which seemed small in the cavernous room. Jimmy walked to the window, peeked through the blinds, and admired the view. Despite only being on the third floor, the window provided an impressive panorama of the city and its bright autumn lights.

Jimmy continued to take in the room and then fell back into the dark leather chair. He leaned forward and replaced the apple with a remote control he picked up from the coffee table. He melted into the chair and put his feet onto the table.

"Nice." Jimmy arched his back and stretched his arms. Reaching into his front pants pocket, he pulled out his multi-folded copy of the contract. He shook it open, looked at it briefly, and tossed it onto the coffee table. Placing one hand behind his head, he flipped channels on the remote with the other and reflected on the night's events. He glanced at the contract crumpled on the table and scoffed quietly.

"I have food to eat, a nice place to stay, and a big TV to watch. And Paul is calling all the shots. Perfect."

Jimmy changed channels, his eyes blinking slowly. "Are you kidding me? All these channels and nothing good to watch. Come on." He grimaced. "I'll have to talk to Paul about upgrading his package." Finally, Jimmy settled on a rerun of *Murder, She Wrote*, faded into the cloudy softness of the chair, and quickly fell asleep.

THREE

THE OBNOXIOUS CLANKING OF A bell-hammered alarm clock was the most insufferable sound Paul could imagine—that's why he used it. Setting on the dresser across his bedroom, the clock required him to get out of bed to turn it off. Some mornings he appreciated it more than others.

Paul rolled out of bed and his knees hit hard on the cool oak flooring. He quickly scooted on his knees across the room and reached atop the dresser to turn off the device. Allowing himself to bask in the newly found silence, he offered a quick morning prayer, asking for increased compassion and patience in dealing with Jimmy. He wanted to do the right thing, and he wanted a clear conscience, but it wasn't an act of kindness. Not really. Paul was helping so he could say he did.

After sluggishly rolling over and completing his morning exercise routine of push-ups and sit-ups, Paul grabbed his clothes and proceeded to the one bathroom in the apartment for a shower and shave. The tidy apartment was located in what had been an old hotel, beautifully rebuilt and transformed as part of a downtown revitalization plan a few years earlier.

Hearing a rustle from the living room, Paul walked over to see Jimmy laying in an uncomfortable position on the leather chair with his feet extended onto the coffee table in front of the muted TV. Paul carefully removed the remote from Jimmy's hand and clicked a couple of buttons before turning off the TV. Feeling a chill and seeing that Jimmy had no cover, Paul placed a blanket over him and continued to the bathroom. "So much for not getting any drool on the leather," Paul said, a grin on his face.

* * * * *

Even though it was still dark, the day was full of possibilities. Emily awoke eagerly with a smile on her face. Following her regular routine, she got ready and grabbed a plain bagel with strawberry cream cheese as she rushed from her apartment. To the skeptical and sleepy, her cheerful attitude sometimes seemed contrived and even intolerable. While others drank multiple cups of coffee just to feel functional, Emily was moving at full speed by the time she hit the office at 7:30. Her supervisor in Jefferson City had once asked her to "tone down the morning energy to an acceptable level." At the time she had laughed, considering the request as a form of compliment. When she later realized he was serious, she apologized and did her best not to seem too cheery around him.

Arriving at her cubical, Emily unzipped her portfolio and removed a file from her credenza, spreading three stacks of paper neatly across her desk. She had spent the last two weeks verifying every conceivable detail on a boneheaded case hardly worthy of the FBI's attention. As the new girl, the unwanted assignment had fallen on her shoulders, but today it would be over. By completing this perfunctory task, Emily hoped to prove that she was not only a competent investigator but also a team player.

The phone on Emily's desk chirped with its usual three-pulse ring, indicating the call was internal. She cheerfully answered, "Good morning, this is Agent Mathews. May I help you?"

Paul smiled widely when he heard her cheerful voice. "Good morning to you," he returned with enthusiasm. "Hey, our lunch didn't really turn out very well yesterday. Are you available today? It's going to be a beautiful day to get outside for a while."

"How did you know I was here already?" she asked playfully. "Wait, I have a better question, Paul. What time do you come in?"

"Oh, I've been here for a little while, and I just figured you seem like a morning person, so I thought there was a decent chance you'd be in early too," Paul admitted.

"Well, you figured right. I actually wouldn't mind coming in earlier, but I think my colleagues would frown on it. They'd think I'm trying to make them look bad."

"Yeah, I had someone get upset with me once for coming in early, but I figure they can get over it. So how about it? Lunch?" Paul asked again.

"Regular time?" she asked.

"Sounds great. I'll see you then."

Emily admired the way Paul blew off comments or criticisms from others around him. He didn't seem to worry about what others said or thought. Paul simply did what he thought was best and let the natural consequences take hold. Emily also felt confident and steady, but not like Paul.

* * * * *

"Whoo-eee!" Jimmy squealed, stretching. "I'm never sleeping on that chair again," he mumbled. He sat up and tilted his neck from side to side, releasing audible cracks each time he adjusted.

He grunted to himself with satisfaction, recognizing the kindness with which the blanket had been placed over him. Standing, he pulled the blanket off his warm body and set it back on the not-so-comfortable chair.

"What's on my agenda today? Not much," Jimmy said. He walked to the refrigerator like a cripple, the feel of pins sticking into the bottom of his foot. Though uncomfortable, it was a feeling he somewhat enjoyed. Looking for his morning snack, he rummaged through the refrigerator and then the cupboards, settling on a bowl of generic Frosted Flakes. On the counter he found a note and a key.

> *You will need this key and code to get out of the house for your job hunt. Good luck!*
>
> *PS—Your code is specific to you. Please be careful not to lose the key or code. Remember, I'm FBI. Please use them wisely.*

Jimmy examined the key. Etched into the metal were the words "FBI" and "Do not copy." He shook his head in disbelief. "Paul's a little messed up," he complained.

Picking up his bowl, he started to eat while he walked, the prickly sensation in his foot nearly gone. Returning to his place in front of the entertainment center, Jimmy picked up the remote control and turned on the TV, but the screen was inactive. A box in the corner read, "Blocked." "Come on!" he hollered in exaggerated disappointment. He tried another channel and then another. He scrolled through every channel on the TV. Every channel was blocked. "That guy is definitely messed up!"

* * * * *

The three piles of documents on Emily's desk had been reduced to one. The day's work was moving along more quickly than she anticipated, and she expected to have her report finished by early afternoon. Rick was nowhere to be seen, and coworkers were minding their own business. What more could she ask?

Her phone chirped and Assistant Special Agent in Charge Murphy was on the other end of the call. "Yes, sir. Right away," she responded.

Sliding the work into her portfolio, Emily headed down the hallway to the ASAC's office, confident he would be pleased with the progress on her assignment.

Entering the office, Emily saw Rick sitting in one of the chairs directly across from ASAC Murphy.

"Sir, you wanted to see me," Emily said nervously, glancing over at Rick.

"Yes. I would like to offer you an opportunity. You're new in the office, but from what I've noticed you seem to carry yourself professionally. Agent Stark here," ASAC Murphy said, looking toward Rick, "tells me you can be counted on to do whatever the job requires, that you're a team player. Is that right, Agent Mathews? Are you a team player?"

"Yes, sir," Emily replied with confidence, giving a sideways glance toward Rick.

"Good. I expect nothing less. Have a seat," he said, pointing toward the empty chair next to Rick. "I've asked Agent Stark to head up a small but vital task force, and he has asked that you be a part of his team. Would you have any problem working under Agent Stark?"

Although her mind was instantly flooded with possible problems, she replied, "No, sir." Sitting next to Rick, she put her portfolio against the leg of the chair. The ASAC was not interested in her recently completed assignment.

"Agent Mathews, are you sure?" he asked, looking directly into her eyes as if trying to read their real meaning. "Agent Stark suggests that despite his seniority and dedicated service in this office, you have not shown him much respect since coming to this office. He thinks you may resist him in a supervisory role. Is Agent Stark wrong?" he challenged.

"Sir, I am confident Agent Stark and I can work together in an effective and respectful way," Emily said, returning the ASAC's stare.

"Excellent! You will need to work together closely. I'll be watching. Agent Stark, please brief Agent Mathews on your new assignment."

"Yes, sir," Agent Stark said. He stood, moving alongside the ASAC. "What we have is a potential mess, a political minefield," he began. "As you know, the FBI is responsible for enforcing federal law. We take that seriously, and we follow our investigation wherever it leads. In this case, the investigation is leading us dangerously close to a federal judge who lives across the state line in Kansas. We'll investigate vigorously, but we must also be mindful of the political ramifications to this office if we're wrong."

"Agent Stark, what political ramifications?" Emily asked.

Before Stark could reply, ASAC Murphy jumped in. "Although we're clearly non-partisan, everything we do has political ramifications, especially for those in top command. If we go after this judge and we're wrong, or the case doesn't stick, he can bring a world of pain on this office. The SAC and I would look like a couple of monkeys roping a bull. I don't want that. We have to get this right."

"Understood, sir," Emily said.

Agent Stark continued, "During a recent investigation, the Kansas City Kansas Police Department stumbled across some, . . . well, some incriminating evidence that suggests that for the right price the judge is for sale. From what we've uncovered so far, sometimes his right price is cash, sometimes it's political favors, and sometimes it's, well, sometimes its female companionship." He blushed slightly.

Careful not to let it cross her lips, Emily hid a smile behind her eyes. *Agent Stark is* good. *No way does that make him blush,* she thought.

"That's where you come in, Agent Mathews. You are going to be our 'right price,' " Agent Stark concluded, giving her a subtle wink, obscured from the view of his superior.

"Okay," Emily said slowly. "I'm a little confused. What exactly is my role here?" she asked, careful to hide the concern in her voice.

"Well, we know a good deal about the judge," Agent Stark said. "We have a stack of verdicts and circumstantial evidence tying him improperly to certain gifts and favors. What we don't have is incontrovertible proof, the proverbial smoking gun. This is where you come in. We want to run a little sting, and you'll be our bait."

A brief but uncomfortable chortle of surprise escaped Emily's lips. She glanced to the ASAC, who rocked back in his chair, stone-faced, observing her every move. Emily quickly regained her composure but not before the ASAC recognized her discomfort.

"Is this assignment outside of your capabilities?" ASAC Murphy asked solemnly, still watching her closely.

"No, sir. I am capable. Just a little surprised is all. I've never been 'bait' for a philanderer before," she said, recovering her game face. "May I ask a question?"

"Agent Stark will fill you in on the details later. But understand this is a sensitive investigation. You are not to speak of it to anyone, not even within this office. Are we clear?"

"Yes, sir. Thank you for the opportunity."

"Good, make the best of it." The ASAC stood, signaling the meeting was over. Taking the cue, Emily and Rick both stood and exited the office.

Walking side-by-side down the hallway, Emily noticed the smug grin on Agent Stark's face. "Rick?" she asked.

"You may call me Agent Stark."

"Okay, Agent Stark," Emily corrected. "I'm just curious—why me? Why did you ask for me in this assignment?"

"There are a few reasons, really. How honest would you like me to be?" he asked as they continued walking.

"Be as honest as you can," Emily said, a hint of accusation in her voice.

Agent Stark stopped and turned toward Emily, backing her against the wall. Speaking in a whispered tone, he attacked. "Fine! Let's be honest with each other. You want to know why I chose you? Listen up.

Reason one: you are new to this office. The judge and his cronies don't know you so we won't risk you being recognized. Two: you're pretty. From what we know you are basically the judges type—young, blonde, dumb, nice figure. We'll make some adjustments to your wardrobe, and I think he'll be very pleased. Three: I don't think you have it in you, and I want to see you fail. I intend to expose your weakness, because it puts all of us at risk."

Not knowing how to respond, Emily stood stunned, her eyebrows furrowed. She felt as though she were melting into the floor.

"Honestly, I can get the judge with or without you, but I want to see you get rid of that holier-than-thou arrogance. I want to see if you're really willing to do *whatever* it takes," Agent Stark said quietly but harshly. "I don't know everything you may have to do, but I don't really care. When you fail, I'll advertise it in bright lights, and you'll be relegated to doing background reports the rest of your career. Then I'll step in and save the day. How is that for honesty? Do you have any other questions, *Emmy*?" he punctuated with disdain.

Emily's heart was pumping, and she felt her shoulders straighten as she purposely stood a little taller. She was not going to let Stark intimidate her. "No, Agent Stark. No more questions, but you may call me Agent Mathews. I look forward to having a respectful working relationship," she said sarcastically.

"Sure thing, little lady," he said mockingly. He turned away, leaving her clinging against the wall. "Finish up whatever you're working on. We'll start digging deeper into the judge's files at noon. We'll be in the third floor conference room, number two. Don't be late."

FOUR

Emily exited the elevator and walked slowly toward the conference room like a prisoner to the gallows. Her enthusiasm was temporarily crushed, and she stopped for a brief moment outside the closed door of the meeting room.

"Relax, breathe," she reminded herself, exhaling. Emily was determined not to let Agent Stark see her rattled. She pulled the door handle with vigor, glued a smile to her face, and made her entrance. Besides Agent Stark, there were only two other men in the large room. All were sitting at the long cherry wood table with stacks of files running down each side. Emily didn't recognize her new colleagues. "Hello, I'm Agent Emily Mathews."

"Hi, I'm Detective Collin Cross," one of the men said cordially, springing to his feet with an extended hand for the obligatory shake. "I'm here on loan from the Kansas City Kansas Police Department. Nice to be working with you."

The other man remained seated, slouched over his PDA. "I'm Thrasher," he mumbled.

Agent Stark moved to the head of the table. "I've met with each of you individually to discuss your specific roles here. I'd like to welcome Detective Cross and recognize his value to our team. He was working with the unit that first recognized some of the irregularities with our new best friend, Judge Craven. He will be able to offer some excellent background and analysis. Agent Thrasher here is our technical muscle," Stark said, smiling, "and Agent Mathews is our secret weapon. We have

26

a lot to review and figure out, so let's get to work."

Emily smiled politely. She glanced down at her watch, 12:05 p.m. *Five minutes down, five and a half hours to go*, she thought to herself.

* * * * *

Paul waited patiently outside the frosted glass door of the second floor office suite. As agents swiped their security card to enter or leave, Paul did his best to peek through the cracked door, trying to catch view of Emily. For security purposes, each division had limited access within the building except the main entrance, the commons area, and their own office space. Leaning against the wall like a discarded baseball bat, Paul held the security card, which hung casually around his neck, and wished it would give him access.

It was normal to get busy and run a couple of minutes late, but Emily was already fifteen minutes tardy. Pulling a phone from his pocket, Paul called the building switchboard, asking to be connected with Agent Emily Mathews. The operator rang him through, but there was no answer. After four rings, the usual beep was heard.

"Emily, sorry I missed you for lunch. I hope you're having a great day. Give me a call if you get a chance," he said, leaving his cell phone number. Disappointed, Paul made a quick visit to the basement vending machine and returned to his desk to eat some chips and a dry turkey sandwich.

* * * * *

Agent Stark could be surprisingly polite and even friendly when there were witnesses, but Emily knew it wouldn't last—it wasn't in his nature. Despite making only one disparaging joke about her "blonde intellect," there was a palpable tension in the room. Emily showed no reaction to Stark's inappropriate comment, Thrasher didn't seem to notice or care, and Detective Cross allowed only an uncomfortable grin while Stark laughed aloud.

For the most part, the day was uneventful and passed slowly. The team spent their time reading quietly, comparing notes, and occasionally discussing interesting facts about their suspect.

Detective Cross was tough, just what you would expect from an ex-marine. At nearly sixty years old and six feet four inches tall, he was still in excellent shape, yet he seemed to have a gentle side. To Emily, he seemed fatherly. Cross was a gentleman, a protector. There was no tension, no innuendo, no haughtiness, and being from outside the agency, he had no internal tie to Agent Stark. He was appropriate and professional, someone who could be a true ally.

Mark Thrasher was a different story—a bit of a mystery. In his mid-thirties, he was the youngest of the group, except for Emily. He was studious and detailed but difficult to read. Thrasher was not naturally friendly, and he didn't care to even try. Unless you consider the occasional grunts, he barely spoke. When he did speak, Emily had to listen closely as his raspy whispers were nearly imperceptible. Agent Thrasher was a black man, and at only five feet six inches and two hundred and ten pounds, he looked more like a grumpy, pre-diet Al Roker than "the muscle," as Agent Stark had called him. While it didn't appear that Thrasher and Stark had more than a casual, professional relationship, she couldn't tell for sure. She would watch them both closely.

After half a day of studying Judge Craven, Emily concluded that it might actually be possible for someone to be less desirable than Rick Stark.

Despite being a young judge, Craven already had a great deal of experience serving on the bench, and it appeared he had worked hard to earn his success. After graduating from law school, he clerked for Justice Myers on the Kansas Supreme Court and then moved into a lucrative private practice for a few years before being appointed to his station at the federal courthouse ten years earlier. At only forty-two years old, Craven was dedicated, powerful, and ambitious. He seemed to have a successful career, a lovely home, and a beautiful family.

John Craven married his wife, Susan, shortly after graduating from college. She was an attractive woman, dedicated to her family and her grade-school teaching career. Their daughter was a high school honor student and volleyball player who they were very proud of, and, although their thirteen-year-old autistic son required a great deal of attention, the couple was loving, giving him every chance for success.

At first, Emily found the judge to be a sympathetic character. He seemed like a hardworking family man with everyday problems. She didn't want to believe the accusations against him, but when she saw photos of the judge carousing at a local nightclub, her ire was raised. Nothing was more abhorrent than betrayal, especially the betrayal of person's own family.

Despite the darkness of her subject, Emily enjoyed the analysis and character study of Judge Craven, but grew increasingly anxious about her future role as "bait." John Craven was a charmer who found a way to get what he wanted, whether it was a presidential appointment to the federal bench or the girl at the end of the bar. Emily needed to dissect his wants and needs to truly understand his driving motivations and behavior. For now, she was safe in a conference room merely studying files, her only danger coming from an egomaniacal supervisor. But within the week, her body, her standards, and her self-respect would be at risk.

* * * * *

Emily swiped her card and entered the office suite, returning to her desk for the first time since noon. It was almost 5:30, and her coworkers were bustling in anticipation of going home for the evening. Sitting at her desk, Emily picked up her phone to review her voice mail but was startled by a voice close by.

"Good day, huh?" Joan asked sarcastically with a simple smile.

"I'm sorry, what?" Emily asked wearily, placing the phone down.

"I was just saying I bet my day was better than yours. I don't know what your new assignment is, but the word is you're working with Rick. That can't be fun, especially after your little run-in last night."

"Yes, I'm working with Agent Stark, but everything's fine," Emily said in a flat tone, hardly convincing.

"He went all, 'You can call me Agent Stark' on you, didn't he? I hope you know there's nothing special about you," Joan said coldly but without malice.

"Huh?" was Emily's only response.

"I think he's probably pulled that bit on everyone in this office at one time or another."

"You don't say." Emily sighed, clearly uninterested in the topic. She placed her elbow on the desk with chin in hand and head slightly cocked, resigned to the prospect of a painful conversation.

"I was trying to get your attention yesterday while the two of you were talking. I was giving you the 'be careful' look. You haven't been here very long, but Rick can really be a jerk. He thinks he can bark and bite and treat people badly because he's tight with the ASAC, but one of these days someone's going to bite back. I was just trying to give you a little warning, but you didn't pick up on it," Joan said brusquely.

"I must have missed it, but thanks for trying," Emily said, sitting up straight. "Next time, cue me in on other interoffice land mines before I step on them."

"Yeah, okay," Joan said, no expression on her face or in her voice. "Just be careful around Rick. Usually when he's being nice and polite, he's up to something." She turned and walked away.

"Thanks, Joan. You have a good night."

Returning to her phone, Emily listened to her voice mail. She gritted her teeth when she heard the message from Paul. She immediately dialed his number but only got his voice mail. Programming his number into her phone, she continued to listen to her other messages and then hung up.

Powering down her computer and locking her credenza, Emily grabbed her purse and eagerly exited the building. The air was crisp and refreshing on her face. She stopped just outside the main entrance, allowing the coolness of the evening to reinvigorate her senses and place the events of the day in their proper perspective.

"It's only work. There are bound to be days like this," she said to herself.

"Days like what?" Paul asked. He touched her elbow softly from behind, causing Emily to flinch. He seemed to appear from nowhere. "Sorry, I didn't mean to startle you," he said with a chuckle. "I called to you, but you seemed pretty focused on something."

Emily looked into Paul's brown eyes and was surprised by the excited flutter in her stomach. "That's all right. It's good to see you," she said with a warm smile. "It has been a day from. . . . I'm sorry I forgot about lunch, although I wouldn't have made it even if I did remember."

Paul nodded, pretending he understood.

"What's your schedule like? Do you have some time to walk with me?"

"No, I don't," Paul said, allowing for a pause to add a touch of suspense. "But I do have a better plan. Normally, I love walks, but I missed lunch today, and I'm starving. Would you like to have dinner with me?" Paul asked, formally extending his hand.

"I would love to. Where are we going?"

"I know a great place," he said, his hand still extended.

Blushing slightly, Emily grabbed his hand. "Lead the way."

FIVE

I APOLOGIZE FOR THE LITTLE DETOUR, but what can I say? I'm a disaster. It'll take me a few minutes to clean up and then—some fine dining," Paul said, smiling. He awkwardly removed his apartment door key from his pants pocket.

"You take all the time you need. I can wait. It's the least I can do after your heroic gesture," she said playfully, evaluating Paul's comical appearance. "I hope you have a good dry-cleaner."

Paul's backside was soaked. Muddy water dripped from the tail of his suit coat, and even the back of his hair was inharmoniously pasted with mud and gunk. Straight on, he looked fairly normal—that is, other than his unusual posture. He was slouched slightly, his neck was stiff and outstretched as if trying to escape from his buttoned collar, and his arms were extended straight, somewhat away from his body.

Paul played up his discomfort, exaggerating every motion for Emily's benefit. He was looking for a laugh or at least one of her gorgeous smiles. Emily gladly compensated Paul for his efforts. As if on cue, she produced her radiant smile, helping Paul to temporarily forget about his valiant misfortune.

Entering the apartment, Paul was surprised to see Jimmy standing at the kitchen counter, artfully chopping what appeared to be the makings of a fresh garden salad and some vegetables. The room was filled with the smell of fresh baked bread and the tangy aroma of tomato and vinegar, with polish sausage slowly grilling on the side. Looking up from his labors, Jimmy saw Paul and Emily standing in the doorway.

Something about Paul was amiss, and it wasn't the perplexed look on his face.

"Paul, welcome!" Jimmy shouted with exuberance. "Whoa! Who's your friend?" He winked.

"This is Emily. Emily, this is my friend Jimmy," Paul said simply, still dripping muddy water on the floor.

"Hi, Jimmy. What are you fixing?" Emily asked pleasantly. "It smells great."

"Well, it's going to be a baked ziti. Basically it's like glorified lasagna, except with ziti pasta and four cheeses: ricotta, cheddar, mozzarella, and Parmesan. Oh, and I use grilled polish sausage instead of hamburger. The bread will be done in a couple of minutes, and then I'll just throw the ziti in the oven and—"

"Please excuse me," Paul interrupted. "I need to get changed. I'll just be a few minutes." He turned and started awkwardly toward the bathroom.

"Take your time," Jimmy called out, still chopping steadily. "Dinner won't be ready for another twenty-five minutes." Glancing again at Paul, Jimmy looked for a response, but none came. "Wait! What happened to you?" Jimmy exclaimed, noticing for the first time Paul's mud-caked suit.

Paul still didn't answer as he disappeared into the bathroom.

* * * * *

"Jimmy, would you like any help with the food?" Emily asked.

"I would love some, but first, you have to tell me, what in the world happened to Paul?"

"It was sweet actually," she said with a modest grin. "We had just left work and were crossing the street on the way to the parking garage. There was this huge hole on the crosswalk near the curb. It looked like there had been one of those big steel plates covering it, but it had probably been jarred off by traffic. Paul jumped over it and then grabbed my hand to help me jump over too, which I did. So we're both standing on the sidewalk near this huge hole as traffic passed by. Did I mention the hole was full of muddy water?" Emily asked, a knowing look on her face.

"Ha! That's classic. So a car came driving by and splashed him? I thought that only happened on TV," Jimmy said, wildly amused.

"Yeah, kind of, but worse. So we had both jumped onto the sidewalk when a city bus started to turn the corner."

"A city bus? You're kidding."

"It didn't even occur to me what was about to happen, but before I knew it, Paul grabbed me, wrapped his arms around me, and shielded me from the bus. I heard a splash, and then Paul slowly unwrapped from around me. I don't think I got a drop on me, but well, you saw Paul. He was my gentleman hero," Emily said, smiling at the thought.

"I'll tell you what, Paul is a class act," Jimmy said, more impressed with Paul's girl than the heroic act. Jimmy had no idea Paul was such a sly dog.

"Yes, he is," Emily agreed.

Emily attempted to be subtle, but her casual glances at Jimmy turned into a hard stare. Something about him was familiar. She looked at him closely trying to stir her memory but nothing. She knew him, but she couldn't remember from where or when.

Together they completed the salad and vegetable preparation. Jimmy then pulled the French bread from the oven, replacing it with the main dish.

"Jimmy, do I know you?" Emily asked. "It seems like I know you, but I can't remember."

Let the good times roll, Jimmy thought. He closed the oven and set the timer. "Oh, I don't know. I think I'd remember a pretty girl like you. Maybe I just have one of those common faces," he offered. He found it impossible that she would have recognized him from the brief and distant meeting on the street the day before.

"I don't think so. Your look is familiar, sure, but it's the way you talk, and laugh, and carry yourself. Even some of your phrases seem really familiar." Emily watched Jimmy closely. "It will come to me," she said, and just as she said it, it did.

SIX

As Paul turned off the steaming shower, he was surprised to hear raucous laughter coming from the other room. He dried his hair with the undersized bath towel and glanced painfully at his suit, piled like trash in the corner of the bathroom floor. He had been so anxious to clean up and avoid making a further mess, he had failed to bring a change of clothes with him into the bathroom. Wrapping himself in his navy-blue towel, he cracked open the door.

The roar of laughter increased, and he looked to see where Jimmy and Emily were located. Paul opened the bathroom door all the way and then silently crept out, retreating to his room unnoticed. Moments later, fully dressed and clean, Paul returned to the room where his friends waited on the sofa. When he entered, the oven timer beeped.

Jimmy quickly arose from his seat next to Emily and turned toward the kitchen, ready to retrieve his main dish from the oven and assemble the meal for serving. "Feeling a little better, champ?" he asked.

Emily swung around in her seat, looking over the back of the sofa, surprised he was able to entirely remove the filth that had covered him. "Hey, looking good," she said, smiling.

"Thanks. I feel much better," Paul admitted, glancing at the small table with three full place settings.

"Your timing's excellent. Dinner will be ready in two minutes," Jimmy said. "Of course I didn't realize you would have anyone with you, but I wanted to make you dinner as a small token of my appreciation. I hope you don't mind. There's plenty for the three of us."

"Well, it isn't exactly what I had in mind for tonight . . ." Paul said, looking toward an appreciative and smiling Emily, "but it looks fantastic. Thanks, Jimmy."

Paul walked to the couch where Emily sat and offered his hand. "I told you I knew a great place. I just didn't know it was mine. Ready to eat?" he asked as he helped her up.

"You bet."

* * * * *

Paul and Emily sat at the table while Jimmy acted as both the waiter and entertainment. He quickly prepared their plates while humming a made-up tune. He served his friends and then sat down.

Before starting the meal, Paul blessed the food and then in the same breath continued. "I see you two are getting to know each other," It sounded more like a question than a statement.

Emily glanced at Jimmy. "Actually, we're getting reacquainted," she said, waiting for a reaction. Paul had just taken a large bite of his meal and was unable to speak, so Emily continued. "I was helping Jimmy finish up with dinner, and there was something about him that seemed so familiar. It was on the tip of my tongue, but I just couldn't place it. It was driving me crazy."

"Yeah, she didn't seem familiar to me at all, so I just thought we had a crazy stalker lady on our hands or something," Jimmy said with a wry smile.

"But then it hit me. College institute!"

"So, you two know each other?" Paul asked in amazement.

"Yeah, isn't that something?" Emily said. "I mean, we didn't really know each other socially, but we were in the same class for a semester, and we know some of the same people. In fact, back in the day, I had a bit of a crush on Jimmy."

Jimmy looked shocked. Paul looked horrified.

"Really?" Jimmy asked with satisfaction. "I can't believe I don't remember you. It's just, I'd think I'd remember a hottie who had a crush on me."

Paul gave Jimmy a sideways glance. "You had a crush on Jimmy, huh? How long did that last?" he asked, trying to hide the defensiveness in his voice.

"Well, at the time, just about every freshman girl in the class had a crush on Jimmy. He was handsome, outgoing, a smooth talker, and smart. He was getting ready to leave on his mission, and he seemed so spiritual. That kind of thing is really impressive to a girl who just joined the Church," Emily said quickly.

"Well, sure . . . I mean, it's great! I'm just a little surprised is all," Paul said, unconvincingly.

Jimmy sat in his chair quietly eating his food, an obvious smile hidden behind the chewing motion of his mouth. It had been a long while since anyone had wanted him.

"I'm kind of surprised I didn't recognize him immediately," Emily continued. "His mannerisms, speech, and even his looks are exactly the same—clean cut and handsome," she said casually, unaware of Paul's discomfort. "I guess seeing people out of context can make it tough to place them."

Paul had become the third wheel on his own date. Jimmy was focused on Emily, becoming more interested in her with each graceful smile and kind word. She only knew him as the desirable college student and future missionary. She didn't know him as the loser he portrayed and thought himself to be. Emily focused on Jimmy, lost in the memories of the crush from her early college days. As the two old acquaintances continued to talk, Paul surveyed the room, hoping to find inspiration for how he could change the subject and progress the conversation without appearing ill at ease.

After a moment he settled on a strategy. "Jimmy, this meal is fantastic! Thank you," Paul complimented. "Have you worked as a cook before, or is this an old favorite?"

"Nah. This is something my mom used to make. I just tweaked it a bit. I like to experiment a little but don't really get much chance. This is fun for me though. I'm glad you like it."

"Good experiment. Maybe you should apply for work at a restaurant or diner. You have a real talent. So did you have any luck in the job search today?" Paul asked in his most innocent voice, hoping to dull Jimmy's luster in Emily's eyes.

"Oh yeah, I had a great day! Thanks for asking," Jimmy said. "Unfortunately, I didn't find work today, but it's partly because I spent the afternoon buying the food and preparing this meal. I'm sure tomorrow will be better."

"Well, all you can do is try, and dinner really is great," Paul said.

Jimmy glared at Paul, cramming the last bit of food into his mouth and swallowing hard. He stood, cleared his dishes, and placed them in the sink. *Yeah, Paul is definitely a class act*, he thought. "I need to get going. I have some things to do, but Emily, we need to do this again. You're truly a *delightful* woman," he said, accentuating his flirtatious words with a wink.

"Thanks, Jimmy. I would love to catch up some more. I had a great time."

"Then it's a date. Now, you two have fun tonight, but not too much," Jimmy said with a sly grin.

Paul ignored Jimmy's comment. As he watched Jimmy leave the room, he grinned to himself, but as he turned back toward Emily, he was met with a disapproving look.

"What?" Paul asked with an uncomfortable laugh.

"You know exactly what," she said, gently shaking her head. "I can't believe you tried to embarrass him that way. And after he went through all that work to make you a nice dinner."

"I don't know what you're talking about," he said, attempting to act innocent but failing miserably.

"Look, you and I both know what you were trying to do. Don't pretend you don't. I hate to break it to you, but you're a terrible liar. I can see right through you."

"I didn't mean anything by it, but I did want to talk with you more privately. I just wanted to spend time with you, not you and Jimmy. You had just started to tell me about your day when I was attacked by the mud puddle," Paul reminded. "It seemed like you had a bad day and wanted to talk about it."

"I do, but I'm not sure how much I can say. You know how it is. But before we change the subject, can I ask you about Jimmy?"

"Sure."

"Well, how long has he been staying with you? What's he been up to? What's his plan?" Emily asked in rapid succession.

Paul cringed at Emily's interest in Jimmy. *Not good.* "Well, you're actually going to laugh. Remember our homeless friend from yesterday?"

"Of course," she responded, not recognizing the connection. "That was Jimmy."

"No way!" she said in amazement. "You're kidding. I would never have recognized him. I can't believe he's the same person."

"Well, he is. He was asking me for a place to stay, and I agreed to help him. I knew him growing up, but we were never close. I was shocked to see how far he had fallen. When we were younger, he seemed to have it all. He was in total control of his life, and now. . . I'm helping him, even though the whole situation makes me nervous."

"When I knew him he was just like tonight—charming, fun, smart. It's hard to imagine what could have caused him to. . . Do you know what happened?" Emily asked, a touch of sadness in her voice.

"I have no idea."

"Is there something we can do to help him? I don't mean just giving him a place to stay. I mean, I know that's important, but what I'm really asking is . . . well, is there a way we can help get him back on track, pull his life together?"

"Honestly, I don't know," Paul said. "He has to want to change and I can't tell if he does. I don't know if you've seen it, but he tends to put on quite the act. I can't tell what part of him is real and sincere and what part is just trying to play me. Part of me wants to give him a place to stay until he moves on in a few days and be done with it. But another part feels responsible for him. I can't really explain. I feel like I'm doing the right thing, but it doesn't feel like enough."

"Is it possible you're doing the right thing but not for the right reason?" Emily suggested. "I'm not trying to psychoanalyze you or any- thing. I'm just asking the question. Are you doing this to help Jimmy, or are you doing it so you can say you did?"

"The funny thing is, I've been asking myself the same question, but I'm not sure. How's that for clarity? I analyze data all day long at work, but I can't even figure myself out." Paul gave an uneasy chuckle.

"Whatever the motivation, you're being a good friend to him, so don't beat yourself up about it. If he starts to annoy you, just put on a happy face and bear through it. From what I hear, even difficult people can be treated with respect." It sounded good, but Emily reflected briefly on her encounter with Agent Stark. "Well, most of the time," she clarified.

"You're right. I just hope I can do it."

"Look, if I can smile and be polite to some of the people I work with, I know *you* can."

"Emily, you always seem to be happy and positive. The most upset I've ever seen you is when you gave me that 'death look' after I trashed Jimmy," Paul joked.

"You know you deserved it," she replied. "But really, it can be a challenge for me. I'm working with a guy right now who is . . . agh! He drives me nuts. He's a power-hungry jerk who's trying to make my life miserable because I wouldn't go out with him. Now he's supervising me on a new assignment."

"If he's being inappropriate, you need to say something," Paul said protectively.

"That would be a disaster. He has friends in high places, and I'd just come off looking like a little girl. He even told me he's expecting me to fail in my assignment, but that's not really the problem. I think I can handle him. What I'm really nervous about is my actual assignment."

Paul huffed as he thought about Emily being treated that way. "Who does this guy think he is?" Paul asked. "I want to—" Paul stopped instantly when he saw Emily fold her arms. It reminded him of the way his favorite Primary teacher used to correct him. "Sorry. What I mean is, can you tell me about your assignment?" Paul asked calmly.

Emily smiled, appreciating his effort. "No, not really." She paused as she considered how much she should say. Surely Paul didn't want to hear her problems, but he was more likely than anyone to understand. "Paul, can I ask you a question?"

Paul nodded.

"Have you ever considered how far you would be willing to go to do your job?"

"What do you mean?"

"Well, if accomplishing your assignment meant setting your personal standards aside for a while, would you do it? In other words, do you think it's a sin to do something you know is wrong, even though your job requires it and it's important in accomplishing an important mission?"

"I don't really know how to answer that. I guess with my assignments analyzing financial statements, I never really considered it a probability that I'd be placed in that kind of situation."

"Honestly, I never expected to be in the situation myself, but now I am, and I'm not sure what I should do."

Paul looked into Emily's eyes and then lowered his head. "Well, I think there are a couple of things to consider. One, how will God view the behavior? Two, what impact will the behavior have on you personally? You know, will it influence your personal standards or your self-esteem? Or is it behavior that may become addicting? Not knowing what you're talking about exactly, I don't really know how to answer any of these questions," Paul admitted sympathetically.

"I could be in a situation that requires me to do things I would normally never do. Hypothetically, if I don't do them, I could put myself and my team at risk. I would totally fail in my assignment."

"All I know is that whenever we do something we know is wrong, for whatever reason, we become a little bit desensitized to that behavior. It makes it a little bit harder to make the right choice the next time we are faced with a similar decision."

Emily's eyes were shining. "I don't know what to do."

"I know you'll make the right choice, even if you don't know what it is yet. I'll be here for you whatever that choice is," Paul said.

"Thanks, Paul. Hey, I know it's dark, but what do you say about taking that walk we talked about earlier? We could walk around the Power and Light District and get some fresh air," Emily suggested.

"That sounds good."

As they walked the city streets, Emily placed her arm around Paul's waist and rested her head on his shoulder. His heart pounded so strong, he was afraid she would feel both his excitement and anxiety. Holding her tight against him, Paul walked in silence.

SEVEN

To EMILY, THE WEEK HAD been the longest in recent memory, even though it was only late Thursday morning. The team had spent their days sequestered in the conference room, evaluating, profiling, and preparing the information gathering operation on Judge Craven.

Emily sat at the middle of the large conference room table, a small stack of case files to her left and another to her right. Opened in front of her was a single file, with a small heap of pictures stacked neatly on one side, and a profile page setting alone on the other. She had studied this file numerous times, and while it certainly painted an unflattering picture of the Judge, it was still incomplete. Emily cocked her head back and looked at the fluorescent bulbs in the light fixture over the center of the table. After a moment she adjusted her stare to a less blinding object —a picture on the wall directly across from her.

"Does anyone else find this strange?" Emily asked.

"What?" muttered the anti-social Agent Thrasher in his deep voice. He always seemed to be reading or typing or just listening, but he seldom participated in the team's conversations.

"Well, we know the judge spends at least one night each weekend hanging out at his favorite nightclub, without his wife obviously. Do you know any wife who would let her husband out that much at night?"

The others laughed in recognition.

"Seriously. I wonder what he tells her. Or maybe she knows and is just sticking with the marriage for security and convenience. Do we know why he's really out each weekend? Is he simply carousing, or is there something else to it?"

Detective Cross was interested. "You think he is up to something more than simple philandering?"

"We know he's up to more than that," Agent Stark blurted. "We wouldn't be investigating him if he was just a bad husband."

"Yes, I understand that," Cross said, clearly annoyed, "but is his night life tied more directly to his corruption than we originally thought? Is that how he makes his contacts? What do you think, Mathews?"

"I'm not sure. The guy is definitely a manipulator, so maybe he has a great recurring alibi for where he goes late at night, but it's hard to imagine. Besides, he's a recognizable public figure. Doesn't he realize he'll be seen, or does he just not care?" she asked. "And if he doesn't care, why not?"

"Let's look at what we know," offered Detective Cross as he rose from his seat. "We know that in a multitude of random cases, he rules contrary to what is expected by his fellow judges and prosecuting attorneys. We have cases ranging from corporate financial fraud to cyber crimes to interstate prostitution with no apparent connection, *and* the precedents he uses to support his rulings appear to be severely overstated. We know he has healthier bank accounts than one would expect based on his federal salary and his wife's teaching income. We know he likes the ladies. We've got photos. We know he's well connected. He's still close with the governor of Kansas from their days clerking for the Kansas Supreme Court, and he has significant relationships with many of the most high-powered politicians and attorneys in the area. We also know he's a regular at his favorite nightclub, The Wall. What do these facts tell us?"

"The guy is slime," Agent Stark accused.

"Yes, but is he even slimier than we're giving him credit for? Is something else going on here?" Emily asked rhetorically. "And if so, what is it?"

* * * * *

Jimmy slowly rose from the comfort of Paul's spare bed. He looked at the clock on the nightstand and fell back into the bed face first. Eyes closed, he stretched his entire body. Propping himself up, he sat on the edge of the bed, contemplating whether starting a new day was worth the effort. He could merely close the blinds and resume his sleep, but he glanced at the clock again, frowned, and stood. It was nearly 11:00 a.m. His sleep had been fitful since first waking to the sound of Paul's hideous alarm at 5:30. Although he had managed to will himself back to sleep, his mind had been stirring most of the morning. Jimmy rubbed his eyes. "I blame you, Paul," he muttered, walking to the door. Entering the living area, he glanced briefly toward the kitchen. "Breakfast will have to wait," he said with a low, groggy rasp in his voice.

Jimmy walked into Paul's bedroom and quickly scanned the area near Paul's bed. Not finding his intended target, he began a more methodical search around the room. Then, on the floor near the dresser, he found it. He bent over and picked up the obnoxious bell-hammered alarm. With the alarm clock in one hand, Jimmy walked to the window, unlocked the latch, and lifted the large pane. Looking briefly at the street below and satisfied he could cause no harm, Jimmy hurled the alarm onto the sidewalk three stories down. It hit with a metallic thud. "What the?" he muttered, disappointed the clock did not shatter into a thousand pieces. It looked like the clock was still in one piece. "That is one evil clock."

The phone rang, distracting Jimmy from his vengeful thoughts, but he was content to let the answering machine pick up. The machine beeped as he walked into the kitchen. "This is Federal Protection calling about an alarm at your location." Jimmy quickly picked up the phone and searched his mind for the cancel code to the alarm.

"No, sir, everything's fine. I just opened a window. The cancellation code is 'Jimmy cracked corn.' Yes, I'm Jimmy. Yes, sir, I thought it was funny too. You have a nice day," Jimmy said, and hung up the phone. He shook his head and laughed at himself. "Real smooth."

The words were still hanging on his tongue when the phone rang again. Reflexively, Jimmy grabbed the receiver, not waiting for the answering machine to pick up. "Hello? Oh, Paul. Yeah, good morning."

"I'm glad I caught you. I wanted to call and apologize for the other night. I shouldn't have submarined you the way I did. I was a little jealous of you and Emily enjoying each other so much. I acted like a jerk, and I'm sorry," Paul said nervously.

"Oh, don't fret about it. No worries," Jimmy said with a deep frog in his throat. "You just caught me," Jimmy lied, still standing in his pajamas. "I'm on my way out to pound the pavement again. I have a couple of places I want to apply today."

"That's great. Keep up the good work. I was also calling because we really haven't had a whole lot of time to talk one-on-one—you know, about other goals and hopes you have for yourself, that kind of thing."

"You haven't written another contract, have you?" Jimmy asked, cringing.

"No. One contract is enough." Paul laughed. "But it does occur to me that maybe there's more I can do to help, more than just give you a place to stay for a little while."

"Ah, that's really generous but—"

"We can talk about it later, but I want you to think about coming to church with me on Sunday." Jimmy didn't respond. "I know what you're probably thinking, but deep down you know it's where you ought to be. You were a missionary, so you know how it works," Paul said with a chuckle. Jimmy's silence persisted. "Jimmy, you still there?"

"Yeah, um, sorry . . . I just don't know. I'm not really the churchy type anymore. You understand."

"No, not really," Paul said. "Church is where you need to be. You've been coasting for long enough and you need to re-engage. It's time to buck up and try a little harder. Finding work and a home is great, but you need to find more than that. Think about it, and we can talk later. I need to get back to work. Catch you later," Paul said quickly and hung up the phone, not giving Jimmy a chance to reply.

Phone still in hand, Jimmy looked down and gritted his teeth. "Crap!"

* * * * *

Just blocks away from the FBI field office stands the Richard Bolling Federal Building, which includes the U.S. Courthouse. Named after former-Congressman Richard Bolling, the eighteen-story building houses nearly twenty-eight hundred federal employees from various organizations and agencies, and boasts many of the same amenities as other large buildings making up the Kansas City skyline.

Despite its size, the building is not particularly impressive. There are no Greek columns or copper domes, no marble facade. Its glassy exterior is quite average amongst its peers. Each entrance has a standard security check point requiring each employee or visitor to present valid ID and pass through screening before being granted limited access within the building.

The building was Judge Craven's kingdom—secure, comfortable, and a place where everyone treated him with appropriate deference. Despite his haughtiness, the judge was sufficiently friendly. His smile seemed genuine, and he used it often to put others at ease. Judge Craven appeared to come straight out of a shampoo commercial, with his clean shave and perfect hair. His Armani suits were pressed precisely, and his tie was knotted with a triple Windsor, which appeared overly large, yet fashionable. His Italian shoes gleamed and cuff links sparkled.

After a full day of reading briefs and making the required appearances in court, Judge Craven sent his secretary home, partially closed the vertical blinds, and lowered the lights. Only a dim haze from the fixtures above was allowed to mingle with the sliver of light entering from underneath the door. Pulling a decanter from his bookshelf, the judge sat comfortably in the executive leather chair. He sipped his bourbon slowly. The office was ostentatious, even a bit cliché, but that's the way he liked it. Behind closed doors, sitting in the shadows, Craven became nothing more than a silhouette positioned against a backdrop of the city skyline, which intruded from between the small cracks in the blinds.

He pulled a cheap prepaid cell phone from his briefcase and dialed slowly. "Can you talk?" he asked in monotone.

"Briefly. You'd better have a handle on this thing. There's only so much I can do to protect you," the voice whispered harshly.

"I know exactly what I'm doing. Don't forget who you're talking to," Craven said with a wicked grin. "Are we still on for tomorrow night?"

"Yes. Ten at The Wall."

"Good, I am looking forward to this."

EIGHT

STILL IN HER WORK CLOTHES, Emily stood in front of the full-length mirror hanging inside her bathroom door. She tucked a tendril of hair behind her ear. Staring at herself, she evaluated her slender legs and then raised her skirt to mid-thigh and turned for a different view. Observing her curved waist, she ran her hand firmly down her hip and then with both hands patted down the front of her skirt. Taking note of her posture, she stood more erect, curved her back slightly, and extending her chest outward. She unbuttoned her blouse once, then again, and stood in a pose for a moment before returning to her usual stance.

Emily attempted to look herself in the eye in the mirror but quickly lowered her head. She exhaled deeply and then stared at herself again. She practiced a subtle smile, raised an eyebrow, and then winked awkwardly, attempting to discover a coy look she could use in her fast-approaching undercover debut.

"Pathetic," she muttered.

Emily had always considered herself an attractive woman, and she received plenty of attention from men, but she had never thought herself seductive or sexy. For the first time, Emily wondered if she would physically be able to pull off her undercover assignment. The judge was experienced with beautiful, seductive women, and he had an expectation for the women in his company. What would it take to be alluring enough to interest the judge? Could she even do it? *Judge Craven is certain to spot me as a fraud*, she thought. Emily's heart pounded as her anxiety grew. Though the meeting with Judge Craven tomorrow night should be safe, Emily's shoulders were tight and her stomach uneasy.

Leaving her place in front of the mirror, Emily exited the bathroom and slammed the door in frustration. Searching her closet frantically, she ripped multiple outfits from their hangers, throwing them on the bed in a heap. She tried on one outfit and then ripped it off, discarding the unwanted garment in the middle of the floor. She went through all the other outfits, holding them up against her body, but she was equally disgusted with each one. Her wardrobe looked appropriate for church but not a nightclub. Nothing in her wardrobe would do for what she intended tonight.

* * * * *

"Paul, are you listening to yourself?" Jimmy asked calmly in a reversal of their usual roles. "Relax, brother. Lower the excitement level a little. Why are you so worked up?"

Jimmy reclined comfortably on the couch in front of the entertainment center. His television show was still playing even though Paul had muted it. Paul sat on the edge of the chair, leaning toward Jimmy and attempting to engage him in conversation. Paul leaned back and laughed uncomfortably, recognizing his error in approaching Jimmy in such a forceful way. "You're right. I need to calm down a little, but can't you see why I'm so frustrated?"

"Are you frustrated with me or with yourself?" Jimmy asked accusingly, still watching his muted program. "You know better than I do that you can't change minds and hearts by decree. I'm not your servant, and *you* are not my father. You can't force me to do what you think is best. See, I think you *want* me to make different choices, but you're frustrated because you can't *make* me do it," he said confidently, turning from his show to view Paul's reaction.

There may have been some truth to Jimmy's argument, but Paul was not yet ready to concede. Shaking his head, Paul inhaled deeply. "Don't you want more out of life than this? This can't be how you envisioned yourself growing up. You were sharp. You looked like you would have it all, and now you have nothing. And that's not even the worst part. You have nothing, but you don't even care. I just can't understand that."

"You know, you really stink at having 'missionary moments.' But I have really felt the Spirit here tonight, and I have committed to myself that I'm going to change my ways," he said mockingly.

"Fine," Paul responded, resigned to his failure. He pushed a button on the remote, returning the sound to Jimmy's program. "I shouldn't have interrupted your important show. I don't even know why I should care. It's your life. You can do what you want," he admitted. "Just answer one question for me: what happened to you? Honestly, I'd like to know."

Jimmy let out a small laugh as he continued watching his program. For a moment he said nothing.

"You know, Paul, you really ought to get a DVR. It's the best. You can pause live TV or record multiple shows. That way, if you're distracted or interrupted, you never have to miss a thing. Yep, it's the best," he said coldly, ignoring Paul's question.

"You're really something, Jimmy. I'm feeding and housing you, and you're too lazy to even keep up your friendly little act. Forget I asked. You can be a failure if you want."

Jimmy glared at Paul, gritting his teeth. There was a slight furrow to his brow. "Hey, this was really fun," he said, plastering a phony smile across his face. "We should do it again sometime." Jimmy paused. "How's that for an act?" he asked, standing abruptly and walking toward the apartment door.

"You're going out? It's already after 10:00!"

"Sorry, *Dad*. I'm extending my own curfew tonight," Jimmy said as he slammed the door shut behind him.

* * * * *

There was a definite briskness to the night air. Despite a daytime temperature hovering in the high sixties, the night's chill was enhanced by a steady breeze. Judge John Craven leaned in and kissed his wife, holding her face in his hands as he stood in front of the open doorway to their suburban home. "I'll be late, honey."

Susan bit her lip. "John, is this absolutely necessary?"

"We've talked about this. Everything is moving ahead as we planned. It's been a long time coming, but we're finally near the end. We need to be patient and alert, and everything will work out."

"I trust you, but I don't understand why you have to take all the risks. Why can't the others . . . ?" She halted, recognizing her husband's stern gaze.

"Remember, honey, the greater the risk, the greater the reward. When we're finished, our lives will never be the same. I promise. Now, I don't want to be late for my meeting. There are some final preparations to be made."

"John, be careful. I love you," Susan said, fighting back tears of worry.

"I will," he said, kissing her on the cheek. "Don't wait up."

John Craven walked down the short driveway to a waiting black sedan with darkened windows. As he approached the vehicle, the rear door swung open. Susan stood in the open doorway and watched the car slowly pull away from the curb and out of sight.

* * * * *

The stink of stale beer and cigarettes permeated the dimness of Julio's Main Street Cantina. Jimmy sat alone at a small round table in the front corner, hidden behind the entryway. He was content with his solitude. Another 1970s rock classic blasted over the speaker mounted precariously on the wall above his head. He grinned as he considered the incongruity of the "Cantina's" name, the Eric Clapton music playing and the décor of sports memorabilia. "A true melting pot," he said, unable to hear his own comment over the music. Jimmy swashed his nearly empty beer bottle, attempting to determine how many more sips he could take before running out.

The place was hopping for a Thursday night, and Jimmy was unable to get his server's attention for another drink. Carefully navigating his course, he weaved between tables and through people across a compact dance floor. The bartender handed him a new bottle, and Jimmy quickly returned to recapture his out-of-the-way seat, one of the few remaining in the establishment. Jimmy had never been much of a drinker, but tonight he wanted something to help him relax. He leaned his chair back into the corner and closed his eyes, holding the neck of his bottle loosely in one hand.

As his eyes reopened, Jimmy's gaze became instantly transfixed on a woman entering the bar. From behind, he enjoyed her well-proportioned figure, the low loose scoop revealing much of her bare back, and the elegant fit of the short red dress. She seemed a bit overdressed for the environment, but he certainly appreciated the improved scenery. He watched her closely as she sauntered to the bar and surveyed the scene, looking for an available seat. Jimmy's eyes scanned the room quickly. He was not the only one watching. Single men were staring. Even men with dates were attempting to catch a quick glimpse without being noticed by their companions. Jimmy watched her every step as though she were moving in slow motion.

He admired her athletic legs and perfectly shaped hips, the tight fit of the dress around her torso, and the loose neckline teasing her ample chest. The woman approached a nearby table but when she sat, Jimmy's view was obstructed by a large cardboard advertisement hanging low from the ceiling. He stared more closely and then averted his eyes when he thought himself too obvious. He quickly returned to staring when he realized the obstruction of his view, aided by the dim lighting, would offer him sufficient coverage from detection. He watched carefully as she sat tall in her chair and gently crossed her bare, slender legs. Jimmy slouched over, his head nearly sideways on his table, struggling to look past walking patrons and hanging advertisements. From this angle he had a good profile view of the woman but felt his neck pinch trying to maintain the awkward position. She sat alone, although she glanced around the room frequently, overly self-conscious for a woman of such beauty.

For a few minutes, Jimmy continued to drink his beer between slouches and peeks. As he watched from under the hanging cardboard sign, she turned in his direction. He quickly blocked his face with an arm, trying to act casual, which was difficult considering his odd position. She couldn't see him, but he saw her clearly for the first time. Jimmy's mouth and eyes opened wide in shock as he recognized the object of his careless desire. *Emily! What are you doing here?* he wondered with disappointment.

Rising from his seat, Jimmy had not taken a single step toward

Emily's table when a fit, well-dressed man approached her. Jimmy sat and resumed the awkward position with his cocked head on the table, watching her every move.

The man, smiling at her side, offered what Jimmy imagined to be a borrowed pickup line from a 1980's romantic comedy. He cringed at the thought. Emily smiled alluringly, motioning the man to take a seat across from her at the table. Instead of taking the offered position, the man grabbed the chair, moving it closer to his intended target. Sitting uncomfortably close to Emily, his leg casually touched hers. "This guy's got no skill," Jimmy scoffed, his words muffled by the music.

Jimmy watched them talk and laugh but became agitated when the man placed a hand just above Emily's knee. She flinched visibly at the touch and appeared embarrassed at her uncontrolled reaction. She attempted to downplay her startled response, and the man appeared to accept her apology. Wasting no time, he again placed his hand on her thigh, and she again was startled. Emily's new friend didn't seem to care about her unease, but she did. Emily placed her lowered head in her hands, propping her elbows on the table.

"Enough of this," Jimmy said. He took one last gulp from the bottle, placed it back on the table, and walked with purpose to rescue Emily's honor.

"Hey, Emily, it's good to see you," Jimmy greeted warmly, approaching the table. Emily lifted her head to see Jimmy standing near. The relief and gratitude that shone in her eyes suddenly changed to a look of fear and embarrassment. "Sir, you may now remove your hand from my date. Thank you," Jimmy said dismissively.

The handsome man muttered something into Emily's ear to which she simply nodded. Looking askance at Jimmy, the man stood and walked away, returning to his previous lookout position at the bar.

"Jimmy, what are you doing here?" Emily whispered firmly.

"Me? Didn't Paul tell you? I'm the unsavory type. My kind lives in places like this," he joked. "You, on the other hand—you really don't belong."

"It's really not what it looks like. You won't say anything to Paul, will you?" Emily pleaded. "That would be so embarrassing."

Jimmy studied her expression carefully. "I'll make you a deal. I won't say anything if you don't. I'm the one actually breaking Paul's house rule #13 right now—or maybe its #14. I don't really care." Jimmy did his best to remain focused on Emily from the neck up, ignoring her appealing but immodest dress. But then, as if in a trance, his eyes wandered.

"Hey! Eyes right here," she said, framing her face with her hands. She leaned in close as if to tell Jimmy a secret, covering her chest with both hands in the process. "I'm embarrassed enough to have strangers see me like this. I wasn't planning on revealing this much of myself to friends."

"Well, what were you planning exactly?" Jimmy asked, laughing. "I mean that is some dress. It hugs every little curve and—" Jimmy stopped abruptly, realizing he was saying too much. "Here, follow me." He stood, pointing to his hiding spot in the corner. "At least over there no one else will be staring, and believe me, right now, everyone is staring."

Emily blushed and gently brushed the hair from her face. She followed Jimmy to his table. They sat in awkward silence for a moment, at least as silent as it could be in a bar with music blasting from the speaker overhead.

"Okay, I'll go first," Jimmy said. "I'm here because . . . well, because Paul drives me nuts, and I needed to get out of there for a while. I saw this place the other day, and it's only a couple of blocks from the apartment, so I figured, why not? There's another place up the street, but it seems kind of yuppity. But this," he said, looking around, "this is my kind of hole."

"Yeah, that yuppity one up the street is where all the FBI guys go, but they wouldn't be caught dead in this place. I'm sure there must be other bars in this city, but I don't know where," she admitted. "So, Jimmy, is that your beer?" Emily asked, nodding toward the bottle.

"Nah, I don't know whose that is, I just, you know . . . well . . . yeah . . . it's mine," he finally admitted, removing the bottle from the table and setting it on the floor. "I mentioned rule #13 right? That's the no alcohol rule. I kind of broke it tonight."

"You know, Jimmy, it's actually a really good rule."

"Yeah, there are lots of really good rules, but I don't do too well with a lot of them. What about you? You know, being here tonight, dressed like that, letting strangers . . . you know. . . . Does that fit into *your* rules? Because if it does, I'm in."

Emily frowned. "No. That's not who I am, but it's something I've got to do. I can't really explain," she said, shaking her head.

"You don't have to convince me. I can see you're uncomfortable. Honestly, I have no idea what you're up to, but be careful. I know you're a smart girl, but you're too good for this."

"No, Jimmy, you don't understand. Really, it's not my choice. There's something I have to do and I'm so bad at it, I just needed to practice tonight . . ." She groaned in frustration. "What's the point?"

"First of all, Emily, there's always a choice. You know that. It might not be easy, but you always have a choice. You decide what you do, how you dress, where you go. Trust me, I know. You remember how I used to be, right? I was a pretty good guy. But then I started doing things that didn't fit who I was. Look at me now. This is who I am. It's who I've become." Jimmy sat quietly for a moment. "Man, I'm depressing."

Emily smiled appreciatively. "You're right. I would normally agree with everything you're saying, but this is different. I'm not going to turn into a girl that hangs out in bars, dressed like . . . like this," she said, gesturing to her clothing. Jimmy took the opportunity to sneak another peek but caught Emily's stare when his eyes returned to her face.

"Sorry," he said, smiling. "You really are hot. Look, I'm not trying to go all Paul on you or anything, I'm just suggesting that maybe there's another way to accomplish whatever it is you're trying to do."

Emily smiled, but her teeth quickly clenched as she tried to hold back her emotion. "If there's another way, I can't figure it out. I've spent the entire week trying to think of options. I don't know what else I can do. Seriously, this is the only way."

"Hey, easy," Jimmy said softly. "I just don't understand it. I can tell how hard this is for you, but would you—?" Jimmy stopped, unable to complete his question.

"What?" Emily prodded.

Jimmy thought for a moment. "Never mind."

"No, what is it?"

"Would you do me a favor before you go ahead with whatever you're planning?"

"Maybe. What is it?" she asked with a slight sniffle.

Jimmy sat quietly, looking around the room uneasily. "Would you pray about it?" Jimmy could hardly believe the words coming out of his own mouth.

Emily seemed nearly as shocked as Jimmy. She laughed nervously. "I don't know, Jimmy. This isn't really the kind of thing I should pray about."

"Why not?"

"Well, you know, with it being work related and all. It seems like I should at least be able to come up with my own answers for work. Besides, what kind of answer should I expect? I don't really think I'm going to get permission to break commandments or lower my standards."

"Look, I'm not trying to tell you what to do. It's just an idea, and it doesn't really matter if it's work related. If it's important to you, you should pray about it."

"I suppose you're right," she admitted, wiping a tear from her cheek.

"So you'll do it?"

"Yeah, I'll do it. I guess I should feel stupid for not praying about it already. Thanks, Jimmy. That's the best suggestion I've had all week."

Jimmy fidgeted and laughed at himself. "You know me—I like to hang out drinking before offering spiritual guidance, but you're welcome."

Emily smiled appreciatively at her friend. "I didn't really take you for an expert on prayer. No offense."

"What can I say? I'm full of surprises."

"I guess it's my turn to help you. What did Paul do that drove you to drinking tonight?"

Jimmy sat quietly for a few moments, contemplating the events and conversation of the night. "He was honest with me," Jimmy said, reflecting on his answer.

"Hmm, sounds pretty rough. What are you going to do about it?"

"Excellent question. I don't know." Emily watched Jimmy fidget in his seat. "I suppose I could change, but I'm not even sure I want to. What if I try but fail? I guess you could say I'm lacking a little confidence."

Reaching across the table, Emily grabbed Jimmy's hand and held it between hers. "I know what you mean. But if you decide you want to try, and I hope you do, I'll do my best to help you."

Jimmy enjoyed her caring touch. "A fine pair we make. What do you say you walk me home so we can talk without all this noise?"

Emily nodded in agreement.

"One last question. Where did you get that dress?"

Emily smiled, ensuring she and Jimmy maintained eye contact. "The mall."

NINE

STEPHENS!"

Having just entered the office suite, Paul was nearing his cubical when the sound of his name being called from across the room startled him. Special Agent Jerome Dallas was a large, intimidating man with a powerful voice. The entire office glanced briefly toward Dallas but quickly resumed their work.

"You picked a rotten day to show up late," his boss said harshly.

"I apologize, sir. I had some problems with my alarm this morning. It won't happen again," Paul promised, glancing at his watch. "What can I do for you, sir?"

"Besides being on a plane in two and a half hours on your way to Oklahoma City, not much."

"Sir? Oklahoma City? Why am I going to Oklahoma?" Paul asked. Though it was common for agents to be loaned out to other offices for special assignments, it had never happened to Paul.

"You've been requested to help analyze the records of a local bank down there. The bank was robbed, and they want your expertise."

Paul tapped his leg eagerly. "They asked for me? How—?"

"They think it may have been an inside job and the catch is, the bank president and the Special Agent in Charge of the office down there are lifelong friends. The SAC wants to avoid any appearance of impropriety, so he asked for an outside man to be lead analyst on the investigation. So, actually, no, they didn't ask for *you* exactly, but they did ask for my best financial analyst. He wasn't available, so I'm giving them you. Sorry for the short notice," Dallas said, his stern mouth turning into a smile.

Paul's eyes lit up. "Thank you, sir. I won't let you down."

"You'd better not," he growled. "Now get moving. Grab your stuff and quickly stop by your place to pack a bag on the way to the airport."

"Sir, how long should I expect to be there?"

"I would think at least a week or two, but I guess that depends on how good you are, doesn't it? The office down there will send a car to pick you up at the airport. Now are you going to get going, or are you just going to stand around chatting all day?"

Rifling through his materials, Paul grabbed a manual, a planner, and a couple of personal items. As he eagerly left the office, he pulled his cell phone from his pocket, dropping his manual on the floor. Before picking it up, he finished dialing and waited for Emily to answer on the other end. She never did. He left a brief message and anxiously continued to the parking garage across the street.

* * * * *

Agent Thrasher unfolded his arms and pounded his hands on the table. "Guys! SHUT UP!" he screamed. Agent Stark and Detective Cross stopped bickering instantly, surprised by their usually calm and silent partner. "Agent Stark, you are in charge here. Please maintain some decency and control. And Cross, we've got to be on the same page here. We're almost ready to send Agent Mathews to meet with Judge Craven—and we can't even stop arguing amongst ourselves? We'd better get it together, and fast. I don't want Mathews hearing this junk. Her confidence is shaky as it is," Thrasher said.

Detective Cross lowered his head sheepishly. "Thrasher, you're right. Stark, you call the shots, but if I hear you make one more comment about what you want to see Mathews wear or do, I'm going to knock your teeth out. I mean that literally. Sorry, Thrasher. I think Stark and I understand each other now. Right, Stark?"

Agent Stark leaned against the wall with his hands in the front pockets of his slacks, trying hard to appear relaxed. "Where is Mathews anyway? Putting a woman in a room full of clothes and makeup is always risky. We may not see her 'til tomorrow," he said, laughing at his own joke. Instantly, he caught the sharpness of Detective Cross's glare. "What? We're getting to crunch time, and we need to run through the game plan one more time. She needs to hurry up."

Thrasher continued typing gracefully on his computer and then pulled a small wallet-sized case from his satchel. "I'm ready." He opened the case to reveal a thin, round transmitter, about the size and weight of a penny. "Place this on Agent Mathews and we'll hear everything she, or anyone around her, says."

"Are we all set with the video?" Stark asked.

"The club has tremendous video surveillance for security so we've tapped their feed. I'll be able to see everything from the club's cameras and hear Mathews right on this laptop."

"Good. What kind of range will you have?"

"Two hundred yards, easy. We'll set up in a van down the street from the club."

"And I'll be in a car at the rear. I won't have video, but I'll be able to hear the audio," added Cross. "We'll have eyes on the only two entrances and exits, so we'll see anyone coming or going."

"I think we're set. This should be a walk in the park," Stark said, pacing slowly in front of the door. "Cross, would you please go find Mathews? She's the only part of this little equation I'm worried about, not that her part requires any skill," he scoffed. "As long as she can strut her stuff in a trashy little outfit, we'll be fine. The judge won't be able to resist Mathews throwing herself at him."

The conference room door opened forcefully, and Emily entered with confidence. The corner of the door crashed into the side of Agent Stark's face, despite his sluggish attempt to avoid it, and it scraped along his face until it hit his ample nose. He fell to the ground like a rag doll. Thrasher looked up from his notebook for a moment and then returned to his work, despite Stark's writhing in pain. Embarrassed at the disturbance she caused, Emily dropped to her knees beside Stark. His cupped hands caught most of the blood flowing from his nose; the rest seeped gradually into the carpet.

"I'm sorry, Agent Stark! It was an accident. Do we have something for the blood?" Emily asked frantically.

"Don't worry about it," Cross said, dropping a box of tissues onto the floor near Stark. "He'll survive." Detective Cross lowered his hand, helping Emily stand. "Just leave him alone for a few minutes, and he'll be fine." Taking a step back, Detective Cross appraised Emily's appearance. "Wow! Agent Mathews, you look lovely."

Thrasher glanced toward Emily and stared for a long moment. "Genius."

Emily stood near the end of the table where Agent Stark was now attempting to stand in a bloody, tearful mess. Contrasted against the ugliness of Stark, Emily was radiant. Her natural blonde hair was pulled back into a simple ponytail, dropping to the base of her neck, which was adorned with a simple gold chain and diamond pendant. An elegant pale-yellow silk dress modestly complimented the shape of her body. On her wrist was an expensive, yet simple gold bracelet-watch. Her ensemble was completed with satin shoes matching the yellow sash around her waist. Emily exuded class and elegance.

"What is that?" The tissue covering his nose and mouth muffled Stark's protest. "That's not the program. We know what Craven goes for, and that's not it. Get back down there, put on something sexy, or trashy, or whatever. Change clothes, and let's get going," Stark said sharply.

"You want sexy, you got sexy," argued Detective Cross. Thrasher simply nodded.

"Look, I know this isn't what you expected, but think about it. What is our goal? For me to get noticed and then gain the judge's trust enough that he might slip up and say something damaging, right? I don't doubt that he likes women dressed in revealing clothes. But everyone dresses that way. If I want to stand out, I need to be different. Do you think he would notice one more chick dressed in a halter-top and mini skirt at the bar, let alone confide in her? Or would he be more willing to relax around a classy woman, someone more like him?"

Stark looked at his watch, then at Emily, and again at his watch. Thrasher and Cross positioned themselves behind Emily as an expression of solidarity. Stark jabbed a finger in Emily's direction. "If this doesn't work, its on your head."

"Agreed," she said.

"Mathews, I want you to talk through your approach on the judge with Detective Cross, step by step. I don't want any more surprises. Thrasher, just keep doing whatever it is you're doing on that computer, and put that bug on her somewhere. I'm going to get cleaned up and put some ice on my nose." Tossing the bloody tissue onto the floor, Stark replaced it with a new fresh tissue. The bleeding had nearly stopped. "I'll be back in a bit."

As Stark closed the door behind him, Emily, Thrasher, and Cross looked at one another. Cross rolled his eyes dramatically, and they all indulged in a brief laugh before refocusing on the task before them.

* * * * *

The video feed from the six stationary cameras located in the ceiling of the club provided outstanding picture onto Thrasher's laptop. "If you can manage it, you either want to be here at the bar," Thrasher explained, pointing at one of the six pictures on the screen, "or here," he said pointing at a table near the back of the room. "The angle of the camera is best in those spots. We'll have a great view."

Although her confidence had been greatly enhanced after following Jimmy's advice, Emily sat in the van with her eyes closed, picking at her fingernails. "I can do this. I can do this," she mouthed inaudibly. She took a deep breath. "God, please help me."

"It's time. Cross, you in position?" Stark inquired.

"Set."

"Mathews, are you ready?"

"I'm ready," Emily said without hesitation.

"Hey, Mathews, you go get 'em. You'll do great," Cross said.

Emily smiled. "Thanks. Just watch my back."

"Got it."

"Okay, folks, here we go. We're in play." Stark opened the van door and Emily exited.

* * * * *

By 11:00 p.m. Emily was growing impatient. Sitting at the bar, her back toward the camera, she finished her third soda. A white wine spritzer, courtesy of a random pickup artist, sat on a napkin in front of her. To give the illusion that she was drinking alcohol, she poured a small portion of the spritzer into her last soda glass before discarding it. The club was bustling, and men from around the room were noticing her distinct beauty. Attractive women were plentiful but their attire was predictable. They were desperate for companionship. On the other hand, Emily looked like a woman secure with herself, seeking a higher class of gentleman.

"Is everyone else as bored as I am?" she asked casually, taking another sip of soda.

"Yep," came a low mumble.

"Me too."

Detective Cross rubbed his eyes softly and then forced them open wide. "Yeah, well, hang in there. At least you know you're a wanted woman. The line that last guy used was actually pretty good. You paying attention, Stark?"

Emily laughed quietly, appreciative of Cross's derision of Stark. "There sure are a lot of lonely guys around here," Emily said. "Being the object of their desperation is not really as flattering as you might think."

"Quit jabbering. The guy's late. Let's give it another fifteen minutes. Then we'll call it a night," Stark said, tossing peanuts into his mouth. "Stay focused and keep your eyes open."

"Yes, boss."

"Wait a second! Whoa, whoa, whoa. Okay, here we go! We've got a silver Mercedes AMG approaching. This is our guy. Vanity plate *KING 1*. What a putz."

TEN

PULLING INTO THE FIRE LANE directly in front of the club's entrance, Judge Craven left his engine running as he stepped out of his sleek Mercedes AMG. Even though valet parking was not a standard amenity of the club, a Wall employee greeted the judge immediately, hopped into his car, and parked it around the side of the building. The gesture of respect in performing such a service for one of the club's most valuable patrons far outweighed any real usefulness. Parking his own car, Craven could have been at the entrance nearly as quickly. But that wasn't the point. It was about prestige, power, and respect. It was a statement of his superiority to both patron and employee, a statement he was willing to pay for.

There was no long rope line or brawny bouncer standing at the door. Couples trickled out, happy to have found temporary companionship. A more steady flow of expectant patrons waded in the front entrance, paid their cover charge, and received a fluorescent stamp on the hand, indicating they belonged. Naturally, this process was not for Judge Craven. An unfortunate server had once challenged the judge when she noticed his hand stamp was missing. With a simple wave of the hand, Judge Craven had summoned the club manager, and the insolent employee was immediately escorted from the building.

Few employees knew John Craven's name. They simply knew him as "the Judge," and that was good enough. As he entered the building, bypassing the cashier/hand-stamper, he nodded to the club's assistant manager.

"It's good to see you, Judge. Please let me know if there is anything I can do to make your evening more enjoyable."

"Thank you. It is good to see you too, Marcus," the Judge replied pleasantly. "May I have my regular table this evening? I am expecting a guest."

"Of course. It will be just a moment while the table is prepared." Marcus hurried away.

Evaluating the evening's crop of women, Judge Craven stood for a moment inside the doorway. It was the usual. The Wall catered to a professional class, but despite the high income and educational level, most of the customers were looking for transitory companionship and a way to escape the responsibilities of their daily lives. Many were doctors, bankers, attorneys, or various management types. It was a more sophisticated nightclub, but it was a club nonetheless. Professionals flocked to the Wall each weekend, hoping to recapture a piece of their youthful, carefree party days. They dressed like mature people trying their best to be trendy and sexy, wearing the latest fashions and drinking the most stylish beverages, while gyrating to the most obnoxious music. But the Judge was different.

Waiting impatiently near the door, Judge Craven was dressed as he always dressed when he wasn't working. Whether he was home, at a restaurant, shopping, or at the club, the Judge wore a similar outfit: a light button-down collared shirt, khaki pants, and the traditional navy sports blazer. Brown Italian shoes were his norm, and he always wore a Rolex. Judge Craven stood out from the others in the club, but that was the point.

"Judge, if you would like to follow me, your table is ready," the assistant manager said nervously, nearly out of breath.

Craven looked at his watch, and his lips turned down slightly. "Thank you. I was beginning to worry my table may not be available for me this evening."

"My apologies for your wait, sir. I have a glass of bourbon waiting at your table."

"Excellent. I have almost always appreciated your efficiency and care. In fact, why don't you stop by my table in forty-five minutes. I have a new friend I would like you to meet. Her name is Emily. I would like every courtesy shown her."

"Of course, Judge. I would be privileged."

* * * * *

The lightness of Emily's silk dress wisped gently above her knees as she sauntered across the room. Judge Craven picked up his bourbon, preparing to take a seat at his table when Emily walked by. She looked at the Judge deliberately as she approached, pausing slightly with a pleasant smile while she made eye contact. Craven watched her closely. As she passed, she slowed even more, turning her body subtly and glancing back in his direction. He inspected her with great interest, and she continued on her way to climb the large, circular staircase to the wide catwalks encircling the room overhead.

High above, Emily positioned herself where she had a clear view of the Judge, and more important, where he could observe her. Even in dim lighting with the occasional strobe, her presence was unmatched. In her classy pale yellow dress and simple accessories, Emily stood out like a full moon on a clear dark night. While the vast crowd simply faded into the darkness, she illuminated the Judge's view.

After spending an acceptable amount of time on the catwalk, Emily made her descent, hoping her prey would take the bait.

"You're doing great, Mathews. Keep working it," she could hear Stark's monotone in her earpiece.

The Judge watched as she moved effortlessly in his direction, but despite his leering eyes, he did not appear ready to make his move.

"Hold on, Mathews . . . slow down a little. We want this fish to bite. You've got to sell it," Stark reminded.

From the corner of her eye, Emily could see a small man moving quickly in her direction. As he came near, she stepped casually into his lane of travel, bumping her shoulder into him, knocking him off stride. The unsuspecting man's drink crashed to the floor along with Emily's purse.

Bending down, Emily reached to the floor to retrieve her purse. She looked up to the man who was still standing there, stunned. "I'm so sorry. I'm such a klutz. Are you all right?" she asked with feigned concern.

The small man appeared to be embarrassed at nearly being knocked over by a petite woman. "Yeah, I'm fine. But you might want to watch where you're going next time," he said.

Judge Craven approached Emily from behind. "Miss, that was quite a collision. I am sure our diminutive friend here will be all right. How are you?"

"Oh, I'm fine. But it looks like I have whatever he was drinking all over my shoes and purse. One of the hazards of nightlife, I suppose? Thank you for your concern," she said as she arose, smiling sweetly. "I'd better get my things cleaned up."

"Please. Join me at my table, and I will take care of your things."

"Are you a mobile dry cleaner?" she asked with a wry grin.

"No, just a man who knows there are better things to attend to than cleaning up messes. I suggest you concentrate on having a good time, and we will find someone to help take care of this little mishap. You will be my guest. I am sitting right over here," he said, motioning toward his table.

Emily paused, taking in the Judge's unusual manner of speech, but then accepted his outstretched hand and walked with him toward his table. "Your guest, huh? I'd love to. You know, I've been watching you. I must say, you seem different than the other men here, more sophisticated, more . . . complicated."

"You are observant in your flattery. Please, my name is John."

"It's nice to meet you John. I'm—"

Before Emily could say her name, the Judge began speaking, seemingly uninterested in her introduction. "I say 'my guest' because I spend a good deal of time here at the club. I feel comfortable here. Sure, I am a little different from the others, but it's boring to be like everyone else. This is a place where I feel I can stand out. It is a diversion for me, a way to unwind from my daily duties and concerns." Craven raised his hand high, motioning to a server.

"Yes, Judge?"

"My friend has had a little mishap. I am hoping you can help us. A careless man nearly knocked her over and spilled his drink on her purse and shoes. Would you please have them cleaned for us and bring some slippers for her to wear?"

The server looked perplexed, not sure where she would find slippers, let alone how she would have the shoes and purse cleaned, but she knew the wisdom in giving the Judge whatever he asked for. "Of course, sir.

I'll be back shortly with the slippers and to collect her things to be cleaned."

"Oh, wait just a moment. Would you also bring my guest a glass of white wine? An elegant drink for an elegant woman."

"Yes, sir. Right away."

"Thank you, dear. You are very gracious." Judge Craven dismissed the server and returned his gaze to Emily. "Here, let me help you." Moving next to Emily's seat, he bent over and put one knee on the ground. Emily focused her mind, determined not to betray her nerves with a flinch. He lifted her leg with one hand, gently holding her calf and ankle. With the other hand, he removed her high heel. He slowly repeated the process with the other shoe, caressing her lower leg.

"You're quite the gentleman. It's been a long time since I've encountered someone as, as, *gallant* as you," Emily complimented. "So, you're a judge?"

"Yes, but that is boring. We can talk about that later. I would like to talk about you. Tell me about where you are from, your family, your occupation. I have only two requests: I don't want to know your name, and I want you to be completely honest with me—none of this storytelling, trying to impress one another. We are who we are, and we should be honest with each other. Do you agree?"

"I do. Games are tedious." Emily began to recite the cover story she had practiced with Detective Cross, telling in detail of her phantom family living in Nebraska. She had just begun discussing her management job when the server returned, holding plain white slippers and a glass of white wine. Placing the wine glass on the table in front of Emily, the server exchanged the slippers for the shoes and purse.

"Thank you, dear. I'm very impressed with your speed in accomplishing such an unusual task. I'll be sure to mention it to your supervisor."

"Thank you, Judge." The server nodded and departed.

Holding the slippers in his hand, Judge Craven assumed his previous position, one knee on the floor next to Emily. He placed the slippers on her feet and again gently massaged her lower legs. Emily remained still, biting the inside of her lip. She was pleased with her ability to keep her gag reflex in check.

Judge Craven was an odd man. Sure, he was creepy and arrogant, but it was as though he had to constantly prove how special and powerful he was. He spoke formally, but his extreme clarity appeared to be with great effort, and his rare use of contractions seemed contrived. Emily had been around snobs many times, and the disdain rolled off their tongues naturally. Judge Craven's condescension, although pervasive, was forced and seemed to require deliberate calculation. Perhaps he simply enjoyed feeling superior, and like a sadist, reveled in the discomfort he caused in others.

Emily tried forcing herself to smile at the Judge, but her lips deformed with disgust. His odd manner, combined with his calculating mind and malicious abuse of power, was intimidating.

After caressing Emily's lower leg, Judge Craven stood up, leaned in front of her, and softly kissed her on the cheek. With Emily's eyes distracted by his close proximity, Judge Craven picked up the glass of wine, poured it onto Emily's dress, and then knocked the glass over on the table, making it appear to be an accident. The placement of the Judge's spill was perfect. The liquid landed directly on the small transmitter hidden in the sash around Emily's waist.

Harsh static crackled in Thrasher's headphones. "Whoa, Mathews. We have a problem. We lost sound. I can't hear you," he said anxiously. Emily swallowed hard but remained composed.

"Mathews, nod if you can hear me," Thrasher said. Emily nodded subtly, still trying to concentrate on the Judge. "Okay, I can't hear you but we still have eyes. Touch your ear if you're fine to continue." Emily's hand shook as she slowly reached up and touched her earring.

"I apologize for my clumsiness. Please forgive me," the Judge pleaded. He passed two extra cloth napkins for Emily to dry her dress.

"Trust me, I know how accidents can happen. This just isn't my night."

"No, it does not seem to be." Judge Craven sat in silence for a moment, grinning as he continued to watch Emily dab at her dress.

"Hello, Judge. I see your guest has arrived," the assistant manager said, standing next to the table.

"Marcus. Thank you for stopping by."

"Emily, it's a pleasure to meet you. You look lovely tonight. I'm the assistant manager here, so please let me know if there is anything you need, anything at all."

Emily's head snapped up. The perpetual dabbing motion with the napkin stopped. *How did he know my name?* she wondered. She sat in silence, her mouth open slightly, looking to the assistant manager and then at the Judge.

"Thank you, Marcus. I will let you know if we need anything further." Judge Craven stared coldly at Emily while Marcus walked away. Emily sat in stunned silence, her mind racing, evaluating the gravity of her situation. She opened her mouth as if preparing to speak but nothing came out.

"Emily, you are exquisite. Since we will be working closely together, your loveliness will be a much appreciated perk." Judge Craven's glare intensified. "But I am disappointed. You have not been honest with me, have you? Maybe now we can speak candidly."

Emily's heart raced as she watched the Judge with dumbfounded alarm.

Judge Craven smiled broadly. "Keep smiling," he reminded Emily. "Your associates may not be able to hear, but they can still see us. Believe me, you do not want them to be suspicious. If you do your part, they will remain safe in the van down the street and in the car at the rear of the building. Please, act like everything is going according to your original plan."

Emily's eyes narrowed. Was she feeling fear or merely contempt? The plastered smile on her face was not persuasive, but the Judge seemed to appreciate the effort.

"Listen closely, and I will explain how this will work. All you need to do is listen and look like you are having a pleasant conversation. Surely you can accomplish this simple feat."

Emily nodded. "What do you want from me? You must know I won't help you, whatever it is."

"You do not listen well, do you? This deficit must be a real challenge for you at the FBI. For your sake, I hope your skill improves dramatically. Now be quiet," he said firmly. "When you leave here, you will report to your friends that you were able to make a real connection with me despite the unfortunate accident with your transmitter. You will tell them we have another casual date here, Tuesday evening. I would have liked to meet again sooner, but unfortunately your team acted more quickly than I expected, and I have a meeting I must attend tomorrow.

Yes, Tuesday at 7:00 will do fine. When we meet, I will buy dinner, and we will have a pleasant conversation. You will flirt with me convincingly, and I will return the sentiment. I will then drop hints for your friends, which will aid your investigation. Are we clear so far?"

"What? No. That makes no sense," Emily said, her mind swirling with panic.

Judge Craven stared at her coldly.

Emily gasped for air as though all the oxygen in the room had just been sucked out. Her head shook with confusion. "I don't understand what you want."

"Let me explain it this way, so it is simple to understand," the Judge said, before pausing in contemplation. "All I am asking you to do is meet with me again, which you already plan to do. I am also offering to provide you with the information you hope to gain. Of course, I have my own reasons for doing this, but I do not plan on explaining them to you at this point. I am not asking you to do anything immoral or illegal. I am simply asking you to follow your own plan. Just understand that if you fail to follow through, or if you discuss this conversation with anyone, you will pay a heavy price."

The Judge sipped slowly from his bourbon. "You may wonder what this 'heavy price' is. I have already mentioned the safety of your team and that threat continues. But if that does not properly motivate you, maybe I can find something that will. For example, it would be unfortunate if something happened to your new boyfriend. I also have a local address for your parents' home and your married sister and her kids. Unfortunately for them, they do not really live in Nebraska, do they? I imagine the loss of any, or all of these individuals, would be painful to you. Think about it. You risk losing what is most important to you, or you can allow me to make you look good at work. The choice seems simple to me."

Blood rushed to Emily's head, causing her temples to pulse with fear and anger. She imagined climbing across the table to yank out his perfect hair by the fistful, but she controlled herself. "So you're saying," she started, her chest heaving with deep breaths, "that after you give me the information I need to build my case against you, we will be done with each other? Through?" Emily asked skeptically.

"I never said that. Consider the period between now and Tuesday as more of a test. However, I am sincere when I say that going forward, I intend to be a great source of information for you in many future investigations. I am offering my knowledge and connections. You know I am dirty, but big deal. Do you think I am the biggest fish you will ever go after? If I am, you are a failure, and you may as well quit now."

The two rivals stared each other down like poker players searching desperately for a tell, but neither flinched. The Judge raised his hand and a server quickly appeared at the table. "Would you please check on Emily's shoes and purse? She is preparing to leave."

Within moments the server returned, and Emily quickly stepped into her clean shoes and clung to the purse like a child's safety blanket.

"Emily, you are a lovely woman, and I understand your apprehension. This evening could not have met your expectations in any way, but you must listen to me. Be careful and do as I say. Your life and the lives of those you love depend on you. You may leave now."

Stunned at the Judge's sudden dismissal, Emily stood abruptly. Slowing her escape, Judge Craven grabbed her by the shoulders and kissed her squarely on the lips. He held her close, both hands behind her waist. "Please remember, I knew you were coming tonight, I knew where your radio transmitter was hidden, I knew where your partners were staked out, I know where your loved ones live, and I will know if you say or do anything contrary to my instructions. You will be tempted to trust a coworker or a friend, but before you do, ask yourself how I know. Until Tuesday." Judge Craven released his hold and gracefully motioned toward the door with his upturned hand.

Emily's adrenaline was pumping. She was ready for a fight but didn't know where to direct her anger. The Judge, obviously, but who else? Stark? The rest of her team? She exited the room hastily and didn't look back.

ELEVEN

THE VAN CARRYING THRASHER, STARK, and Mathews rode smoothly through the downtown streets of Kansas City with Detective Cross trailing closely behind. It was well after midnight, but the streets were still active with weekend excitement. Stark was speaking, but Emily didn't seem to notice or care, and Thrasher was quiet as usual. Emily sat silently in the front passenger side seat, her heart still racing. Deep in thought, she considered her next move before the Field Office debrief. Emily repeated Judge Craven's words in her mind.

I knew you were coming tonight. . . . How did he know?

She focused on what he said last and repeated it silently to herself. *How did he know? How did he know?* she wondered.

Emily glanced to the back of the van where Thrasher was sitting on a jump seat, his head back and his eyes closed. She then looked to Stark. Stark's lips were still moving, but the sound failed to penetrate Emily's ears.

Reflecting on the evening's operation, Emily considered the possible involvement of her team. *Could everyone be involved with Craven?* It seemed unlikely. Or maybe just one member was involved. Stark certainly had an ax to grind and seemed generally underwhelmed with moral fortitude. Thrasher had placed the transmitter in her sash. Had anyone else seen where he placed it? Cross was from outside the Bureau. Was that a plus or a minus? Or maybe the leak went far beyond her team. Could ASAC Murphy be involved? Or maybe it was just a random FBI agent with security access.

The questions swirled in her mind, making the back of her eyes throb and her stomach feel queasy.

Who can I really trust? she wondered silently.

* * * * *

The hotel bed was comfortable, but it was not his own. Rolling heavily onto his side, Paul peeked through his nearly closed eyes, hoping to see the time on the clock near his bed. He was pleased to see it was only 3:30 a.m. There was still plenty of time to rest before his long weekend of work. As his head sank into the long pillow, he quickly began to drift out of consciousness when the phone rang. Realizing the phone had been attempting to rouse him, he fumbled toward the nightstand, seeking the blue glow from his pulsing phone. Answering, the only greeting he was able to manage was, "Yeah," in a gravely bass tone.

"You know who this is. Please call me back at this number right away, and use the hotel phone." The phone went dead in his hand.

Paul sat at the edge of his bed, surprised, but mostly asleep. He stared wearily at the phone, unable to recognize the number, but the voice was familiar. Standing, Paul turned the small knob on his bedside lamp, casting a yellow light across the room. "Emily?"

Blinking his eyes rapidly, Paul contemplated the brief call and Emily's unusual earnestness. Accessing the recently received calls, he retrieved the phone number from the screen. Following Emily's instructions, he dialed the number using the hotel room phone.

"Emily, what's going on?" he asked, the gravel nearly absent from his voice.

"I'm sorry, but I don't think your cell phone is safe. I don't know if the hotel phone is being monitored or not, but can you get a clean phone?"

"Yeah, sure, give me about a half an hour."

"Good, I need to talk to someone I can trust. Please be quick, and call me at this new number."

Paul reached frantically for a pen and paper from his hotel room desk and jotted the number as it was recited.

"Emily, just tell me if . . ."

The phone went dead.

Paul quickly pulled on his jeans, a long sleeved T-shirt, and his shoes. He grabbed his wallet and keys from the nightstand, bolted into the well-lit hallway, and made his way down to the sub-level parking garage.

Climbing into the black FBI-issued sedan, he left the parking spot, squealing the tires, and raced around the corner, bouncing forcefully up the ramp toward the street level exit. "What are you into, Emily?" he mumbled to himself as the car burst onto the deserted street.

* * * * *

The engine was off and the chill from the outside air was seeping gradually into the vehicle through the console vents; an ominous haze began to creep around the bottom of her vehicle. Slightly reclined, but with eyes opened wide, Emily sat in her red Nissan, waiting eagerly for Paul's call. She answered instantly when the phone rang.

"Paul, thank you. I'm sorry for the cloak and dagger routine, but I don't know what to do. I'm in trouble. I'm not really sure what you can do to help, but I need to talk to someone I can trust." Emily spoke rapidly, barely breathing as she raced through her introduction.

"Whoa, hold on, Emily. Try to relax a little. First, tell me, are you hurt?"

"No, I'm fine."

"Okay, good. Where are you?"

Slightly annoyed by Paul's questions, she continued to speak at her frantic pace. "I'm sitting in my car in a Walmart parking lot. The lot is virtually empty, and I'm positioned so I can see anyone that comes or goes."

"Slow down. Are you in danger? Is someone after you?"

"No, I don't think so. I don't know. I'm fine. I'm fine for now."

"Good, now take a couple of deep breaths, and try to calm down just a little. I want to understand what's going on. Can you tell me what happened that's upsetting you?"

"I probably shouldn't, but I'm going to tell you anyway, unless you tell me to stop. You need to understand, telling you may be putting you in danger. I'm sorry, but I don't know who else I can talk to."

"Emily, don't worry. I'll risk it. Please, tell me slowly."

Beginning with the night's events that were most fresh in her mind, Emily shared the details of her alarming encounter with Judge Craven.

Paul simply listened. Backtracking to the day she received her assignment, Emily described her relationship with each member of her team, raising the possibility of involvement with Judge Craven.

Paul attempted to keep his voice calm and even, analytical not emotional. "Now, do you believe the Judge is truly able and willing to follow through on his threats, or is there a chance he's just trying to scare you?"

"No way he's bluffing. He is absolutely capable. Sure, he's creepy and weird, but there is something more to him. I don't know how to describe it exactly. He's not like anyone I've ever known. I'm not trying to be dramatic, but he's frightening. He's motivated, driven. I believe every word he said."

"Okay. Where do you think he's getting his information? What's your gut reaction?" Paul asked.

"Honestly, I don't know. Based on his operational knowledge, a member of my team would be the obvious suspect, but I just don't see it. Stark is definitely a jerk, but I don't think he has the capacity to pull off something like that. Thrasher, well, he just seems really dedicated to his work, and Cross? We brought him in. He's not even FBI, and he's been protecting me from Stark since day one. There must be someone else."

"So, where does that leave us?"

"I guess it leaves us with a crazy judge who has an inside man. The guy even knew I started dating you. He knows where you live. Whoever it is, he does his homework."

"All right, we have to assume that everything you do or say will be noticed. Maybe we can use that against them," Paul suggested. "But for now, I think you're playing this the way you should. You said exactly what the Judge told you to say in your debrief, so if the leak is a team member, or a superior, you're protected."

"There may be a lapse in his info, though. When he threatened you and mentioned where you live, he thought you were vulnerable—still in Kansas City. Maybe there's a delay in his information. He had no idea you were sent to Oklahoma today. Then again, neither did I until I called the apartment looking for you."

"If there's a lag in his info, maybe we can exploit that," Paul said. "So, you called the apartment? I bet Jimmy appreciated the late night call. I guess you didn't get my message."

"No, sorry. I listened to my messages after I spoke to Jimmy, but he filled me in on what was going on with you. Congratulations, by the way."

"Yeah, thanks. But I wish I were in Kansas City with you. I'm worried about you. What are you planning to do? Where will you stay? You can't sleep in the Walmart parking lot every night."

Emily sat quietly, contemplating the question. She had wondered the same thing. "Well, after talking this through with you, I think I'm probably pretty safe. After all, I'm part of the Judge's plan. I doubt he would do anything to threaten that. But still, it would feel strange staying in my apartment. I'd feel like I was being watched or listened to the whole time. I'm actually thinking of getting a hotel room for a few days."

"You know, it may be a little weird, and it's definitely not the ideal, but you could stay at my place in my room while I'm gone. My security system is probably better than a hotel. You can even lock the bedroom door to protect yourself from Jimmy," Paul said, an obvious smile behind his voice. "I even have clean sheets in the closet, but it's up to you. If you feel comfortable with it, I'll set it up. If you're being watched, they probably won't think twice about you spending a few nights at my place, no offense. They just don't know the kind of woman you are."

Paul squinted, lightly rubbing his tired eyes as the first sliver of daylight blinded him through his rearview mirror.

"I don't know. I doubt the bishop would approve," she said with an uncomfortable laugh.

Paul was happy to see she was getting her sense of humor back. "No, probably not, but then, you really couldn't tell him the reason for it, could you? But this is a matter of safety. Any place you go, you may put others at risk. This way we only risk Jimmy. I can live with that," he said with a laugh.

"I know—you're right. Jimmy and I get along well, so I don't think he'll mind. But it is ironic."

"How do you mean?"

"Moving into an apartment with a man as I take him back to church for the first time in years."

Paul laughed. "Well, maybe. Good luck getting him back to church though. I already tried to talk with him about it and failed miserably."

"Don't be so sure. You may have more influence than either one of you would like to admit. He told me about your missionary moment from the other night. I've already asked him about church, and he agreed to come. You kind of warmed him up, and then I moved in for the kill. You know, kind of a bad cop/good cop routine."

Paul was stunned. "I'm impressed. I'll be even more impressed if he actually does it."

"Well, if he doesn't, I'll pound on his door until he changes his mind."

Paul laughed appreciatively. "You know, it's probably cheesy, but aside from the fact that I have to be to work in a couple of hours, and my back is hurting from reclining in my car, I wouldn't have wanted to spend my time any other way. I'm glad you called."

Emily's voice suddenly choked. "Thank you, Paul. You're a true friend. You've helped me more than you know."

Paul smiled widely. "Now you get over to the apartment and get some rest. I'll let Jimmy know you're coming. Remember, there's nothing you can do for the next couple of days, so there's no need to worry. Relax. Things are seldom as bad as we think."

"Good night, Paul. Thanks again."

* * * * *

Hanging up the phone, Paul's eyes narrowed and his lips tightened as he reflected on their conversation. Emily was in real trouble. Worse, there was nothing he could do to help.

TWELVE

THE BEEFY CHICAGO NATIVE REMAINED still, his white knuckles at ten and two on the steering wheel of the motionless Cadillac Escalade and his gaze fixed in front of him where the elevated Missouri River should be. Sunrise was near. Just yesterday, the weather had topped out north of seventy degrees, but the late night temperature had plunged under forty. Already, it was evident the day would heat up again; a muggy smell dominated the riverside air. Clouds seemed to seep from the ground, casting a further veil of shadow on the already gloomy morning.

The sun peeked out from the horizon across the river, but the dense fog would not allow the early rays to penetrate. Gordy surveyed his surroundings, wondering how quickly the fog would burn off but not holding his breath that it would be any time soon.

Parked on the soft dirt frontage road just south of an abandoned glove factory, Gordy glanced repeatedly at his diver's watch. He was certainly no diver—never been once in his life—but the oversized timepiece was manly and tough.

Despite being born and raised in Chicago, Gordon Harrison considered himself a true Kansas City'an. He even liked the Royals, a genuine test of loyalty for an unwavering baseball fan. Gordy had spent the last forty years proving himself within the syndicate, working at all levels within the organization with great success. For the past ten years, he was cochair of the syndicate, directing its enterprises with his trusted partner.

Gordy was a simple man. He drove a nice vehicle and lived in a comfortable home, but he lived far below his capability, content with the few luxuries he indulged in. Instead of acquiring possessions, he was motivated by success and power.

He remained surprisingly fit for his advancing age, but was average in most other ways—his height, his manner of speech, his dress—and except for his diabetes, he was in reasonable health. A tattered ball cap sheltered his thin white hair, and a plain navy blue jogging suit covered his broad body. He waited in his Cadillac, his fingers tapping the wheel incessantly.

The meeting had been called abruptly. Details of the syndicate's operations were leaking out, and although fear of an excruciating death would keep most mouths shut, it was always dangerous when the police pinched knowledgeable associates.

From his left, Gordy saw a flash of light, which disappeared again in the dense fog. He watched vigilantly, and then, as expected, the headlights reappeared as they approached slowly, mere yards from where his vehicle was parked. Cloaked in fog and darkness, Gordy turned a knob, flashing his brights twice. Immediately after the second vehicle stopped, a third emerged, flashed its lights briefly, and then parked to his right, creating a triangle. One man emerged from each vehicle and stood at the front, lights shining from behind.

"Gordy, it is good to see you. It has been a while, has it not?" one of the men said loudly, as if worried the fog would dampen the sound. The man stood erect, poised. Looking down at his fashionable Italians, he was disappointed that they were being dirtied by . . . dirt.

"Yes, it has. With all due respect, this is a meeting for the partners. What are you doing here?" Gordy asked.

"I invited him," the third man said. "I thought that given his expertise, he might be particularly helpful with this discussion."

"Fine, you called this meeting. Let's get on with it!"

Gordy's partner was significantly younger than he and had a long career in front of him. While Gordy seemed to concentrate on the substance of administrative planning and action, his partner was more focused on the glamour and horror of organized crime. Together, they proved a winning team, one complementing the other. While Gordy was "organized," strategically looking forward with ambition, his partner provided the hard "crime," reigning in the syndicate with fear and order. It was unclear if they were blood relations, but they were family, nonetheless.

"As you say, Gordy. Let's get on with this. We've got a real problem. The police have a source in our organization, and it's hurting us. It's time to put an end to it, and I'm prepared to do whatever it takes."

"Good. What *are* we doing about it?" Gordy asked.

"Our associate has brought some interesting facts to my attention. You see, regardless of the particular enterprise, or the employees involved, every damaging leak in the last six months has had one thing in common. You!"

"What?"

"Besides me, you're the only one with access to the details in every case. You are the problem, Gordy," his partner accused coldly. "I always thought you were too smart for your own good, but I never expected you to run an endgame around me, trying to force me out. I thought we had a good partnership going here." The man paused. "I can't tell you how disappointed I am, Gordy."

Gordy's breathing was heavy but quick. "What in the world are you talking about? Have you gone crazy?"

The partner didn't respond.

"I'm not pushing you out. Whatever this pompous clown is telling you is meant for his own benefit. He's obviously the one playing you. Can't you see it? I have always been loyal to you *and* the syndicate. I brought you in. You owe your station to me. I got you here, not him. Who are you going to trust? This guy?" he said derisively. "It's a simple question, partner."

The third man stood quietly, his head lowered, both to examine the dirt on his beloved shoes as well as to hide his sizeable grin.

"You're right, Gordy. It's a simple question. Unfortunately for you, it has a painful answer," his partner said. Turning back toward his SUV, he gave the dreaded nod. Three large men dressed entirely in black emerged from the rear doors. One held a sawed-off shotgun at his side. The others were unarmed.

As Gordy saw the men cut slowly through the fog, he instinctively backed up, knocking hard into the front grill of his Escalade. Like a pinball, he bounced off the grill, turned, and lunged toward the driver side door. Before he was able to pull the handle, the first man in black placed a heavy hand on his shoulder.

"Cousin, what're you doing? Let's talk about this," Gordy pleaded.

"I'm sorry it has to be this way, Gordy. Really, I am," he said, slowly turning away.

With another nod to his henchmen, the partner ordered Gordy's murder. Two large men forced Gordy's arms behind him, while the other slammed the shotgun stock against the front of his head. Gordy went limp, collapsing into the arms of his attackers.

The partner approached his other associate, who was still staring at the ground. "I'll meet you later as planned," he said. Climbing into the front passenger side of the SUV, he waited for the gruesome deed to be done.

Judge Craven climbed into his own dark sedan with pure satisfaction on his face. His plan, along with Gordy Harrison, was being executed perfectly.

* * * * *

"Jimmy? Are you in there?" Emily hollered through the front door of Paul's apartment. She beat loudly with the side of her closed fist. Waiting for a response, her head sagged, and her eyes closed for a moment, but then she began beating again. "Hello? Jimmy! Ugh, forget it." Moving toward the elevator, Emily stopped when she heard the apartment door open.

Jimmy's head peeked carefully around the corner of the opened door. He had classic bed head and appeared to be shirtless. Emily hoped he was wearing pants but couldn't be sure. "Emily, what are you doing here?" he asked, rubbing his eyes.

"Paul was supposed to call you to let you know I was on my way. I guess he didn't get a hold of you."

"I heard the phone ring a couple of times, but I usually let the machine get it. I mean, it's not even my place, you know? But I'm up now, so what do you need?" he asked, attempting to smile, his eyes half open. Despite his effort, the sleepy welcome lacked authenticity.

"Well, I wish you had talked to Paul," she said. Considering an appropriate course of action, Emily maintained her position down the hallway near the elevator, only occasionally glancing toward Jimmy.

"Sorry I woke you up." She shifted toward the elevator and then paused, before turning again to Jimmy. "Look, I'm really tired. I've been working all night, and I need a place to crash for a little bit. Would you mind?"

"No, no, not at all. Come on in. Is something wrong at your place?"

"No, I just need to stay out for a while. Set off a bug bomb. You know how it is," Emily explained, walking toward the opened door. Jimmy stepped out slightly, proving he was dressed from the waist down. Emily's eyes bulged and she caught herself staring at Jimmy's chest. She averted her gaze to a point on the wall behind him. His upper body was surprisingly chiseled. Emily was thankful he was at least wearing long flannel pajama pants.

"Well, are you coming in?"

"Uh, I'll just wait here for a moment while you finish getting dressed," she said, hoping her blushing cheeks did not betray her.

"Oh, yeah. Just a sec." Jimmy ran to his room, quickly pulled on the previous day's T-shirt, and appeared once again at the door. "Sorry about that. You can come in now."

"Jimmy, if you don't mind, I'm just going to lay down for a while and take a quick nap on the couch."

"Sounds good. Make yourself comfortable. I'm going to go back to bed myself. Sweet dreams." Returning to his own room, Jimmy plopped onto the bed, his head sinking into the pillow. His eyes closed, and he quickly fell back to sleep.

Laying her head on the stuffed armrest of the couch, Emily curled up and closed her eyes. Although her body was shutting down, eager to renew, her mind was not. The same tired thoughts irritated her mind, keeping her from rest. Sitting up slowly, she warmed the goose bumps on her arms with her hands and then stood with a sigh.

Strolling to the window, Emily pulled the blinds closed, darkening the room instantly. Then, wandering into Paul's room, she noticed what appeared to be an antique alarm clock. It was scratched and dented, and the glass face was missing. "Hmm, interesting piece."

Emily's eyes shifted from side to side. She felt like a snoop. Opening Paul's twin closet doors, she found a stack of fresh linens, including a thick flannel comforter. Grabbing the blanket and a pillow from his bed, Emily returned to her location on the cold leather couch.

Wrapping herself in the blanket like a cocoon, she laid her head gently down. She focused her thoughts on the warmth of the blanket and the darkness of the room, enjoying the slight hint of Paul's cologne on the pillow. Expelling all other thoughts from her mind, she was sleeping peacefully within moments.

* * * * *

Awaking with a start, Emily bolted upright on the couch, the comforter still wrapped safely around her. For a moment she had forgotten where she was. She stood gingerly, dropping the comforter to the floor around her feet, arching her back and stretching both hands high above her head. She rotated her body and stretched her feet, standing temporarily on the tips of her toes. As she turned toward the kitchen, she saw Jimmy smiling at his usual place near the stove, preparing some fresh ingredients. "Oh, hi, Jimmy," she said, with an embarrassed grin.

"It's good to see you back in the land of the living. You feeling better?"

Her smile was full. "I feel great. What time is it?"

"Well, my dear, it's nearly 5:00 p.m. You've been out for a while. Hungry?"

"Starving. What are you making?" she asked, trying to view the ingredients on the cupboard from her place behind the couch.

"Pizza, an American classic. And you woke up just in time. Now you can choose the toppings for your own personalized pie. I've got pepperoni, sausage, mushrooms, green peppers, onions, black olives, and my absolute favorite, pineapple."

"No cheese?" she asked incredulously.

"Well, of course cheese. That just goes without saying. It also has dough and tomato sauce. I might even brush a little egg yolk on the crust for color," Jimmy said, insulting her question.

"It sounds good, but I'm not sure about the pineapple. Maybe I can try a piece of yours." Emily's eyes were bright and her smile ready. She strode to the counter and began placing ingredients onto her pizza. "Fresh pizza dough, impressive," she said with raised eyebrows. Jimmy and Emily stood side-by-side assembling their pizzas, each deliberately placing their toppings.

"I spoke to Paul while you were sleeping. He told me you'd be staying here for a few days while some water damage is being repaired at your place. Something about a leak?" Jimmy paused, looking for a response or at least a reaction. "He didn't say anything about fumigation."

Emily continued to assemble her pizza, pretending the comment was too insignificant to warrant a response. "So how long will they take to bake? I'm ready to scarf it down right now." She pinched an olive, a piece of pepperoni, and a small amount of cheese, stuffing it quickly into her mouth.

"Whoa, hold on there. It'll only be about twelve minutes, and there will be plenty of leftovers for later on."

"Actually, I won't be staying another night after all," she said with a matter-of-fact tone. "But I appreciate the offer, and being able to take a quick nap—"

"Quick nap? That was more of a hibernation."

Emily laughed and stuck another olive in her mouth. "I think I'm going to get a hotel room. It just feels a little strange, you know? It doesn't seem right staying alone in an apartment together. It's too compromising. I wouldn't want anybody to get the wrong idea about you."

Jimmy smiled as he watched her closely. She was beautiful even when she lied.

THIRTEEN

LIGHTNING CRACKED AND RAIN POUNDED against the window. Jimmy loved the ferocity of a good lightning storm. Back in college, a major tempest had raged through town while he was golfing. The course was cleared and golfers returned to the clubhouse to wait out the weather; after all, holding a shaft of metal high above your head in a lightening storm is not the pillar of intelligence. Jimmy smirked at his foolishness in playing out the remaining six holes. He smiled at the thought, knowing well he would do it again.

Within the course of the day, the temperature had ranged from thirty-eight to sixty-seven degrees and fluctuated from intense fog with no visibility to clear warm sunshine, to blustery winds, cold, hard rain, thunder, and lightning. The only thing predictable about the weather in Kansas City is that it's unpredictable. With no mountains to shield the region, the energy generated from competing wind currents was responsible for the famous Midwest tornados and damaging straight-line winds.

Just before dusk, the first menacing thunderclouds rolled over the city. The Doppler radar showed an intense line of storms, which seemed to be unending, stretching from Texarkana through the KC metro area. Warm, thick rain slanted almost sideways into the window-pane as Jimmy and Emily sat at the small kitchen table. The TV was on, but they were barely paying attention, only occasionally looking up between rolls of the dice for a weather update. To Emily it felt like they were weathering a hurricane on the Gulf Coast with the sounds of rain and thunder punctuated by the occasional flicker of the interior lighting.

After the first power outage, shortly following their feast of personalized pizzas, Jimmy had rummaged through some cupboards and found two flashlights and fresh batteries. The lights flickered again, and then once more before they cut out entirely. Emily smiled as she sat blindly in the darkened room. Then, a distant flash of blue light illuminated her face. The gentle rattle of dice hitting the table in a controlled roll was the only sound when it hit. Two seconds after the lightning flash, the windows clattered and the entire building seemed to moan at the percussion. Taking advantage of the darkness and the loud distraction, Emily waited for the thunder to subside before sweetly calling out, "Yahtzee!"

"Whatever! You should be ashamed of cheating the way you do," Jimmy protested amiably. He clicked on his heavy Maglight and pointed it to the table, but Emily had already collected the dice, removing any possibility for the verification of her suspicious roll.

Emily held a flashlight under her chin, her expression intense like a storyteller at a campfire. "What do you mean? I can't believe you would accuse me of cheating. Jimmy, that really hurts." Unclear whether she was honestly offended or merely playing him for effect, Jimmy wondered how he should respond. Mercifully, before he could embarrass himself by speaking, Emily's face broke into a schoolgirl grin. He joined happily in the joke. The dormant lights overhead flickered briefly as a precursor to the permanent restoration of electrical power. The lights again brightened the table, ruining the intimate ambiance of the room.

"You know, you have a pretty good poker face—or should I say Yahtzee face? You're hard to read sometimes. I haven't quite figured you out yet," Jimmy commented, partly in complaint, partly as a compliment.

"Thank you, sir. I try. But you know, you're a little bit of a mystery yourself. You put on a bit of an act, smiling and underachieving, but that's not who you really are. I'm on to you."

Jimmy cocked his head, placed his clasped hands on the table, and looked Emily directly in the eyes. "Okay then, who am I?" he challenged.

"I think you're a man with great potential and possibility, but you're also someone who has been broken."

"I'm broken? Time for the trash heap."

"I don't mean broken, like a bicycle's broken and won't work. I mean *broken*, like how a wild mustang's will, or fight, is broken. A part of you has been beaten down, and somehow you've been trained to give up. If there's a chance you may fail, why bother making the effort?" Emily matched Jimmy's earnest stare, refusing to blink. "So how far off base am I?"

Jimmy lowered his eyes. "Maybe I'll start calling you Doc. Should I lie down on the couch and tell you about my mother?"

"See, that's another thing. I made an observation that you found uncomfortable, so you brushed it aside with a smile or a joke. That tells me I must be closer to the truth than you'd like. Maybe you feel embarrassed or guilty about something, or maybe you're just not comfortable with me."

"No, come on. I feel more at ease with you than I can remember feeling with anyone in a really long time. But think of the moment in your life you're most ashamed of. Sure, you're a good person, but everyone has something they're not proud of. How excited are you to talk about it? Even with friends and family, I doubt you lead off your conversations talking about your most shameful moments."

"Well, you're right about that. You saw one of my unflattering moments the other night at the bar. But we talked about it, and I can move on. It's not going to cripple me."

"Unflattering? That dress with the . . . the—it was definitely flattering," Jimmy wisecracked as he attempted to keep his hands from motioning inappropriately.

"Funny. I agree, most people aren't interested in baring their soul or airing their dirty laundry to just anyone. We don't want to burden others with our failings. Besides, we want people to like us. If everyone knew all the rotten, mean, thoughtless things I've done in my life, I don't know how many friends I'd have."

"Exactly."

"Then again, if I never share my fears and worries or my hopes and dreams with anyone, I probably won't have many close relationships either. In other words, it's possible to share too much, but I can also share too little."

"I'm just not convinced. Is there really a benefit in dragging someone else down into my depressing little world?" Jimmy challenged.

"Look, I'm not saying you need to talk about it with me. It just seems that talking with someone may help you work things out in your own mind. I'm a friend, so if you want to talk, I'm here. If you don't, that's fine too. But if you're like me, things usually seem better after I talk them through. I seem to gain more perspective."

Shifting uncomfortably in his chair, partly due to the topic of conversation and partly due to the hardness of the wooden seat, Jimmy thought carefully. "I guess I don't even know what to say. Do I start talking about my family life when I was three? Or how I didn't get the bike I wanted for Christmas when I was ten? Should I start with a family tragedy or an embarrassing moment from high school? I'm not trying to be difficult. I just don't think any of those things caused me to be who I am today."

Emily moved her chair back gently, stood, and moved toward the kitchen. Grabbing a clean glass from the oak cupboard, she filled it with ice and water from the refrigerator. "Need a drink?" she asked, looking back at Jimmy. He shook his head to decline the offer.

"My guess is you have a pretty good idea about how and when things really started changing for you. Am I right? You mentioned shame and depression. Did one lead to the other?" Emily asked, still standing at the counter.

Nervously biting his lower lip, Jimmy shook his head, a hint of aggravation in his voice. "You really want to know what happened to me? Why I'm a mess? Why I've done nothing with myself? You want to know why I'm a failure? Is that it?"

"Yeah, I want to know. I want to know why you're choosing to be a failure. You're the one that told me the other night that everything we do is a choice, remember? Sorry if this hurts, but I'm just being honest."

"Fine. But I don't want you to be disappointed. My story is really nothing special. Others have been through harder times than I have, but if you want it, I'll give it to you."

* * * * *

Leaning into the monitor atop his borrowed desk, Paul read rapidly, occasionally typing to modify or clarify his search on Judge John Craven. His dry eyes hurt. His contact lenses seemed glued to his eyeball, and he wondered if they would ever be separated. He rubbed his eyes gently, hoping to wipe away the exhaustion. When that didn't work, he opted for removing the lenses altogether and discarded them in the trash can. Time was too precious to waste it on issues of comfort and long distance sight. There was too much to do.

Except for the soft blue glow from Paul's monitor and the two security lights at either end of the long rectangular room, the Oklahoma City Field Office was dark and nearly empty. Apparently at 7:30 p.m. on a Saturday evening, every federal employee had other places to be, other things to do—everyone except for Paul and a couple of guys from the cleaning crew.

Arriving at his temporary assignment early in the afternoon the day before, Paul had waded deep into his new assignment, analyzing the records of the subject bank, eager to get the job done and impress his local counterparts. Despite working long hours on Friday and the sleep deprivation caused by his early-morning phone call with Emily, Paul planned another extended evening. What else was there to do? Watch TV at the hotel? Besides, a little peace and privacy was just what he needed. Paul continued to read, searching for answers.

* * * * *

Moving to a more comfortable seat on the leather couch, Jimmy and Emily prepared for conversation. With a family-size bag of Fritos on the table and glasses of water set thoughtfully upon coasters, they were prepared for the long haul.

"Now keep in mind," Jimmy reminded her, "you asked for this."

Emily didn't say a word. She took a quick sip of her water and continued holding her glass in both hands as she watched Jimmy.

"Let me start by catching you up from when we knew each other. You remember me from college. Things were going great. I had lots of friends, school was good, and I was pumped to leave on my mission. I always expected to serve a mission, but I'm not sure if I was excited because my testimony was strong, or because I was ready for some grand international adventure. I'd never been out of the States, and suddenly

I was getting ready to go to Ecuador. It's pretty wild when you think about it. But, to make a long story short, I had some good experiences, but mostly I just survived. I was glad when it was over. I figured I would be back in control my own life again, do what I want, and do it with people of my own choosing. Good plan, huh?"

"Sure, I guess. But I thought a mission was supposed to be a time of spiritual growth. You're describing it like a prison sentence."

"Well, kind of. But again, what's our new favorite phrase? 'We always have a choice'? If it was a prison sentence, it's only because that's what I chose to make of it. It was tough at times, a lot different from what I expected, but I let it wear me down. That was my mistake. It didn't seem like anything I did mattered, so I gradually stopped trying. When my mission was over, I was ready to jump back into college life and get on with things."

"So you came home and started back at school. Were you still going to church?"

"Oh yeah. I loved church. I had a pretty good testimony, and the best-looking girls were always church girls," Jimmy said with an exaggerated wink and grin.

"You're kind of a brat sometimes. You know that?"

Jimmy smiled. Of course he did. "So I came back and spent the next four semesters doing pretty well. I wasn't breaking any records, but my GPA was decent, and I was on course to finish in another year. I had lots of friends and a sweet girlfriend. Life was really good."

Jimmy paused, took a sip of water, and then shoved a handful of Fritos into his mouth. Except for the mellow crunch from his chips, the room was silent. He took a deeper drink from his glass. Jimmy was making every effort to appear relaxed, but really he was stalling.

Remembering the last kiss on his sisters' cheeks awakened the raw emotions long hidden inside. His family tragedy never seemed to end; in fact, it felt like he was still living one.

FOURTEEN

WITH THE BLOOD OF THE deadliest Kansas City organized crime syndicate splattered across the upholstery of the black Escalade, Alex waited patiently for the scene of carnage to be found in the bottoms near the river. He anticipated the frantic call from Gordy's widow after being notified of her husband's grisly shotgun suicide. He role-played the conversation in his mind, knowing it would be critical to express the appropriate level of shock and sadness at his partner's violent passing.

Alexander Nicas was the grandson of Greek immigrants. His grandparents settled briefly in New York City and then moved to Chicago before making a permanent home in Kansas City during the late 1920s. Their story was similar to that of countless immigrants. They came to America seeking a more prosperous life, but the Great Depression challenged their plans. Grandfather Nicas sought opportunity and took advantage of every opening that presented itself. Finding unsavory but steady work as a mid-level thug in the Kansas City mob during the late 1930s, he gained just enough affluence to acquire a real taste for it, setting in motion a family tradition that would be difficult to end.

Thin, wire-rimmed glasses imitated Alex's wiry physique. His olive skin, strong Greek nose, and thick black hair were not unattractive, but his usual puckered expression and foul temper were. Nicas was a textbook example of a Napoleon complex. From his scrawny days of middle school to his undersized days at high school, Nicas had a lot to prove, at least to himself. Lacking in athletic skill and size, he compensated in competition with covert aggression. He didn't just attempt to slow down or stop his competitors; he hurt them any way he could, with a well-placed elbow, a knee, or an "accidental" head butt to the nose. At five feet four inches tall, he never really grew, and he never lost his taste for the success achieved by his brutal hands.

The chandelier above the expansive dining room table dazzled his surroundings as he finished eating his lobster tail and baked sweet potato. Unlike his foolish partner—that is, his former partner—Alex Nicas had a lust for the luxurious and opulent. The seventy-five hundred square foot, three-story brick estate on forty-one gated acres just outside the city limits screamed wealth to anyone who passed by. The perfectly manicured grounds resembled a nineteenth-century English garden, and the corners of the estate were dappled with timber. A nine-acre pond was just large enough for his two teenage children to Jet Ski during the humid summer months. The detached six-car garage, with an upper level for servants' quarters, more closely resembled an automotive museum than a garage. The scene was picturesque, and the life was incredible.

Despite the reality of their working partnership and the incongruity of each partner's actual wealth, to view their homes side-by-side, one would incorrectly presume Nicas to be king, while Gordy was merely a knight. While Gordy sought and gloried in power and position, Nicas appreciated the more tangible trappings of his supremacy. In his mind, power and position merely afforded one the capacity to enjoy life more richly than everyone else. With Gordy relegated to worm food, Nicas had achieved sole reign of the city's organized crime operation. Now, he really was king.

He savored the final bite of lobster as he received word of the anticipated phone call. Looking at his watch, he marveled that the scene had taken so long to be discovered. A thin smile crossed his lips. He thought of the discomfort law enforcement must be experiencing, sloshing around in the muddy river bottoms. For his purposes, it could not have been a better day. He finished chewing his food and took a couple of short sips from his crystal goblet. Shifting into appropriate character, he took two deep breaths, grabbed the handset, and answered sympathetically to the widow's sobs of despair.

* * * * *

Is it possible we are all just one personal tragedy away from being ruined emotionally, damaged beyond repair? Emily remained silent as she contemplated the question. Dabbing her swollen eyes, she wiped away a tear before it ran down her cheek. Her eyes were red and full as she looked compassionately into the eyes of her heartbroken friend.

In detail, Jimmy described the fateful events of the wintry early-morning accident, which had extinguished the lives of both sisters. His descriptions were precise and detached as though he were describing the events from a movie or a book. But as he backtracked to describe the last blown kiss from his rebellious little sister, Meg, his chest heaved and his eyes squinted tight, in a futile attempt to block the tears before they poured down his cheeks.

Jimmy leaned forward and buried his face in his hands. Between soft sobs, Jimmy apologized for his lack of composure. "I warned you it was a depressing little world," he said with a forced smile.

"You don't need to apologize Jimmy. Just hearing you tell it makes me bawl," Emily said between sniffles. "I'm really sorry for your loss."

"You know, I think about the funeral, and I feel like pulling a pillow over my head and hiding under a blanket. I can see my sisters' caskets sitting next to each other draped in flowers, and then I see the small casket holding Meg's unnamed baby." Jimmy's voice failed him.

"The baby survived for a while?" Emily asked in horrified amazement.

"The EMTs were pretty amazing, but the baby only lived until the end of the day. Of course, Meg was already gone, and my mom couldn't bring herself to name the baby."

Emily imagined the three caskets lying solemnly in a chapel, crowded by the remaining family. Tears flowed down her cheeks and her lips quivered. "Jimmy, I . . . I . . ."

"I know it's horrible and all, but I feel guilty. It's like I'm enveloped with despair, and I don't think I should be, but I can't shrug it off."

"Jimmy, there's nothing wrong with being sad."

"I know, but it's like I have no faith. I was raised believing that families can be together forever, that after this life we would still be a family, but I just can't get over it." Jimmy smeared the tears across his cheek, first with one hand and then the other. He sat taller in his seat, looking again at Emily. He was embarrassed he had made her cry.

Emily's reddened eyes looked kindly toward Jimmy. "Jimmy, having faith that you'll be reunited with your family doesn't mean you won't feel the horrible pains from their loss. You shouldn't feel guilty about that. But do you still believe you can be together as a family?"

"Honestly, no. Not really."

"Why not?"

"Emily, you don't really want . . ." He paused briefly. "I've only told you part of the story."

Emily was stunned. Could the story get worse? She took a long sip of water, hoping to refill her emotional reservoir. She wondered how Jimmy could go on, but it was clear he needed to. Grabbing the blanket from the arm of the couch, she placed it gently over her and tucked her legs beneath as she prepared for another round of torment.

Jimmy dried his eyes and steadied his breathing. Once again his voice was strong. "I believe families *can* be together. I just don't think my family qualifies. I told you about Meg. She was a rebellious little punk. She drank, did some drugs, was immoral, and frankly she couldn't care less about anything having to do with church. I don't think she'd been to church for well over a year, and if she did go a couple times, it was only because my parents forced her."

"Jimmy, I'm not exactly sure what your point is. Are you saying your family can never be together because Meg was a hellion?"

"Well, yeah. We're taught over and over that mortality is a probationary state, a time where we must prepare to meet God. That's why the prophets are always preaching repentance, right? Meg will be judged like everyone else, and frankly, it's hard to imagine Shelly and Meg ending up in the same place. We talk about this life as a test of our faith and devotion to God, a time to prove ourselves. As much as I love Meg, it's hard to believe she gets the same grade as Shelly. Does that make sense?"

"It does," Emily replied. But it didn't really, at least not completely. Emily's mind raced, looking for a smart, doctrinal thought that could help return hope to Jimmy, but her mind failed her. Thoughts of faith and works rolled through her head as she tried to assemble a rational argument about why there was still hope for Meg, and therefore the entire family, but she was unable to formulate her thoughts in a way she could communicate.

"And then there's Dad. I've never seen anything so pathetic. You should have seen him. At the viewing, he was nearly catatonic, no tears at all. Nothing. He didn't speak to anyone, he just mumbled every once in a while, and he left Mom to greet all the friends and family. Before the service, he even hid in the bathroom for a while. I had to go find him before they wheeled in the caskets. During the funeral, he just stared blankly. I don't think he heard a word that was said. I looked over at him every once in a while. He was clearly grieving; his eyes kept shifting, taking in each of the caskets, one by one. He looked like he had aged twenty years overnight. The lines in his face were deep, and his hair was suddenly white. He had just turned fifty years old, but he looked seventy. I don't think he'd been eating much. In fact, he kind of looked like a gaunt crypt keeper you might see in a horror movie. It was a little creepy but mostly just sad."

"So what happened? How's he doing now?"

An uncomfortable chuckle escaped Jimmy's lips. Once again, he struggled to suppress his pain. His eyebrows furrowed deeply as he squinted his eyes and puckered his lips. "Not so good." Jimmy wiped a tear from the corner of his eye. "Four days after the funeral, Mom came home from shopping. She clicked the garage door opener, but it was busted so she just parked in the driveway. She unloaded the groceries and started calling for Dad, but he didn't answer, so she started looking around."

"Where was he?" Emily interrupted.

"She couldn't find him, so she figured he'd gone for a walk or something and was about to go look for him. She decided to finish putting the groceries away first, so she went into the garage to put some meat into the deep freeze." Jimmy paused, taking a sip from his water as he mustered the courage to finish his story.

"It's okay. Go on, Jimmy," Emily prodded gently.

"When she opened the door, she saw a rope hanging from the garage door opener."

Emily gasped.

"Dad was collapsed on the floor underneath. It was almost five at night, but he was still wearing his bathrobe. His neck was covered with rope burns and scratches from trying to get free. Mom was a mess, but she called 911. The ambulance came and got him, and he stayed in the hospital for about a month. Aside from his partially crushed larynx, the doctors couldn't find much wrong with him, but he seemed to get worse. The hospital even had to feed him through an IV for a couple of weeks before he agreed to start eating again."

Creases covered Emily's forehead as she tried to hold back tears. "So did something happen that reminded him life was worth living?" she asked hopefully.

"I don't know. Maybe he just got hungry. He's never talked about it, and I've never asked. Mom had found a note beneath him on the garage floor. In the note, he apologized to Mom and me for quitting like he did. He said he knew Shelly and the baby would be fine, but he wanted to be with Meg, so she wouldn't be alone." The sobs overtook Jimmy's voice, and he was unable to speak, despite repeated attempts.

After a few moments, his tearful words were understandable once again. "He said this way he could be with Meg and watch over her, and the rest of us could be happy together. That was wishful thinking. Not much happiness going on around here. Of course, Mom and I were glad his attempt failed, but I think he was pretty disappointed. Even now, he's sad all the time. He barely talks, and he has a wheelchair he sits in. I'm not really sure why because I know he can walk. I think he just doesn't want to. He lost his job, so they moved back to Kansas City."

"That's horrible," were the only words Emily could muster, but Jimmy didn't mind.

"You know, it's possible none of this would have happened if I had just gone with my sisters that morning. If I was driving, maybe . . ."

Emily's heart throbbed. She desperately wanted to say something comforting, something useful, but she didn't know what. She couldn't relate to the agony and pain Jimmy had been through. She wanted to, but she couldn't. Sympathy was the best she could offer, and she hoped it would be enough.

Looking to Jimmy, she could see he was still fighting his emotions. He struggled to regain control, looking everywhere except directly at her. She studied his face and his expressions. Something was different. Clearly the sting was still sharp, but beyond the sorrow, he looked mad.

Bending her head sideways, she placed her nose directly in front of his, but he continued to avoid eye contact, gazing instead upon a chip that had fallen to the floor. As one last remnant of moisture trickled down his face, Emily reached softly with her hand, wiping it from his lower cheek with her fingers. Her touch lingered, softly caressing his face as her thumb moved slowly toward the corner of his mouth. With her other hand she tenderly held his face. Holding him close, she waited patiently as his eyes slowly arose from the floor. First, his gaze rested upon her tear-softened lips. Then he allowed their eyes to connect. Emily pulled him closer as she kissed him high on the cheekbone just below the eye. Her lips then moved to the soft flesh of his cheek where she pressed a little harder and then a supple, nearly imperceptible graze on his lower lip. Jimmy's face showed no reaction, but he didn't shy away.

Emily's fingers moved to his neck, her hand resting across his ear. She stroked his hair, pulling his head to her body, placing it at rest on her shoulder. Her left arm was wrapped around his back, holding his neck comfortably. Her other hand relaxed on his upper body as he leaned into her. Jimmy closed his eyes, relishing the soft comfort she afforded. Emily remained still, holding him tight and moving her hand softly back and forth across his chest. The living room lights were bright, but she dared not move to dim them. It was late, but she didn't know how much time had passed since they began their discussion. She gazed through the window into the stormy night. Her eyes transfixed on the water drops cascading down the glass, one drop joining another on its way down the pane. Her vision became unfocused, and her eyes closed as she drifted calmly into sleep.

* * * * *

Not even the cleaning crew remained. Paul was completely alone in front of his computer monitor. The pace of his reading had slowed considerably. His eyes were so heavy, he felt a panic come over him, like a hypoglycemic needing food. He closed them briefly, allowing them to rest for just a moment.

Shooting open again, his eyes focused to reacquire the information on the screen as he continued to read. The words, the sentences, and the paragraphs seemed to run together. Paul's exhausted mind scrambled to make sense of the gibberish in front of him. He could not let up. Emily needed him, and he wouldn't let her down. The words on the screen melded into an unfocused backdrop of black on white, and then just black. His eyes closed, and his head slumped forward, his hands still on the keyboard in the ready position. He didn't want it, but sleep had forced itself upon him.

FIFTEEN

Susan Craven woke up early Sunday morning and rolled over in bed to face her husband, her arm reaching to land on his side. To her disappointment, John's side of the mahogany four-post bed was already empty. From the slight indentation of the mattress and the mussed blankets, it was clear he had been there, at least for a short time, but he was gone now. At 5:30 a.m. the room was still dark, and the harsh weather once again beat against the window. Leaning to click the lamp, Susan rolled her legs over the side of the bed. A soft yellow glow filled her side of the room, encroaching only slightly onto John's. She walked to the closet door and pulled out a night robe and slippers to warm herself. She looked at the door to the master bath, but she could tell by the darkness underneath that the light was off. John wasn't there.

Leaving the room, she crept quietly down the stairs to avoid any unnecessary creeks in the floorboards so as to not wake her sleeping children. The house was cool and black except for a sliver of blue light emanating from the spare bedroom off the foyer of the home's main entrance. For now, John reluctantly used it as his home office, but he had made it clear to Susan on multiple occasions he needed a more worthy workplace.

The home was located in an affluent suburb of Kansas City, Kansas, and was beautiful by most standards. It was furnished and decorated nicely; expensive rugs and well-placed greenery accented the floors while curios full of Lladro figurines and beautiful artwork covered the walls.

A six-foot privacy fence surrounded a small, well-maintained yard where Susan tended her rose bushes during the summer, but aside from her activity in the modest flower garden, the family did not use the yard. Each summer a hammock was tied between two close trees in the corner, but every summer it went unused. Susan hoped John would find time to relax and enjoy the outdoors, but he never did. When John was home, he was content to stay inside, either at his inadequate desk or comfortably ensconced in his recliner stationed in front of the large plasma screen.

Despite the beauty and comfort of the home, Susan knew John was dissatisfied. He wanted more. He expected more.

Susan stood at the office doorway to the left of her husband's desk. She leaned her head inside, smiling widely at her unaware partner. Crouching in his seat, John was so focused on the monitor in front of him that he didn't notice Susan standing nearby. The sound was low and barely audible, but to her, it sounded like a television news report. His eyes were gleaming with excitement, and a sliver of grin turned the corners of his mouth.

Images of a black SUV and police cruisers played on the screen in front of John as a newscaster reported the grisly events of a suicide near the river bottoms. Clearing her throat, Susan tapped lightly on the door frame as though she had just arrived. John looked up, startled to see his wife. Instinctively he clicked the left button on his mouse, muting the sound and changing the screen.

"Good morning, dear. You're up early," he said pleasantly. John stood and walked toward his wife, meeting her at the corner of his desk. He grabbed her waist and pulled her against him and then embraced her more firmly as they kissed.

Snuggling her head against his shoulder, Susan wrapped her arms tight around him. "Couldn't sleep?"

"I had a few items to check on this morning, but all is well. I didn't want to disturb you. You look so angelic when you sleep."

Smiling at his shameless compliment, Susan tilted her head back. "I miss you, you know. I'm hoping we can all spend the day together. No meetings or urgent phone calls, no activities with friends—just the four of us. What do you think?"

"It sounds fine. Will the kids go for it?"

"I wasn't planning on asking. I'm going to be dictator mom today—but in a nice way."

John smiled at his wife. He was different around her. His speech was even less formal around Susan, but that didn't mean he wasn't always calculating or planning.

* * * * *

Jimmy's neck hurt and his right arm tingled; he was still on the couch in the same position from the night before. A ray of early sunshine shone through the window as the rain fell peacefully. Except for the tiny ray of natural light, the room was black. Not a single light shone from the electronics in the entertainment center. The power was out and Jimmy wondered about the time.

Emily's left arm was cradled behind him, her other arm sprawled across his chest as she leaned into the corner of the sofa, deep in a restful sleep. He remembered Emily's kindness and comfort from the night before, her soft kiss and gentle embrace, but he didn't recall falling asleep in her arms. He was surprised by the compromising position, but he appreciated the tenderness.

Knowing she would be horrified at the impropriety of falling asleep with him in her arms, Jimmy needed to remove himself so that when she awoke, she would find herself appropriately alone. Gently, Jimmy lifted Emily's hand from his chest and set it softly in her lap. Scooting carefully to the edge of the cushion, he placed his entire weight forward and stood. His back popped once as he straightened, making a gentle cracking sound, but too minor for Emily to stir. Noticing her blanket had fallen to the floor, he bent to pick it up, but instead of taking a risk in waking her, he left the blanket where it lay and walked on the balls of his feet across the large room to his bedroom door, shutting it behind him with care. Once inside his room, Jimmy stretched his numb arm and rolled his neck before lying quietly on his bed.

A moment after Jimmy was in his room, Emily's eyes burst open. She had suddenly noticed an uncomfortable chill. She picked up the king-sized comforter from the floor and wrapped it around her. The flannel comforter draped from her shoulders, and like a royal robe, it flowed behind as she walked to the kitchen counter. Emily looked to the microwave, but the clock was dark. She looked slowly around the room and released an audible sigh, relieved to notice Jimmy's absence. She walked to his door and tapped lightly with her finger. No answer. Turning the knob, she opened the door a crack. Emily was pleased to find Jimmy there, sleeping comfortably in his own bed. The latch clicked softly as the door closed.

Underneath his blankets, Jimmy still wore the clothes from the night before. His eyes were open as he thought about his delightful friend and the significance of the evening they spent together.

Punching in the code Paul had given her, Emily deactivated and reset the alarm system as she left the apartment. Figuring she had only a few hours before church started, she headed to her own place to clean up and get ready. Today was an important day.

* * * * *

Arriving back at Paul's apartment, Emily was surprised to find Jimmy sitting at the counter eating a breakfast of eggs over easy with toast and grape jam. He was still in his pajamas, but she knew that any consciousness before 8:00 a.m. was a bit of a milestone for Jimmy. His hair was sticking out in every imaginable direction, and his drooping eyes made Eeyore seem vibrant. Emily smiled contentedly as she noticed a large glob of jam on his T-shirt. He didn't care enough to bother wiping it away, and the newly acquired stain was recognized only as a necessary sacrifice to pre-noon life.

"Good morning, bright eyes," Emily greeted cheerfully from the doorway. "Nice to see you up and about. You getting ready for church?"

Jimmy's eyes widened. Being unemployed and not attending church had left him losing track of the days. They all meld together into one uneventful mass of time. "Oh, is that today?" Jimmy asked innocently, a small crust of bread falling from his mouth.

"Yes, Jimmy. Church is on Sunday, every week, just like it's always been," she said.

"Great! I was afraid I'd missed it," he said with a chuckle. "That was a close one. I'm ready—let's go."

Emily grinned at his schoolboy frivolity and charm and marveled that the man in front of her was the same person from last night. The contrast between his happy-go-lucky, casual approach to life and the sincerity of his anguish was totally inconsistent. Fortunately, she could now see through his lightheartedness like a rain-covered window. The view was a little off-kilter, and some of the details blurry and misshapen, but the overall picture was clear.

Holding out her elbow for Jimmy to grab, she called his bluff. "Okay, let's hit it."

A fleeting look of confusion crossed his face, replaced almost instantly with his usual sly smile. "You know, I almost forgot. My suit's at the cleaners. I'm so sorry, Emily. I bet it'll be ready by next week though."

"Now you're just being obnoxious. You let me worry about the wardrobe. Go hop in the shower and shave. I'll lay out your clothes."

Jimmy knew he was beaten. He had pushed it as far as he felt he could without offending her. Shoving the last bite into his mouth, Jimmy headed for the bathroom.

He emerged twenty minutes later, clean and dripping wet in Paul's bathrobe. He walked into his bedroom to find one of Paul's navy pin-striped suites laid across the bed, a white shirt and pale yellow tie off to the side. "This isn't going to fit," he hollered through the door.

"Sure it will! Now quit whining and get dressed."

They were both right. Jimmy's broad shoulders made the fit of the jacket a bit snug and his arms were a touch too long for the sleeves, but with the belt cinched tightly, the slacks fit at the waist and barely hit the floor near his heel. "Hey, you got any shoes?"

"Nope, sorry. Yours will have to do. Come on out. Let me take a look."

Jimmy finished tying the knot in his tie and put his shoes on. He looked in the mirror and nodded with satisfaction. He pointed at himself and winked. "I'm back."

Jimmy stepped from his room. Emily seemed just as impressed.

"Looking good!" Emily said with a pleased smile. She looked him over from head to canvas toe and moved closer to adjust his tie. "You know, the long pants actually help hide the shoes. I doubt anyone will even notice."

Jimmy puckered his lips, lifted his right leg onto the stool, and placed his elbow on his knee, chin in hand, doing his best *GQ* impression. It was then Emily noticed the socks.

"Jimmy, you can't be serious. You've heard of the unpardonable sin right?"

Jimmy nodded, unsure where she was going with this. "You cannot wear white socks with a dark suit. It's un-American. There may even be a law against it," she said, smiling.

Jimmy laughed casually, lowering his foot back to the floor. "Sorry about that. I had no idea I was in the presence of the Gestapo's fashion police. It'll never happen again. I promise." Jimmy walked to the door and punched in his code. "All right, let's get this show on the road."

"Seriously, you need to change your socks first." Her look was resolute. Was she joking with him again? He didn't think so.

Looking down at his feet, he gradually lifted the pant leg, revealing the white sock. He flinched with exaggerated response to its brightness. "I see what you mean. How could I have dared? Hey, wait just a minute." Running into Paul's bedroom, Jimmy rifled through his sock drawer and found the perfect pair. He yelled back to Emily. "Don't you worry, I'm going to fix this." He put on the socks and then stepped into his shoes.

"Well?"

"That really could have been a disaster. I really appreciate the thoughtfulness and care with which you clothed me today, and let me add—"

"Be quiet and let me see the socks," she said curtly.

Jimmy stretched his leg outward and slowly revealed the bright red and green Christmas socks with candy canes and reindeer.

The look on Emily's face could be summed up in one word—disgust. She sighed. "Come on, we're going to be late."

"What? I can sense you're displeased. 'Tis the season and all. Well, I guess, not yet. At least they're not white. That really would have been embarrassing."

Emily didn't respond. She walked out the door, moving quickly to the elevator. Jimmy hustled to catch up. "I really am going to have to talk to Paul about his selection of socks though. Candy canes and reindeer? That guy's full of surprises."

SIXTEEN

SLOUCHING INCONSPICUOUSLY BEHIND THE WHEEL of the maroon Ford E-series van, Mark Thrasher focused on the couple emerging from the downtown apartment building. Positioned fifty yards down on the opposite side of the street with a clear view of the building entrance, he pulled his ball cap low, his peering eyes barely escaping from underneath the rim. Being discovered from such a distance was unlikely, but this kind of visual surveillance was new to Thrasher. He much preferred his regular seat, deep in the secure bowels of the van, listening and watching in anonymity via his electronic gadgets.

It was unusual to be working alone, and although there was a slight thrill, Thrasher's nerves were getting the best of him. His portly physique and nervous bladder were not meant for such work. Although he was a relatively young agent, he was not terribly fit, nor was he a risk taker. Watching his target subjects approach the small red car, he winced at the pain in his flexed lower abdomen. The subject was on the move, and Thrasher wished he had not indulged in the last two cups of coffee from his thermos. He started the engine and waited, pulling out slowly only after the red Nissan made its first turn.

Struggling to keep a comfortable distance along the deserted city streets, Thrasher maintained visual contact with the red car. He was relieved when the car merged northbound onto I-35. With more traffic to hide amongst and fewer turns to mimic, he eased off the gas, falling further behind in the right lane, and positioned himself to follow easily when an exit was made. After just seven miles on the interstate, the red

Nissan exited at Vivion Road with Thrasher safely in the rear, a large pickup truck between them.

Preparing to turn left, the lead car stopped slowly as the light changed from yellow to red. The massive gray Chevy peeled off to the right at the top of the ramp, leaving the maroon van exposed, directly behind the Nissan. Thrasher's heart leapt as he looked to the vehicle directly in front of him. He could see his subject's bright eyes in the narrow rearview mirror as he came to a stop behind her. Quickly, he tilted his head down, revealing only the front of his cap. He hoped the driver didn't see him.

With no noticeable recognition, the Nissan turned left onto Vivion, and right at North Jackson, pulling responsibly into a church parking lot. Thrasher breathed a sigh of relief as he pulled to the curb a good distance down the street. He had a clear view of the lot exit. Removing his cap, Thrasher rubbed his head as he killed the vehicle's engine. His cover appeared to be intact.

* * * * *

"Good to see you." "Welcome." "Hey there." "Good morning, brother." "Hello." "Hi, how are you this morning?" "We're glad you're here." From the moment Jimmy and Emily entered the building, the greetings and extended hands seemed to collapse around Jimmy like a gang mugging at Disneyland. Most congregants were already in the chapel finding a seat or talking as they waited for services to begin, but a large contingent remained in the foyer as if waiting for the opportunity to pounce. Emily smiled warmly at the members of her ward family, impressed with the broad and friendly greetings extended to Jimmy.

With a slightly raised hand, Jimmy politely waved and nodded to the sea of unfamiliar faces surrounding him. It had been ages since he stepped inside a church, and Jimmy was taken aback at first, surprised by the intensity of his reception by complete strangers. But after a few moments, his attitude changed, and he seemed to bask in the attention, firmly shaking the outstretched hands and responding to the welcoming mass with warm greetings of his own. Pausing briefly from the adulation of his fans, Jimmy leaned closely into Emily's ear. "I didn't know I'd have groupies," he said with a smile. "This is kind of wild. Talk about nice people." Emily smiled broadly in agreement.

Surveying the gathering throng, Emily took a mental note of all those present: the elders quorum president and high priest group leader, the mission leader, the ward executive secretary, the Relief Society president, the young men's president, and, of course, the full-time missionaries. Even the bishopric was in full force, as if all were present for the sole purpose of greeting Jimmy. The greeting was so over the top, Emily nearly allowed an embarrassed laugh to escape her lips but caught herself before drawing undue attention. Softly touching the bishop's elbow, Emily drew his attention away from her friend.

"Excuse me, Bishop. What is this? Were you all having a meeting out here in the hall?" she asked partly in jest, partly in confusion. "I mean this is nice, but were you just hanging around hoping someone would show up today?" Of course she knew that was unlikely.

The bishop was a large man, with an exceptionally round head, nearly bald except for the thin grayish blond hair standing upright in an attempted crew cut. He towered over his two counselors and most others around him, but he had a gentleness about him that was unlike anyone Emily had ever met. He was only forty-eight years old, but he seemed grandfatherly. She had heard stories of his stern calls to repentance and fiery sermons, but she had never seen that side of him. She knew him only as the teddy bear that would tear up during the sacrament prayers or virtually any Sunday hymn.

The bishop placed a hand on Emily's shoulder. "This is an important day for your friend. We're just here to help him feel welcome."

Emily nodded, confusion furrowing her brow. Bishop Taylor explained further. "Brother Stephens called me early this morning and told me you'd be bringing Jimmy today. He explained that Jimmy hasn't been to church for quite a while and that his experience here today could be critical in his reactivation."

Emily nodded. "Brother Stephens? You mean Paul? He called you? How did he know? *I* wasn't even sure Jimmy was coming until I practically forced him out the door this morning."

"Well, I guess Paul has great confidence in your powers of persuasion. He knew you were serious about getting Jimmy here, so I doubt he had much of a question about your success." Bishop Taylor looked quickly at his watch. It was only five minutes until sacrament meeting started. "If you'll excuse me, Emily, I need to get into the meeting."

"Thank you, Bishop. Would you . . . ? I mean, is it possible you would have some time to meet with Jimmy today during church? He has some questions that I don't know how to answer. Some tough stuff about his family and repentance and judgment—you know, your specialties."

Bishop Taylor smiled kindly, impressed with Emily's earnest care for her friend. "Emily, I'll be happy to meet with him. I need to move a couple of things around, but have him outside my office after sacrament meeting, and we'll talk. Deal?"

"Deal," she agreed.

* * * * *

Feeling unworthy, Jimmy allowed the sacrament tray to pass by without partaking. He felt awkward, like he didn't belong, and it was only a matter of time until others became wise to his infiltration. His eyes darted uneasily back and forth across the vibrant and sometimes irreverent congregation. Locking eyes with a four-year-old girl sitting two rows in front, he forgot about his temporary social discomfort. The girl's short curly blonde hair perfectly framed her massively chubby cheeks. She widened her eyes with a large smile and then narrowed them quickly with an exaggerated frown and then back to a smile. Jimmy mimicked the expressions to her great amusement. The girl looked cautiously, but noticing her mother's head was lowered and not paying attention, she pulled her mouth wide with her thumbs while her chubby fingers pulled down her rolling eyes. Jimmy's broad smile only encouraged the child as she immediately assumed a new pose.

The child's mother became suddenly aware of her daughter's antics. Jimmy averted his eyes, glancing sideways at Emily to avoid detection as the agitator of the girl's irreverence. Emily had been watching. Her head now bowed, Emily's lips continued to curl up at the lingering mental image of Jimmy and the girl. With Emily's eyes now closed, Jimmy took the opportunity to admire her stunning features. He breathed contentedly, slow and deep. She was inspirational.

* * * * *

"Yeah . . . uh-huh . . . no. I haven't been able to clean up any more of the recording. I'm working on it right now. . . . Yes. I'm still outside the church. . . . I don't know. They've been in there almost three hours. How much church can a person take? Yeah. I'll get back to you."

Ending his call, Thrasher returned his full attention to the high-powered notebook computer and replaced the headphones over his ears. Despite his extensive efforts to decipher the nightclub recording, it was dominated by harsh static with only a few audible fragments. On his screen, he reduced the treble levels by a third and increased two levels of bass, isolating the peaks in the Judge's voice. Through the fuzz and static all he could hear were the same words already translated, in what seemed to be the Judge's voice.

"suspicious.................. your part .... act like ...
according ... original plan"

It was unclear what he had, but it didn't sound good. Agent Mathews and the Judge were involved somehow, but he needed more sound, more clarity. Thrasher continued adjusting the various sound levels on his computer, hoping to find the magical combination that would unlock more of the unusual conversation.

* * * * *

Bishop Taylor sat tall behind the large oak desk, an artist's rendering of the new Kansas City temple directly behind him. His scriptures sat on the corner of the cleared desk next to a small canister of Jolly Ranchers. His clasped hands rested at the desk's center as he leaned toward Jimmy, waiting for an answer.

Jimmy was unsure how to respond. It seemed like a trick question, but after a long moment of silence, Jimmy gave the only reply he could. "No, of course I'm not smarter than God. I never said I was."

"You sure act like it," the bishop challenged in a calm but firm tone. "You've spent the last two hours telling me about your family tragedy. According to you, that tragedy somehow justifies you in being lazy and hopeless, that because your rebellious sister died and your father attempted suicide, your family is lost forever. That *is* what you're saying, right?"

Jimmy felt uneasy and small. "Well, it's not really like that. I . . .

I'm just trying to explain my circumstance, and I was just hoping you might be a little more understanding. But you seem more interested in calling me to repentance and blaming me than in helping."

Bishop Taylor's unblinking eyes drew Jimmy in. "Listen, if I didn't care about you—if I wasn't trying to help—I wouldn't have spent the last two hours talking with you. Just like your friend waiting outside my office, I care enough to listen, and I give you enough credit that you can handle a little honesty. You're a smart guy, but you've been playing the sympathy game for too long. You need to get over yourself."

Jimmy scoffed.

"I'm not trying to be rude, only direct and honest, and I'm sorry if that offends you. But it's time for you to stand up and start acting like a man."

Jimmy was stunned. He had never been spoken to this way, certainly not by a priesthood leader he was seeking counsel from. "I'm sorry, Bishop. This was a mistake. I'm sorry I wasted your time. I'll let you get back to whatever else you have to do." Jimmy stood abruptly and took a step toward the door but was stopped by the bishop's next question.

"Jimmy, don't you want to know why I asked you if you thought you were smarter than God? The question's ridiculous, right?"

"Yeah, I guess," Jimmy responded, like a fifteen-year old boy talking to his father. His outstretched hand paused at the door as he turned his head back.

"You've cited scriptures talking about mortality as a probationary state, a time where we prepare to meet God. And you're right about that. You also mentioned judgment and eternal families and implied that because your little sister failed, at least in your eyes, and your father is in the process of failing, again in your eyes, your family has no hope of being eternal and happy. I asked if you're smarter than God, because you're casting judgment as though you were."

Returning to his chair, Jimmy grabbed a Jolly Rancher, popped it in his mouth, and then sat. "You're the one that said I was right about probation and the preparation needed to return to God. Now you're saying that's wrong?"

"I'm not saying it's wrong. What I'm saying is that it's possible your understanding is incomplete. Let's use your sister as an example. She was what? Nineteen years old? She was living a wild life, not keeping the commandments, and she died while still involved in her rebellious behavior. According to you, because she was a sinner when she died, she has no chance for the celestial kingdom, and therefore, your family will never be complete. Did I summarize correctly?"

Jimmy nodded.

"Good. Now, do you remember Saul from the New Testament?"

"Uh . . ."

"Okay, never mind. What about the story of Alma the Younger from the Book of Mormon?" Bishop Taylor asked, lifting his hands from the desk and leaning back in his chair. He watched the wheels turn in Jimmy's head.

"Yeah, sure. He and his buddies were going around wreaking havoc in the Church. They were pretty bad guys."

"Good. Then what happened?"

"They were visited by an angel—their souls were wracked with torment—and after a while, they repented and changed their ways. They all went on to be great missionaries and leaders," Jimmy answered.

"You're right. That's exactly what happened. In fact, it's similar to what happened with Saul," Bishop Taylor said. "Have you ever wondered why Alma the Younger was so lucky that he had a visit from an angel to help him turn his life around?" The bishop waited for a moment, but there was no reply. "Have you ever wondered what would have happened to Alma if, before his angelic vision and repentance, he had been kicked in the head by a horse and died, still as a pretty bad guy? According to your judgment, he would be lost forever." The bishop paused as he watched Jimmy for a reaction. "He sure was more fortunate than your little sister, wasn't he?"

Glaring at the bishop, Jimmy was unclear whether he was feeling anger or confusion. He thought for a long moment and then accepted the answer in his mind. "Yeah, he was luckier. But God had a special mission for Alma."

"Yeah, that stinks. It doesn't really seem fair, but you're right. God did have a mission for Alma, so he must have been more important than your sister. What was her name again?"

"Meg."

"Right, Meg. He sure loved Alma more than Meg, didn't he? Alma got all the breaks. His father was a prophet, so he probably got some special consideration there too, and Meg got nothing but eternal damnation. Yep, Meg was unfortunate."

"Bishop, I'm picking up on your sarcasm."

"Good, I didn't know how I could lay it on any thicker."

"But I don't understand. I know it's important to keep the commandments, because we will be judged, but you're saying if we don't keep them, we'll still be okay?"

"I'm not saying that at all. Our lives are blessed when we keep the commandments, and we slowly become the kind of people our Father wants us to become. All I'm suggesting is that judgment may not be as clear cut and obvious as we sometimes think. It's true—Meg died as a sinner, but don't we all? I know I won't be perfect when I die. Jimmy, I think it's highly possible that you've been too hard on her and your dad. I think you should trust that our ultimate Judge is perfectly wise, just, and merciful. I think you should recognize that the eye of the Shepherd is always upon us. He is smarter than you and me. He understands the bigger picture. I sure don't have all of the answers, Jimmy, but I do know that God loves each of us. He desires that we all return to Him and through His grace it is possible, if we want it."

Jimmy shrugged his shoulders and shook his head calmly. "Maybe I'm just dense, Bishop, but this is a little hard for me to digest. It sounds too good to be true."

"Look, Jimmy, I'm not trying to trick you, or sell you a magical cure-all potion, or even make you feel better. I'm simply telling you we can all be hopeful as we exercise faith in our Savior, his atoning grace, and his perfect judgment. That's the way I see it. Your sister and your father, just like the rest of us, will have to work out their own repentance, and it will be difficult. I don't know how it will turn out, but neither do you. The best we can do is trust in Jesus Christ, make every effort to be worthy, and repent as needed."

Jimmy nodded.

"Will you do something for me? I want to give you a couple of reading assignments. Will you read them?" Bishop Taylor asked, clearly unwilling to accept no for an answer.

"Yeah, sure."

"Good. First I want you to read Doctrine and Covenants 138,

which talks about the preaching being done to those who have already passed on. I also want you to read 1 Peter 3, especially verses 18–20. And when you read it, ask yourself the question, 'Why did the Savior visit the spirits in prison?' Those verses talk about the people who are in prison and say some were 'disobedient.' Does that sound like a sister you know? If she was in the prison being taught and it was possible for her to be removed from prison, can't we infer that, on some level, repentance is possible after death? Maybe things aren't as bad as you think. Will you read those chapters and think about how they apply to your family?"

Jimmy bowed his head and rested his forearms across his thighs. His head bobbed gently, accepting the bishop's assignment. "Yeah, I'll read it, but what if I can't understand it?"

"Easy. Write down your questions as you read, and bring them with you next week, and we'll talk about them. How does that sound?"

"Fine, I guess."

"Now, Jimmy, once you start to have hope again, because of your faith in God and his Son, you will start to feel the urge to change your ways. To REPENT!" Bishop Taylor said, smacking his fist loudly onto the desk.

Jimmy jumped as he looked up to see the smiling bishop.

"There is hope for your family, Jimmy. And there is hope for you, but it's up to you. It's time for you to escape from the darkness that you've been living in. Now, don't mess it up."

The bishop stood and extended his hand. Jimmy took it reluctantly. Bishop Taylor pulled him close, giving him a strong, manly hug. Jimmy looked up at the large man but said nothing. "You know, you're going to be all right, Jimmy. I can tell. See you next Sunday."

Emily stood as the door to the bishop's office opened. Bishop Taylor was smiling, but Jimmy didn't look as satisfied. She waved to the bishop and approached her friend. "Well, how'd it go?"

"Great. I'm cured. Everything is ship-shape," he said, smiling.

"You're being a brat again, you know. So, you had a good talk?"

Jimmy thought. "I'm not sure whether I want to hit him or give him another big hug."

"Another hug, huh? Ah, it was a good talk."

SEVENTEEN

Looking again in the rearview mirror, Emily tensed and her breathing became uneasy. To Jimmy she appeared to be enjoying the peaceful Sunday afternoon drive while casually inquiring about the details of his conversation with Bishop Taylor.

Emily knew the suburbs and rural routes north of the Missouri River well, and they provided the option of escape should one become necessary. She continued to smile and nod her head, adding the occasional "that's great," as Jimmy shared his enthusiasm and newfound hope for his family. His words hung in the air, and Emily felt a tinge of guilt at the inattention she paid to her friend, but she knew her first priority was their safety. Glancing to her driver's side mirror, it appeared for now the trailing vehicle was keeping its distance, content merely to keep the red Nissan Maxima under observation.

Rural Missouri in autumn is usually picturesque, with its softly rolling hills accentuated by animals grazing in the fields, rustic barns, and colorful leaves crossing the broad landscape, but not this year, and certainly not today. An early frost the entire first week of October confused the Midwest plant life, sending the trees and shrubbery into early hibernation. Even the usually lush green grass was relegated prematurely to its unattractive winter condition.

In contrast to the dreariness Emily felt, Jimmy was reminded of more peaceful times in his life. He sensed the same excitement and anticipation he felt as a child when he knew winter was near. Memories swamped his mind, building snow forts and making snow angels with his sisters and playing outside until his mom made them come in to warm up with hot chocolate. He even reminisced fondly about the damaging ice storms most people complained about. The beautiful ice would weigh down the bushes, trees, and telephone lines as it shimmered in the sunlight. These vivid memories brought a warm smile to his face. Jimmy was oblivious to Emily's dour countenance.

Glancing in the side view mirror, Emily remained subtle in her countersurveillance, but not subtle enough. "Emily? Is something wrong?" Jimmy asked as he noticed her eyes wandering.

"Mm-hmm. Yeah, that's wonderful, Jimmy," she said thoughtlessly, again checking her side mirror. The plastered smile was now absent from her face.

Jimmy tapped his hand softly near her knee, attempting to pull her out of her worried daze. Noticing Emily's eyes dart again to the rearview mirror, he turned in his seat looking plainly at the vehicle behind them. "Is there something wrong about that van? Did you see something?"

"Turn around!" she shouted harshly. "We've got a tail. I thought it might shrug off but—"

"The van? Why would someone be following you? I mean, I guess it's kind of cool. I've always wanted to be followed. What are they doing? What do they want?" Jimmy asked, never waiting for an answer.

"Jimmy, do you mind? I'm trying to concentrate, and no, it's not the van. Well, yeah, the van too, but that's not the one I'm worried about."

Jimmy began to turn again in his seat, but Emily reached over, digging her fingers into Jimmy's left thigh. The message was obvious. Jimmy sat rigidly, looking straight ahead, and set his right hand on his knee and the other soothingly on Emily's hand, which was still clenching tight. "I can see the van. Who else is there?" Jimmy asked evenly, striving to hide his concern.

Emily appeared to relax, but her heart was still thumping in her chest. "Agent Thrasher is driving the maroon van. I work with him. We're actually working the same case right now, but I'm not sure why he's following me. He's been trailing us since I picked you up at Paul's this morning, but I think he's harmless. His surveillance is too clumsy to be a real threat."

"So, who else is there?" Jimmy asked. "I can't see anything."

"Take a look in your side view mirror. There's a slight bend in the road coming up, so you'll be able to see better. It's a black sedan a hundred yards behind the van—a Chrysler, I think." She paused as they continued driving. "It's been following us since we left the church. There, can you see it?"

"Yeah. I got it. This may be a stupid question, but how do you know it's following you and not the guy in the van?"

Emily pondered briefly. "Well, good question. I guess I don't. Grab my cell phone. It's in the front pocket," she said, pointing to her purse near Jimmy's feet. Grabbing the phone from his hand, Emily dialed quickly.

"What are you doing?" Jimmy asked.

"I'm calling Thrasher. I'm going to find out what he's doing and see if he's watching the guy behind us."

"Well, I guess that's one approach. They teach you that in the Academy? Doesn't seem very stealthy," Jimmy muttered, a hint of a grin signaling his amusement at his own dull put-down. Emily's straight face did not reciprocate the smile.

"You got a better idea?" she asked firmly, the stress creeping back into her voice.

"No. By all means, go ahead and call your partner. I just hope he ends up being on our side."

"Yeah, me too." Letting off the gas, Emily listened to the phone ring as the unaware van crept closer toward the small red car. "Come on, Thrasher. Pick up." The phone went to voice mail and she hung up. Hitting the redial she waited again as the phone continued to ring. Finally, Thrasher answered.

"Mathews?" Thrasher asked with his usual brevity.

"Oh, hello, Agent Thrasher. How are you today? I'm taking a lovely drive through the country with a friend, but I needed to ask you a quick question."

"Oh . . . go ahead."

"Who's in the black sedan that's trailing you a hundred yards back? Are they friendly or unknown?"

"Mathews, what are you talking about?" His awkward attempt at misleading innocence was worse than his surveillance tactics.

The red Nissan slowed rapidly with a slight fishtail when Emily slammed the brakes. The unprepared van pushed quickly to a position directly behind it. Once again pressing the gas softly and keeping her left hand on the wheel, Emily leaned past the headrest, looking back through the rear window, and waved the phone with her right hand.

"Now, Thrasher, I don't mean to be critical, but you really need to improve your surveillance skills." With the phone to her ear, all she could hear were some angry mumbles and a clear expletive. "Now let me ask again, because it's kind of important. The black sedan—do you know who they are?"

"Wait a minute."

In the rearview mirror Emily could see Thrasher adjusting his mirrors as he attempted to catch a glimpse of the trailing sedan.

"You didn't know he was back there, did you?" There was no comment. "Look, I need to know if he's following me or you. And I want to know who he is, why he's there, and who's he working for."

"You have a plan?" Thrasher asked.

Emily's stomach was bubbling with apprehension. "Of course."

* * * * *

The black Chrysler closed in as Thrasher's vehicle slowly limped along, jolting forward bit by bit. To give the impression of mechanical problems, Thrasher partially engaged the emergency brake and then stepped harshly on the gas, off and on again, jerking the vehicle violently. He swerved the van just over the center stripe of the road, blocking the view of, and any possible passage by the black sedan.

Pulling to one side and then the other, the driver of the sedan struggled to look past Thrasher's van and was frustrated by his inability to pass on either side. After a long minute, a small intersecting road appeared, and Thrasher engaged his left blinker before turning onto the gravel. As expected, the sedan accelerated, eager to gain ground and reestablish visual contact with Emily's Nissan. When the black car safely passed, Thrasher disengaged the emergency brake and raced the quarter mile to the next gravel road, running horizontal to the main blacktop highway. Although only separated by a short distance, the two roads were obscured from each other due to a line of trees and overgrown brush. Thrasher laid his foot to the gas, racing dangerously to the rendezvous. The van's tires slipped occasionally, spitting loose gravel.

Continuing along the state highway at a decreased speed, Emily followed the narrow, curving road to the east, the tiny black dot ever increasing in the rearview mirror. Hoping Thrasher's straight-line road would allow him time to gain ground before reconnecting to the highway, Emily watched patiently as the mystery car sped closer. "Well, whoever he is, I think we made him mad," she said, speaking loudly enough for Thrasher to hear over the upheld cell in Jimmy's hand. "How are you coming, Thrasher?"

"Moving as fast as I can. I see the crossroad . . . quarter of a mile."

"Good. Now, stay out of sight and approach slowly so you can come up from behind."

"Got it."

Jimmy grabbed the handle above the door and looked to Emily, who gave a brief nod of recognition.

"Okay, Jimmy, you ready? After we stop, grab the Glock from the glove box and hand it to me. Exit your side quickly. I'll be right behind you. Now, don't worry, this is going to work out fine." The look on Jimmy's face made it clear he didn't share Emily's optimism.

Emily eased off the accelerator as a thin dirt road, ironically named Dirt Road, came into view. Down what amounted to little more than a pathway, Emily looked to the spot where she imagined Thrasher should be by now, obscured on the other side of a slight rise. "Thrasher, the sedan is about twenty-five yards behind me, and I'm almost to the intersection. Ready?"

"Ready."

"Here we go."

Emily pulled hard on the emergency brake and gripped the steering wheel tightly with both hands as she turned faintly to the left. The small red car slid across the slippery pavement, which was still wet from the nighttime showers. She adjusted the wheel slightly, causing the car to turn sideways down the road, and came to a stop twenty-five yards past the intersection of Highway MM and Dirt Road. Looking out the driver's side window, Emily noticed the black sedan swerving as it turned precariously from one side to the other.

"Jimmy, go. Go!" Extending the handle of the gun, Jimmy dove from the passenger side seat onto the wet pavement, Emily nearly on top of him. She grabbed the Glock from his hand. Her car was perfectly sideways, positioned on the road safely between Jimmy and Emily and the black sedan. Rising from the ground, Emily peered over the hood of her car at the black vehicle, which had stopped mere yards away with the motor still running.

"FBI! Get out of your vehicle with your hands up," Emily yelled into the light wind. There was no response. Emily stood, lifting a badge above her head, with her gun raised. Looking through the windshield of the sedan, she could clearly see a driver and a passenger but was unable to view deeper into the car. "Get out of the vehicle!" she hollered again.

The passenger side door opened a crack and then swung hard, revealing the barrel of a handgun, which unloaded three quick rounds, one connecting with a metallic clank on the side of the red car. Ducking back behind the Nissan, Emily peeked cautiously through her car windows at the enemy sedan. "Thrasher, where are you? We're taking fire," she yelled frantically into the phone Jimmy was holding. His hand shook so badly that he grabbed his wrist with the other hand in an attempt to slow it down. It didn't work. Both hands jerked with fear.

"Hold on. I'm coming," they heard in response over the speaker.

Peeking at the attackers, Emily saw the car door close as the gunman slid back into the passenger seat. Standing, she unloaded two quick rounds into the front of the black sedan. The engine revved, and the tires spun as the driver wrenched the wheel, expertly turning the car one hundred eighty degrees. In an instant, the large maroon van appeared from Dirt Road, sliding to a stop just past the intersection, blocking the enemy vehicle between the two FBI agents. The driver of the black Chrysler shifted into reverse without hesitation. The wheels turned furiously, hurling the rear of the sedan toward the front of Emily's small red Nissan.

Grabbing Jimmy by the collar, Emily sprinted from behind the car. Pushing Jimmy and diving into the deep drainage ditch, she heard the metallic crash. Raising her head from the ground, she looked up to see her car spinning out of control toward the trench. With little time to react, Emily threw herself across Jimmy, covering him and burying her head in his back as the car came sliding down the ditch, barely missing them.

"Jimmy, are you okay?" Emily shouted into his ear and then rolled off his back into the muddy water. He nodded rapidly and looked with wide eyes at Emily. Seeing he was shaken, but unhurt, Emily scrambled up the embankment to the road. Looking ahead, she saw the van chasing the black sedan, which was still racing in reverse. As the driver attempted another one hundred eighty degree super-turn, Thrasher accelerated into the side of the vehicle, forcing it off the road and across the ditch. The Chrysler crashed sideways into a large walnut tree. In her muddy church clothes, Emily ran down the road with her gun raised.

By the time Emily approached the van, Thrasher was already out and across the ditch, his gun drawn on the two immobile occupants of the black Chrysler 500. Emily was breathing hard as she joined Thrasher.

"These two won't be going far," she said, opening the driver's door. Looking inside, she saw the passenger's gun and one other in the back seat. She then checked the glove box. Nothing. "It's clear," she said, laying the weapons on the soggy ground. Thrasher leaned into the vehicle to check the assailants for pulses. Both were alive but unconsciousness.

"I'll call it in," Thrasher volunteered.

Emily's dress was torn and grungy. Her hair was soaked with muddy water. Streaks of mud rolled down from her temples, and mascara trailed from her eyes. She bent over, her hands on her knees as she tried to regain her breath. "Thrasher, it's really good to see you. Thank you."

Failing to acknowledge her in any way, Thrasher returned to his van to call for medical support and transport.

Jimmy approached the scene quickly, a bit of a mess himself. He stood in awe of the woman by his side. He had never seen such strength and poise in the face of danger, and despite her grim appearance, Jimmy had never been so attracted to a woman in his life.

Although Emily had already recovered her normal breathing, her chest heaved and her fingers trembled. Her adrenaline was also returning to normal levels, but despite her brave face, she was visibly shaken. Jimmy dropped his fingers to his side and searched for the soft touch of Emily's hand. As he nudged her fingers, she grabbed tight and then turned in for a comforting hug. "This is your idea of working out fine?"

he asked, looking into her mascara and mud-streaked face.

Emily laid her head into Jimmy's chest and wrapped her arms tightly around him. "We got the bad guys—no one got hurt—I'm going to get a new car. I'd say it turned out pretty well." Emily's voice weakened as her body slid to the wet ground.

Dropping to one knee at her side, Jimmy noticed a spot of blood soaking through Emily's blouse. Had one of the assailant's shots found its mark? Jimmy's fingers picked at the blouse near the wound, pulling the cloth away from the skin, tearing it slightly for a better look.

"Hey you, Basher! I need some help!" Jimmy yelled, catching Agent Thrasher's instant attention. "We need an ambulance, NOW!"

Tears welled in Jimmy's eyes as he sunk to the ground, holding Emily in his arms. He placed her head in his lap and gently stroked her mud-caked hair, staring at her sweet, pale face and praying desperately for a quick emergency response.

EIGHTEEN

Sunday afternoon in the field office was even more deserted than Saturday had been. "Perfect," Paul said to himself, settling in at his workstation. He paused briefly before logging in. If the FBI was really committed to keeping employee information confidential, they would try harder. At least that's how Paul rationalized the input of the borrowed password he had spied from the Oklahoma City ASAC. After his previous searches on Judge Craven failed to yield the proverbial smoking gun, Paul turned his attention to Emily's teammates, hoping to find a damning link.

Normally he was a by-the-book kind of agent, but extraordinary measures were called for, because whether she knew it or not, Emily's life depended on his investigation. Paul knew he was risking a great deal, so he scanned the screens quickly, hoping to limit his electronic footprint. Once it was discovered that confidential files from Kansas City were surreptitiously accessed, it wouldn't take the ASAC two seconds to identify the culprit. Paul's only hope was that his violation of computer security protocol would go unnoticed, or, at the very least, it would be detected after his mission was complete.

Rapidly scanning performance reviews from the past five years it appeared to Paul that Agent Stark was an average employee. His work reflected adequate success, and he generally received the standard three percent cost-of-living increase each year. He was divorced with two kids, who both lived with Mom, and he didn't date much.

"Real surprise," Paul said aloud as he read the personal notes written by the field supervisor. He then wondered what he would find in his own file. "Come on, concentrate."

Paul refocused and pushed on. Reviewing Stark's credit report, it appeared a large portion of Stark's income paid directly for child support. He lived in a modestly priced apartment and drove a five-year-old vehicle, which was nearly paid off. He had a small bank loan and three credit cards with reasonable balances. He did not live like someone with a padded income.

Switching his attention to Agent Thrasher's file, Paul was unimpressed and moved quickly to Detective Cross from the KCK Police Department, but to Paul's eyes there was nothing out of the ordinary with either of the men. Thrasher and his wife had a standard two income household with appropriate assets and debt, while Cross, like many experienced law enforcement officers, augmented his modest department income by moonlighting his security consulting services with a familiar Kansas City financial firm.

In Paul's experience, white-collar crime paid, and if there was no money trail, there was no crime. The personnel files and finances of Emily's teammates felt like a dead end. Printing a couple of pages out of each man's file, he packed them neatly in his portfolio and closed out his unauthorized computer access. Once again the subject of his focus shifted, this time to Susan Craven, the Judge's wife.

* * * * *

Jimmy sat at the edge of the hospital bed clasping Emily's hand between his, while Thrasher, Cross, and Stark stood near, whispering. Opening her eyes slowly, Emily focused first on Jimmy and then on the others as she took in the coldness of her surroundings.

"Hey," Emily croaked, and then forcefully cleared her throat. "What's going on here?"

"Welcome back to the land of the living!" Jimmy said with a relieved smile.

"Why am I in the hospital? Am I hurt?"

"Well, you have a gash on your shoulder and a couple of cracked ribs, but the doctors say you'll be fine. You overexerted, and with your cracked ribs, you weren't breathing right, so you passed out. How are you feeling?" Jimmy asked, brushing a strand of hair from her face.

Under the watchful gaze of her colleagues, she responded, "I feel fine," and gently withdrew from Jimmy's touch. Looking at the men surrounding her, she held her side gingerly and winced when she sat up. Seeing that she was wearing only a thin hospital gown, Emily pulled the blanket high on her chest and leaned heavily against the headboard.

"Thrasher, how are our suspects? Do we know anything about them yet?"

Agent Thrasher glanced at Stark and then to Cross, who fielded the question. "Mathews, we don't know anything yet. The car is clean. It's not registered, the license plates are phony, and neither suspect was carrying any kind of identification. The vehicle is being processed, and we're running fingerprints now, but so far, nothing."

"What do you mean it wasn't registered? Was the vehicle reported stolen? There must be an owner," Emily stated.

"No. It doesn't exist. We ran the VIN for a title and against DMV and insurance records, but we got nothing. We have no evidence it was ever purchased, registered, or insured. We don't know who it belongs to. It's just there," Detective Cross answered, raising his hands protectively. "I don't know what else to tell you."

"Fine. Well, we can at least talk to the guys," Emily stated, easing her tone.

"Just hold on, little lady. We can talk to them when they wake up. But Mathews, you're lucky you didn't kill them with that little stunt. Why in the world would you run a car off the road? They hadn't broken any laws. Were they threatening you, or did you just get scared?" As a natural irritant, Stark knew exactly how to aggravate Emily. "If I were you, I'd be hoping they don't sue."

Emily's cutting glare accessorized her cool smile. "You think they can sue? Are you insane? I mean, I do feel bad about those poor men being pushed off the road, but I guess they shouldn't have shot at me or rammed my car. On the bright side, if they do sue, we'll at least know who they are, won't we?" Emily smiled and noticed a sly nod from Agent Thrasher.

"Look, we all agree that we need to figure out who these guys are, why they followed Mathews, and who they work for, right? Can we all agree on that?" Cross asked. Heads nodded around the room. "The timing of this run-in is awfully suspicious. Should we assume it has something to do with the Craven case?"

"You're a detective. Do you really think we need to assume anything?" Stark scolded. "I spoke with the doctors, and our two scum buddies will be ready for a good talking to in a little while. Until then, we'll wait for the fingerprint analysis and see if the car yields any clues."

"Fine. If you gentlemen will excuse me, I'm going to get showered and changed." Emily glanced quickly around the room, searching for her own clothing. Grabbing Jimmy's forearm, she pulled him close. "Jimmy, I never thought I'd ask you this, but where are my clothes?" she whispered.

"Trust me, you don't want them," he answered. "I'll see if I can round up some scrubs."

"Thanks. Hey, Stark, can I talk to you for a minute?" Emily asked.

Stark closed the door after the others filed out in silence. "What do you want, Emmy?" Stark asked with his usual condescension.

"I want to thank you for your concern in coming to see me at the hospital. It was very thoughtful," she said sarcastically. "You must have been worried, but as you can see, I'll be fine." She paused to note his predictable scoff and then continued. "Seriously, I just wanted to let you know, I'm not going anywhere, so you need to get used to it. We're on the same team here. Don't let my smiling good nature fool you," she said with a grin. "I've got a little bit of bite left in me, but how about we put all our squabbling aside and just get along. What do you say?" Emily extended her hand, ready to confirm the peace offering.

Running his hands through his thick hair, Stark looked at Emily and shook his head slightly. "It's either you or me, little lady. There's something about you, I just want to—" Stark's teeth clenched as he growled with disgust. "Whether you know it or not, today was the first nail in your coffin."

* * * * *

Four stories above, on the sixth floor of St. Luke's Medical Center, armed sentries stood in front of two closed doors at separate ends of the sterile hallway. Behind each door lay the unidentified wreckers of Emily's Sunday afternoon drive, both with hands cuffed to the metal railings and legs bound to their beds.

In the room at the north end of the hall, the driver of the Chrysler 500 lay with his eyes closed but aware of every movement outside the door. His biceps bulged, nearly filling the usually loose sleeves on his hospital gown, and the veins in his thick neck pulsated through his temple with each heartbeat. A wide lesion had been stapled closed above his right eye, and a large purple contusion decorated his cheek. His shoulder ached, and his left leg had a sharp pain midway between his knee and ankle. He tried to assess the seriousness of the wound, but the restraints prevented him from sitting up or even moving his leg. Despite his general pain and the grogginess from his medication, he was in much better shape than his partner down the hall, who lay unconscious with a concussion and shards of glass imbedded in his face.

The driver waited calmly, feigning sleep, so as not to be hassled by his captors. He knew his people would come. It was only a matter of time.

At 4:15 p.m., two handsome, forty-something doctors stepped out of the elevator and onto the sixth floor. They walked past the nurses, who were chatting and laughing loudly about an emergency room patient admitted the previous night—something about a baseball, a dare, and an extremely wide mouth. The doctors paused as they came to the hallway entrance, each looking at his clipboard to discern which patient was his, and then separated. Now silent, each doctor approached the uniformed guard in front of each door with raised hospital credentials. A few pleasantries were exchanged as the doctors logged in with the guards and entered the separate rooms to complete their evaluations.

Walking to the bedside, Dr. Hadarias examined the deep wound above the driver's eye, and then, retrieving his flashlight pen from his breast pocket, pulled back the patient's eyelids and checked for pupil response. His back was to the door, where the guard waited and watched. With a wink, Hadarias indicated to the constrained patient that the time was here.

The bulging patient waited for his cue, ready to leap to his feet and fight to the death, if necessary. Touching him softly on the shoulder, Dr. Hadarias checked the calibrations on the IV and then looked earnestly at the patient's chart.

"This is all wrong. We've got a real problem here. Guard, can you please check that cupboard? Yeah, the one by the door. See if you can find a small vile with a navy blue label. It'll say 4-uSuKr." The doctor grinned at his idiotic joke as he watched the guard turn to look inside the cabinet. In an instant, Dr. Hadarias removed a syringe from the front lab coat pocket and placed into the IV tube entering the patient's hand. He pressed the plunger, causing the patient to convulse momentarily before complete paralysis set in. The shackled man's face tightened, and his square jaw locked before becoming perfectly still. His eyes were open and aware, wide with terror before rolling back helplessly into his head. Hadarias touched the vacant eyes softly, closing the lids.

"Officer, are you finding anything?"

"No, I don't see a thing."

Hadarias strode briskly to the cabinet, disgust showing on his face, as he rummaged through the medical supplies. "Nothing!" He stopped and looked at his watch for an instant and then to the patient. "Wait here. Don't let anyone near my patient until you see me. Got it?"

The guard nodded as the doctor raced through the door and down the hallway. He turned the corner and approached the nurses' station, slowing to a casual walk and giving a subtle nod to his associate, who was approaching successfully from the opposite direction. Looking at his colleague, Dr. Hadarias took a deep breath and smiled. "You know, doctor, I don't know how that patient got a baseball stuck in his mouth."

"He must have been real stupid and had a big mouth, I guess," the other responded.

"Yeah, but we fixed it."

The duo entered the elevator and disappeared.

* * * * *

Attempting to dull the pain from her cracked ribs, Emily held her side as she raced past the nurses' station, nearly slid into a supply cart, and turned left down the long hallway. Fresh from the shower, Emily approached the north room in her hospital slippers and hot pink scrubs with a soggy ponytail whipping behind her. Agent Stark and Detective Cross were already present, standing outside the room and speaking with the unsuccessful guard while medical personnel hovered around the lifeless body.

"How did this happen?" Emily asked loudly, stopping near the men. The officer guarding the room averted his eyes, and Emily studied him closely. "Do we at least have a good description or some surveillance video of these so-called doctors?"

"Nice of you to join us, Mathews," Stark said, glancing quickly at his wristwatch. "Where's your little boyfriend?"

Emily ignored the question. She accepted the surveillance photos of the doctors. She reviewed the faces closely and then looked at the login sheets the doctors signed.

"Dr. Hadarias was this guy's name," Cross explained pointing to one of the pictures.

"Hmm. Hadarias? What is that, Pakistani? Indian?" Emily asked.

"Indian, I think," Cross agreed.

"Does this guy look Indian?" Emily asked, gently waving the photo of the Caucasian doctor. Emily's eyes met the young uniformed police officer's gaze, and her face softened. "Officer, was there anything unusual? Anything at all you can think of?"

"I wish there was, but he knew our procedure and had credentials. He seemed to belong. I can't believe I fell for his act, but he was good," the officer stated sheepishly.

"*You* can't believe it? Not your brightest day, buddy," Stark commented. "Stick around for a while in case we need you." Stark frowned and nodded his head, dismissing the officer.

"Hey, take it easy, Stark. Frankly, if the kid hadn't been fooled into turning his back he'd probably be dead too, so relax a little." Cross caught Stark's vengeful stare and retaliated with one of his own.

"Are you kidding? With everything that's happened today? We've got nothing. Nothing! This is a disaster," Stark hissed, shaking his head in disbelief.

Emily turned away, shielding a thin grin from her melodramatic colleague. Cutting the tension as if on cue, Emily's gaze was drawn to a scene she would not soon forget. Racing down the hall in a stylish speed walk, Agent Thrasher drew closer, waving a small piece of ivory colored card stock.

"I've got it," he hollered from halfway down the hall. The others turned toward Thrasher, smiling instantly. The round man waved the paper over his head more emphatically for effect as his hips and torso swayed, one foot stepping precisely in front of the other.

Emily smiled at Cross and nudged his stomach softly with her elbow. "You've got to hand it to him. He's got good form."

Thrasher came to a stop next to Agent Stark but continued to wave the paper energetically as he bent over, gasping for breath. Emily had never seen him so animated. Heavy beads of perspiration lined his hair with an occasional drop running down his cheek.

"I've got it," he panted again, handing the paper to Agent Stark.

"What is it? A parking stub?" Stark asked.

Thrasher stood upright, his chest rising and falling dramatically with each breath. "Exactly. It's to the King's Ridge Parking Garage off 4th Street. The guys found it between the passenger seat and the center console of the black Chrysler."

"Thrasher, that's great, but that's a big garage that services quite a few buildings. How are we going to . . . ?" Cross began to ask with puzzlement.

Not waiting for the detective to finish his question, Emily took the paper and held it close to her face. "There. See that thin imprint? It's validated!"

Thrasher's grin signaled his approval. "Yes, exactly."

"Thrasher, I could kiss you," Emily said excitedly, but noting the immenseness of the sweat rolling from his face, she thought better of it. "So not only do we have pictures of our car attack buddies—and their assassins—but we also know where they've been. Prodigy Industrial Group? What's that? Anyone ever hear of it?" Emily asked to blank stares.

"Don't get too excited. It's probably nothing," Stark suggested.

"Maybe it's not much, but it's something. I'll check this Prodigy place out first thing in the morning. I'll show the pictures around and see if anyone recognizes our suspects." Cross clapped his hands together. "We've got a lead."

Emily slapped Cross on the shoulder. "We sure do. I'm going with you."

"Okay, good," Stark agreed. "Thrasher, you wait on the fingerprint ID and work with some facial recognition software. Try to identify our assassins. I'll research this company and find out who they are and what they do, cross-referencing the company and Judge Craven to see if his name pops up anywhere. Mathews and Cross, you two poke around on site and show your pictures. Actually, take a picture of Craven with you too. See if they recognize him. Let's meet up after lunch tomorrow and see what we've got."

The team separated, ready to salvage the few remaining hours of their weekends. Cross and Stark walked at the front of the group. Emily gripped Agent Thrasher's elbow. "I've got some questions for you. I'm hoping you can give me some surveillance tips."

Thrasher grimaced at the look on Emily's stern face. "All right. Let's find someplace private."

NINETEEN

PAUL STABBED HIS FINGER AT the power button, turning off his monitor. He ran his hands roughly through his dark hair, skewing it in every direction. His brown eyes were gray with fatigue—the result of a day's worth of failure.

Reclining in his chair, Paul placed his heavy feet on the corner of the desk. His eyes closed as he thought about Emily. He longed to enjoy the sweetness of her company. Paul sat motionless in the hushed office, the only sound coming from his gentle breathing and the soft hum of the fluorescent security lights.

From inside the front pocket of his black leather portfolio, he heard the gentle vibrations of his cell phone. Placing it quickly to his ear, he listened but heard nothing except another soft buzz coming from his bag. Clapping the phone closed, he grabbed an inexpensive prepaid cell from the other side of the bag. An instant smile brushed away his weariness, because only one person had this phone number. Emily!

Emily lay on the hard bed in an inexpensive hotel room that she had paid for with cash. She held tightly to the untraceable cell phone. As Paul answered cheerfully, her eyes closed as she savored the soothing sound of his voice. "Paul, I can't tell you how good it is to hear your voice. You really sound great."

"Well, thank you. Since you mentioned it, I have been practicing my deep manly sound," Paul said in his richest bass tone, allowing the dark timbre of his voice to resonate in the receiver. "If I wash out of the FBI, I can pursue a career as a media voiceover man."

Emily allowed for a soft chuckle as she imagined the goofy grin that usually accompanied Paul's self-deprecating humor. "Maybe when I wash out, I can join you selling toothpaste or insurance on TV," Emily joked in what was supposed to be a sultry lounge singer voice. "Oh, that was really bad. Sorry."

Paul smiled, impressed that even Emily's worst imitation was still attractive. "I'm glad you called, but I wish I had something worthwhile to tell you. Since we spoke last, I've been trying everything I can think of to find some connection between Craven and a member of your team, but I didn't find a thing. I feel like I've let you down. I didn't want to alarm you the other day, but I'm really worried about you."

"You have good reason to be," Emily said, allowing for a moment of quiet. "I wish you didn't, but you do. Can I tell you about my day?"

"Of course. What happened? Is everything all right? Are you okay?"

"Where should I start?" Emily asked rhetorically, and then paused. "Actually, the day started great, and there is some good news. Jimmy really did well today. Not only did he come to church, but he also had a long conversation with Bishop Taylor. He already seems to be more positive, more hopeful."

"That's great, Emily. I want to hear all about it, but tell me what's really on your mind."

"Well, in a nutshell, the FBI followed me most of the day because I'm under some kind of suspicion, which actually turned out to be a good thing, because my FBI tail helped me elude and capture some bad guys, who were also following me. My car is totaled, I was shot at, I spent a few hours in the hospital, I have broken ribs and a gash on my shoulder from who knows what, and our captured bad guys were assassinated under guard at the hospital before we could interrogate or even identify them." Emily took a deep breath. "How was your day?"

Emily heard silence and then the crash of a chair falling to the floor.

Paul flitted nervously as he attempted to digest the rapid-fire words flowing from Emily's lips. "What? Are you serious? How are you feeling? Are you in pain?" Paul asked. He stared at his wristwatch while trying to calculate how quickly he could be back in Kansas City. His intense anxiety surprised him. His mind could barely focus, and all he could think about was being with Emily—holding her, protecting her. But he was stuck in Oklahoma. Paul cursed the distance between them.

"Paul, it's okay. I'm fine—just a little sore is all. Things worked out pretty well, considering."

Paul laughed uncomfortably. "Considering what?"

"Well, it could have been worse. I'm fortunate to come out of things today with just a couple of minor injuries. Honestly, I'll be fine." Realizing she may have been too abrupt in delivering the frightening events to Paul, Emily slipped her voice seamlessly into a sweet, comforting tone. "Now, I don't mind if you worry about me a tiny little bit, because that means you care, but you don't need to stress. Things here are bound to calm down. I promise I'm fine." Emily sensed she had done little to ease Paul's troubled mind.

Paul stood next to his workstation, the chair on its side next to his feet. He nearly hyperventilated as he held the top of his head. "Okay, now, Emily," Paul began as calmly as he could manage, "I'm freaking out, just a little bit. Please, toss the nutshell away and tell me again, in detail."

Beginning with Thrasher's morning surveillance, Emily confided the events of the day to Paul. She discussed the capture of the men from the black car, their untimely deaths at the hospital, and her conversation with Thrasher, in which he detailed his reasons for following her. Emily paused as an unwanted break of emotion crept into her voice.

"Paul, you must think I'm a basket case. It seems like every time we talk, I'm having some kind of emotional breakdown. Thanks for listening. I always know I can count on you."

"That's right, you can. I'm so sorry I can't be there right now, but I love hearing your voice, and I'm glad you feel comfortable talking with me. I'll do anything I can to help you. Count on that."

For a moment, Emily forgot the pain from her injuries. A tear ran down her cheek, and she sniffled as she recognized Paul's deep concern. His sincerity was comforting.

"Emily, I need to ask you a question."

"Sure, go ahead," Emily said.

"About Thrasher—when I reviewed his personnel file and finances, he seemed to be on the up and up, and from his actions today, it seems like he's trustworthy. What's your take?"

"I agree. In fact, I've already bet on it."

"What do you mean?"

"Well, after the rest of the team left the hospital, Thrasher and I had a frank discussion, and he told me about the fragmented recording he had of me speaking with Craven. Honestly, I'd have been just as suspicious if I only heard the few bits he had, so I told him everything, the threats on the team and my loved ones, and how Craven knew all about our operation."

"What did he say?"

"He was pretty calm for the most part, but ticked off—not at me, but still ticked. He was fairly sympathetic, at least as much as he could show in ten words or less. But, you know, he saved my life today, and his actions prove he's someone I can trust, so I took the gamble."

"Did he have any insight about who might be involved?"

"Not really. Detective Cross and Stark are the only ones with access to operational details. After our talk I think he believes me, but he did say that he needs to convince the SAC who directly authorized the surveillance."

"Hmmm. Okay, changing gears—what do we know about the other guys who were following you? And what about their killers?"

"We don't know much. We have pictures and a parking stub from a garage on 4th Street. The business that validated was called . . . what is it? Oh yeah, Prodigy International, or Industrial—something like that."

"Prodigy?" Paul asked for clarification.

"Yes, Prodigy Industrial. Why, do you know them?"

"No, but I've seen that name somewhere recently. Where did I see that?" Paul wondered aloud, pulling a stack of loose papers from his bag and spreading them across the desk.

Emily listened closely but heard only the frantic rustle of papers. "Paul, can you hear me? Paul?" she spoke loudly into the phone and then resigned herself to waiting.

After a couple minutes of silence, Paul spoke loudly into the phone, causing Emily to pull it away from her ear. "Emily, are you ready for this?"

"What do you have?" she asked, the excitement welling inside her.

"Prodigy Industrial is a subsidiary of a parent company, which has its headquarters in Kansas City." Emily could hear Paul typing furiously on his computer and then the familiar rustle of paper. "The parent company is called Royal Flush Holdings, and guess who receives a stipend for sitting on the board of directors. Go ahead, guess."

Emily thought for a moment. "Judge Craven?"

"It's just as good, and basically the same. It's Susan Craven. I found this today when I was researching the judge's wife. Apparently Susan Craven has been receiving an income for the past seven years as a board member, and in the last couple of years, her stipend has increased significantly."

"Paul, that's great! This gives us at least a circumstantial connection between Craven—or his wife anyway—and our bad guys." Emily listened for a response but heard only typing and the occasional movement of paper. "So we need to review Craven's cases again and look for any connections with Royal Flush or its subsidiaries. This could change everything."

"Emily, I have something else. One of Prodigy's sister companies is a financial firm called Infinity Pecuniary."

"Wow, that's quite the name," she noted sarcastically.

"Yeah, well, I'm familiar with these guys. They're a very reputable company. They're basically a firm of financial consultants with some serious political connections at both the local and state levels. I don't know about national, but it wouldn't surprise me. These guys are rich and powerful. I came across this name recently as well. I didn't think much of it at the time because they're such an established company, but, well . . ."

"What is it?"

"Detective Cross is on their payroll and receives a modest income for his security consulting services," Paul explained.

"Detective Cross?" Emily asked, the disappointment clear in her voice. "He's the mole? Are you saying he's the one connected to Craven?"

"In all fairness, we can't be certain yet. Between Prodigy and Infinity Pecuniary and all the rest of Royal Flush Holdings companies, they employ a whole lot of people, most of whom are legitimate. They're just employees like we are; however, it's not a coincidence I'm comfortable with."

"We'll need more evidence to make a case, and personally, I'm not quite convinced that Cross is connected to Craven. But at least I know to keep my eyes open," Emily agreed.

"So what's your plan? How are you going to proceed? " Paul asked as he ran his fingers through his hair with nervous anticipation.

"I guess all I can do is act. Cross and I are meeting in the morning and going to Prodigy to show the pictures of our car guys and their killers. You know, shake the bushes a little."

"Please be careful, Emily. The connection between these companies is fairly obvious to anyone who knows where to look. Just a word of advice, keep your distance from Detective Cross. If he sees things closing in on him and feels trapped, you don't want to be anywhere near him."

"I'll be careful. By the way, how were you able to look at the personnel files for Cross and the others?"

Paul's eyebrows furrowed as he grimaced slightly. "You don't want to know."

* * * * *

Judge Craven broke the promise he had made to his wife early that morning: *No work, no meetings, no urgent phone calls—today is only about us.* Although they had spent much of the day together engaged in a variety of family activities, he had to accept this phone call.

Of all the people John Craven knew, only Susan possessed the occasional ability of putting him in his place. Maybe it was because she seldom attempted to do so. Or maybe it was because he loved her.

Susan looked firmly at her husband as he reached for his ringing cell phone. "John, you promised," she reminded him with a hint of playfulness and a heavy measure of guilt. Instead of ignoring the call, he ignored her with bruising indifference.

Taking a seat behind his desk, Judge Craven listened intently to his mole's report of the day's events. His eyes narrowed and his thin lips fell into a frown as he contemplated the meaning of the events and the possible effect on his plans.

"The validated parking ticket presents hard evidence and a new line of inquiry for the FBI. I am counting on you to take care of this problem. My new partner and his men are as clumsy as they are stupid.

I want to know the names of the men who were captured endangering Agent Mathews, and I want to know the names of the men who killed them and were stupid enough to have their faces caught on camera. I want them to pay."

"With all due respect, sir, two of the men are dead already. I think they've already suffered for their mistake," the shadowy man offered, more boldly than he had intended.

"Do not be insolent. Surely they have—or I should say 'had'—family. Am I right? Their families will do nicely for the message I want to send Alex Nicas. My new partner's not the only one who can play rough."

"Yes, sir. I'll see what I can find."

"How is Agent Mathews? Will she be fine?" Craven asked.

"Yes, sir. She's as feisty as ever," the man responded.

"And she is remaining silent in obedience to my instructions?"

"Yes, sir, I believe so. If she speaks out or foolishly trusts a colleague, I'll know. But I'll keep a close eye on her. I'll poke around to see if she's been able to make any connections," the man offered dryly.

"And do you think she has?" the Judge asked, leaning forward in his chair.

"No, sir. She's FBI window dressing. She may be the best looking, but she's not exactly the brightest agent in the Bureau. She's no threat. I'll handle Agent Mathews."

"Good. And this Agent Thrasher who helped Agent Mathews capture Nicas's men, will he be a problem?" Craven asked.

"I'm not sure. Maybe. But if he becomes a problem, I'll take care of him."

"I leave it in your capable hands."

"Thank you, Judge."

TWENTY

PULLING INTO THE PARKING LOT, Detective Cross found a convenient spot directly across from Emily. Raising one finger from the steering wheel of his large Ford F-250 extended cab, he wagged it slightly in recognition of his waiting colleague. He left the truck running and stepped onto the chrome tubular running board, descending from the cab with some difficulty. Even for a man his size, getting into or out of his massive pickup required effort.

Emily rolled her window down as Cross approached her small blue rental car. "Good morning, detective. Are you ready to go find some bad guys?"

Cross smiled at Emily's early morning perkiness and leaned down to her driver's side window. "I'm ready, but do you mind if I drive?" he asked, surveying the small rental. "I'm not sure I'll fit in this thing."

Emily grabbed a manila folder and emerged from the car, locking it behind her. Moving to the passenger side of Cross's truck, she opened the door and tossed her items onto the seat. Grabbing a handle, which protruded just behind the door's interior, she swung her leg up onto the running board and then another large step into the cab. "Been to any monster truck rallies lately, Detective Cross?"

Cross grinned, swung his door shut, and secured his seat belt. "Off to Prodigy we go," he said, glancing at his partner. "I'm glad you wanted to come with me. We really haven't had a lot of time to get to know each other without the other yahoos around. I must admit, I don't really get Thrasher. But Stark? I don't know how you put up with that guy."

Smiling in agreement, Emily nodded her head while glancing at the tall ex-marine. "I'm glad you're on the team, Cross. You really make it bearable. Stark isn't even worth discussing, and Thrasher is just . . . well, he's just odd. I'm sure he's probably a good guy, I just can't decipher his anti-social grunts."

Setting his left blinker, Cross waited for an opening and then merged slowly from the parking lot onto the road. "Now, I don't know what to expect from this place. I got online briefly last night to see if I could tell what kind of business they do but didn't find anything worthwhile. What do you know?"

"About the same, unfortunately," Emily said. "Our job is to find out a little bit about the business and the people who work there. I want to see if anyone recognizes our friends. I'm looking forward to rattling the cage a little."

"Perfect. Now we should be coming up on Kings Ridge Parking Garage in a couple of blocks. Let's get 'em."

* * * * *

The sixth floor of the Kings Ridge building was divided into four corporate suites—three of the occupants Agent Mathews had never heard of, but the fourth was Prodigy Industrial. Despite the name's insinuation of industry or manufacturing, the corporate suite was refined and posh. In large gold letters beside the entrance of dark mahogany French doors, Prodigy Industrial Group announced stylishly to Cross and Mathews that they were in the right place.

Emily pulled down softly on the handle but the door would not open. Placing her hands above her eyes, she leaned in to peer through the glass. The place appeared deserted except for a receptionist sitting just beyond the entrance behind a large circular desk. Tapping softly on the glass, Emily motioned for the receptionist to come closer but was ignored.

Pulling a cell phone from her pocket, Emily dialed a phone number she had scribbled inside her manila folder. After two rings she heard, "Prodigy Industrial Group, how may I direct your call."

"Hello, my name is Agent Emily Mathews with the Federal Bureau of Investigation. How are you today?" Emily waited briefly for a response and then continued before receiving one. "What time does your office open this morning?"

"Nine o'clock," came the response.

Emily glanced at her watch—8:55. "Great. In five minutes, when you open this door, I would like to speak with you." Emily peered again through the glass to see the receptionist staring in her direction. With a friendly wave, Emily moved from the glass and turned toward her partner. "I guess we have five minutes."

Within a moment, the door opened a crack, the brunette receptionist peeking from within. She was young and thin, smartly dressed with a strand of pearls around her neck. The words flew rapidly from her lips. "I'm sorry. I wasn't meaning to be rude, but we just don't usually open until nine. If I knew who you were, I wouldn't have ignored you. Honest. If you would like to come in, I'd be happy to help you with anything you need, and I would love to—"

"It's okay. I'm Agent Mathews, and this is Detective Cross. Thank you for opening up a few minutes early. We have some questions we'd like to ask you."

The receptionist stood in the doorway, blocking entrance to the suite. Cross nodded his head, suggesting they move inside.

"Oh, yes, of course. Pardon me. Please come in. My name is Andie. What can I do for you?"

As they entered the suite, Emily's eyes wandered around the lobby, enjoying the lavishness of the furnishings. Just inside the door to the left was a small reception area with four rose-colored high-backed chairs and a small pedestal table in between. Original oil paintings of Kansas City landscapes decorated the paneled wall. Straight ahead, the receptionist desk separated the entrance from the rest of the vast lobby.

"Thank you, Andie. You are exactly the person I'd like to talk to. How long have you been working here?" Emily asked, looking over the attractive young woman.

"Me? Oh, I've been here about six months. It's the best job I've ever had. Everyone is super nice and really generous. I love it here."

"Isn't that nice?" Cross muttered, trying to catch a glimpse around the wall that backed the reception area.

"That's great, Andie. Enjoying your work is important. Feeling appreciated makes all the difference. If you don't mind me asking, how much do you make?"

Andie looked around cautiously and then allowed a toothy smile to envelop her face. "I'm not really supposed to talk about it, but I started at $55,000 a year. Can you believe it?"

"You're right. That's very generous. You must be a very good receptionist. How old are you, Andie?" Emily asked.

"I just turned twenty-one a couple of weeks ago. My friends took me out for a night on the town, and we had a great time. Twenty-one is such an important birthday, don't you think, and—"

"Yeah. That's great." Cross didn't have the patience for Andie's rambling stories. "So you sit here all day long, right? You see everyone who comes and goes right?"

"Of course."

Emily pulled the pictures from her folder and spread them across the wide front ledge of Andie's desk. "Do you recognize any of these people? Please look closely."

Andie looked at each picture, nodding slightly. "Sure, I know these two," she said, pointing to the two men from the black sedan that had followed Emily. "Well, I mean, I've seen them before, but I don't really know them. These other two don't look familiar. Should they?"

"The two you recognize, what is their business here?" Cross asked.

"I don't really know. Before last week I'd only seen them one other time," she answered.

"Last week?" Cross prodded.

"Yeah, they were here. My boss told me they were coming and to just let them in, so I did."

"You must have a good memory to recall such a brief interaction," Cross challenged.

"Yes, I do. But these guys were easy to remember because when they left they were irate. I mean, really mad."

"Yes, I got it. *Irate* means really mad," Cross jabbed.

Andie appeared unfazed by the derisive comment.

Emily studied Andie's movements and facial expressions. "Why were they angry?" Emily asked.

"Oh, this is good. I don't know all the details but—" Andie abruptly paused and raised a finger. "Thank you for calling Prodigy Industrial. How may I direct your call?" Andie answered, tapping the phone at her ear. "Yes, sir. Of course." She tapped her ear again, signaling the call was over. "Would you please excuse me for just a moment?" Andie walked around the reception area and turned left down a hallway, out of the agents' sight.

"Get a load of this place. Nice!" Cross commented, clearly impressed with the office suite. "How much do you think these marble floors cost?"

"Probably more than I make in five years. Hey, Cross, this receptionist is exactly the type of person we want to talk to, so be a little nicer. She may only be the receptionist, but she's also the gatekeeper. Anyone in or out of this office goes by her. Who knows what kind of nuggets of information she may have picked up around this place?"

"Nah, you're the good cop. I'm the cage rattler. It's a good system. And as the bad cop, I don't have to act interested in what she did for her twenty-first birthday," Cross said, winking.

Moments later, the clip-clop of high heels approached. Andie reappeared from around the reception area with a smile plastered to her face. "Sorry to keep you waiting."

"You were about to tell us a really good story about the mad guys from the pictures," Emily reminded.

"Oh, yeah. That's kind of boring. You don't want to hear that, but would you like to see the rest of the office? There's something I want to show you."

Emily and Cross looked at each other, wondering why their talkative new friend was now unwilling to speak. Emily gave Cross a nod of acknowledgment and followed the receptionist. "So, Andie, what are you going to show us?"

As they turned the corner and entered the inner lobby, Andie turned to her right and spread her arm as if unveiling the prize from behind a curtain on a game show. "I want to show you Kansas City," she said, clearly prepared to impress them with the spectacle.

Emily looked in awe at the ten by fifteen foot long model of the Kansas City Missouri Business District. "Wow. Cross, look at this! Traffic lights are changing."

"That is cool. Here's Crown Center and the Liberty Memorial. They even have the restaurant at the top of the Hyatt Regency, and it's rotating. Incredible!" Detective Cross bent low to look through the street corridors between the miniature skyscrapers. "I see the Sprint Center right here, and there's Union Station."

"This is so great, Andie. Where are we located?" Emily asked, obviously impressed.

"We're right here—the building with the large X on top." Andie directed the agents' view with a laser pointer.

"Oh, I thought that was for a helipad or something," Emily said.

"There is a helipad on the roof, but X also marks the spot," she reminded with a smile.

"This is really beautiful. It actually looks better than the real thing," Emily said.

"Watch this." Pushing another button on the laser pointer, Andie dimmed the lobby lights into a dark purple hue, and the lights inside the model windows illuminated, creating a beautiful late evening skyline of the city.

Emily and Cross stood still, appreciating the scene in front of them. "How many people even know this model exists? It should be in a museum," Emily suggested to Andie's satisfaction.

"I'm glad you like it. I think it's beautiful too. My boss had it built about two years ago as a gift for his business partner, and it found its permanent home right here in our lobby. Of course, it's been here longer than I have, but I'm afraid there are few people who have seen it, and even fewer who know it exists."

"Your boss sounds very interesting. Is he in? I'd love to meet him," Emily asked.

"Yes, Mr. Nicas is in, but unfortunately there was a terrible tragedy over the weekend that he's working through. Let me see when he might be available to speak with you."

"Thank you," Emily said as Andie walked down the hall.

Emily and Cross connected wide eyes, and when Andie was out of listening distance, Emily moved close to Cross, placing one hand on his tall shoulder and encouraging him to lean in. "Does she mean Alex Nicas? Mob man Alex Nicas? This could get interesting."

* * * * *

The office had been bustling since Paul's early-morning arrival. Unlike Kansas City, the Oklahoma City office seemed to employ a slightly more eager crew than he was accustomed to. He assumed his usual place at the workstation and stacked documents around his desk for further review of the official bank robbery investigation. After a few more hours of review, Paul marveled at the simplicity of the case and looked forward to the accolades he would receive after completing his work in a mere day or two. The evidence was clear-cut, and a poorly obscured money trail was traced easily to the SAC's good friend, the bank president. As originally suspected, the bank robbery was an inside job, and Paul had efficiently pieced the puzzle together.

Working feverishly, Paul continued to assemble the file for presentation to the Special Agent in Charge, documenting the bank president's involvement. By 11:00 a.m., his task was complete. With a slight swagger, Paul grabbed his files and walked the long corridor toward the SAC's office but stopped before entering the doorway.

The Special Agent in Charge was screaming at the ASAC like a drill instructor at basic training. In between profanities, Paul could tell they were talking about him. The discovery of his unauthorized investigation had happened faster than he expected. A lump formed in Paul's throat, and his palms grew damp with nervous anticipation. He was caught. Hurrying back to his desk, he stacked the evidence files neatly, grabbed his personal items, and put into play the contingency escape he had formulated the night before.

Exiting down the east stairwell, Paul dialed the ASAC's direct line expecting to get his voice mail, but to his surprise, the ASAC answered. Paul had never been a good liar, but tapping every devious instinct he possessed, he gave it his all. While descending the stairs rapidly, he informed his temporary supervisor of his sudden illness and the location of the completed work on his desk, making an unconvincing vomit sound into the phone.

"I don't care how sick you are. I want you in my office, now," the ASAC commanded.

Paul unleashed another fake vomit sound and then asked in his best sick voice, "Can you please give me five minutes? You don't want this on your floor."

"Fine, but not a second longer. We have some things to talk about."

"Thank you, sir. I'll be right there."

His eyes wide with hope, Paul turned off the phone, raced through the parking garage, and finally reached his FBI-issued loaner. He climbed in and drove to the gate, where he showed his ID to the security attendant. The gate lifted, granting him access to freedom on the city streets.

Three blocks away, Paul pulled the car to the side of the street and boarded an OCT transit bus, taking refuge from the traceable car. With his satchel over his shoulder, he sat quietly while his heart raced. What had he done? Legally, Paul's infraction was minor, but his dream career with the FBI was now in jeopardy.

TWENTY-ONE

DRESSED IN HIS NICE BLUE jeans and a long-sleeved polo-style shirt that Paul had purchased for him, Jimmy stepped from the tractor supply parts warehouse and walked down the street toward the corner bus stop. Whistling while he walked, the morning sun warmed him, and he considered the opportunity he was being given.

Jimmy had done warehouse work for about two and a half weeks nearly a year ago, but following the usual plan, he had arranged to be fired at the end of his short stint. He didn't mind manual labor; in fact, he found it invigorating. He just didn't like being told what to do.

Jimmy sat on the bench in front of the bus stop and waited, the broad smile on his face giving way to a more contemplative look. He folded his arms and stretched his legs toward the curb, leaning his head back to welcome the sunshine. Shaking his head, Jimmy thought about his past employment—the sandwich shop, warehouse, oil and lube place, and grocery store, as well as many others. The last few years had been a complete waste of time.

* * * * *

It was obvious Brother Brad Jenkins was doing a favor for the bishop, or maybe even for Paul or Emily. It didn't really matter for whom. It had been a pleasant surprise when Jimmy answered the phone late Sunday night. Very professionally, as if Jimmy had actually applied and was considered a strong candidate for the position, Brother Jenkins requested a job interview with him for late Monday morning. Jimmy found his nicest outfit and spent nearly an hour ironing the wrinkles out of his jeans; he even pressed a firm crease into the sleeves of his casual collared shirt. Ready to charm his way into another temporary job, Jimmy fell asleep sometime after midnight.

The next morning, the interview did not go according to plan. Jimmy sat tall and smiled broadly as often as occasion would permit, and without looking silly, but unexpectedly, he answered every question honestly—uncomfortable questions about his unstable job history and career goals. After twenty minutes, Brother Jenkins excused him to wait outside the office.

Taking a seat in a padded chair, Jimmy's confidence fled, and he reconsidered the wisdom in honestly answering Brother Jenkins's probing questions. Knowing he had failed to charm the interviewer, or even appear to be a worthy employee, Jimmy figured he would be back watching Paul's TV for the foreseeable future.

Brad opened the door to the office and waved Jimmy in, reseating him across from the wide metal desk. Jimmy forced a modest smile and cautiously watched his interviewer. Strangely, Brad appeared to be the uneasier of the two, as he struggled to make a decision about Jimmy's potential employment.

"Jimmy, let me be honest with you. Bishop Taylor told me you're a good young man but that you've had a bit of a rough history. He thinks you're on the upswing. I want to give you a shot, really I do, but I'm not sure I can take the risk. I'm responsible for the people I hire, and I don't want to explain to my boss why I hired a guy who quits after he collects his first paycheck. Can you understand my hesitation?" Brad asked.

Jimmy nodded his head, comprehending well that his previous failures made him unworthy of a chance to prove himself. "Hey, it's no problem. I understand. Just taking the time to meet with me was a nice thing to do, and seriously, don't worry about it. I'm not sure I'd want to hire me either. Thank you for your time, Brother Jenkins." Jimmy stood and offered his hand but was stopped when Brad held tight, making it clear the conversation was not finished.

"Jimmy, I may be uneasy about your history, but I'm impressed with your honesty. If you were trying to fool me into hiring you, you did a lousy job, maybe the worst ever. You told me almost nothing

I wanted to hear, but I think you were truthful. I can't think of any other explanation for some of your painful answers," Brad said with a crooked smirk, sitting down. He motioned for Jimmy to do the same. "Let me ask you one more question. *If* I hire you, will you take this job as an opportunity to work hard, to improve yourself, and advance as a loyal, dependable employee?"

Jimmy bowed his head and hunched over to look at the floor. He was quiet for a long moment and then sat up straight, looking directly into the eyes of his interviewer. "I can tell you this, Brother Jenkins. I'll work hard and do the best I can. I won't quit, and I won't force you to fire me. I'll try to be a good employee for you, and that's more than I've done in a long time."

With an approving nod, Brad leaned forward, placing both arms on the desk. He watched Jimmy while twirling a pencil between his fingers and then set it down on a stack of papers. "Please, call me Brad. Brother Jenkins doesn't really fly around here," he said, grinning at his new employee. "I believe you, Jimmy, and I'm counting on you." Pulling a file from his drawer, he placed it on the desk and paused. "If you can stay for about another hour, I can get your new-hire paperwork completed, and you can start tomorrow morning at 6:00 a.m. How does that sound?"

"It sounds really early, but great. Thank you!" Jimmy said excitedly, grabbing Brad's hand and shaking it vigorously. "I won't let you down, sir."

"Please drop the 'sir.' Brad is fine, really. Oh, and Jimmy, in the morning, please make sure you're on time."

* * * * *

Jimmy broke from his reflective daydream as the city bus approached the curb. Pulling some loose change from his pocket, he stepped up and claimed one of the numerous empty seats. Looking at his Velcro watch, he was eager to get home so he could call Paul and Emily to tell them the good news.

* * * * *

After retrieving his suitcase and personal items from his hotel room,

Paul went directly to the bus station, paying cash for his Greyhound ticket back to Kansas City. He knew the FBI was not likely to kick up much of a fuss on his behalf, so Paul relaxed while he waited for his one o'clock departure. Retrieving his laptop from his carry-on, he opened it and waited a moment for the satellite connection to give him Internet access.

When he typed "Prodigy Industrial Group" into his search, numerous results flooded the screen. The headlines failed to yield any useful information, so he modified his search for Prodigy's parent company, "Royal Flush Holdings and Officers." Again, numerous headlines filled the page, but only one captured his attention. Four entries from the top of the page was a headline that read "Business Leader Commits Suicide," dateline by the *K.C. Business Journal*, two hours ago.

Paul clicked on the link, and a picture of a large elderly man with dyed red hair appeared with a caption, "Kansas City business leader Gordon Harrison found dead from self-inflicted gunshot wound." Paul read the story, quickly scanning the details of Harrison's philanthropic work and personal life. He looked for suspicious details relating to the holding company, which Harrison had led as the CEO. No suicidal motive was revealed, and there was no mention of the company's future.

"That wasn't very satisfying," Paul said to himself. He pulled a printed page from his bag and examined it. Of the company's eleven board members, Paul only recognized Susan Craven's name. "Let's see what we can find out about you guys," he said, mumbling to himself. After a series of cursory searches, it appeared the board members, with the exception of Susan Craven, were all leaders of the various companies within Royal Flush Holdings.

"Okay, Alex Nicas, you're with Prodigy Industrial. What do we know about you?" he wondered aloud, typing the name into his search as he started scanning the result headlines.

"New President to Lead Prodigy Industrial Group," *ITradeKC. com, July 2003*

"Record Earnings for Nicas and Prodigy," *kcbusiness.com, March 2005*

"Indictment at Prodigy," *Kansas City Star, December 2005*

"Nicas Trial Scheduled to Begin," *kcstar.com, April 2006*

"Business Leader Acquitted of Conspiracy Charges," *Kansas City Star, April 2006*

"Royal Flush Positioned to Name Nicas as Successor," *Chamber. KC/MO, 6 minutes ago*

"Now we're getting somewhere. Why in the world would Royal Flush hire a guy like you?" Paul began typing another search but halted as the intercom announced the boarding for his bus.

Packing away his laptop and papers, Paul slipped the strap of his case over his shoulder and boarded the bus. He found his seat and unpacked his gear, returning quickly to his Internet inquiry.

* * * * *

"Congratulations, Jimmy! That's fantastic! I'm so happy for you. Brother Jenkins seems really nice. I think you'll enjoy working with him. Have you told Paul yet?" Emily asked.

"I tried calling as soon as I got home and then about an hour later, but the call went directly to his voice mail. I haven't heard back from him yet."

"He's probably busy with his investigation. Being in a different office and all, it can be kind of hectic," Emily offered apologetically.

Lying on his bed, Jimmy rolled from his stomach onto his back, leaving his opened scriptures, a notepad, and a pen at his side. Placing the pillow behind his head, he crossed a leg over the other upraised knee. "Yeah, I'm not worried about it. That's the good thing about a surprise. He'll be just as surprised when he calls later as he would be if I spoke to him right now. It'll hold." Emily was quiet on the other end of the line, so Jimmy continued, "Do you want to get together tonight for dinner? I'm cooking and taking requests."

"Sure, sounds good. Seven o'clock?"

"Perfect! What would you like?" Jimmy asked.

"It's hard to go wrong with pasta," Emily suggested.

"Awesome. I make a killer shrimp fettuccine. It's a date."

"Uh, yeah, great," she responded, not liking the sound of "date" in Jimmy's announcement, although technically he was right.

"So, how's work going for you today? Are you hot on the trail of the bad guys yet?" Jimmy asked.

Emily looked over her left shoulder in the corridor just outside the third floor conference room, sensing Agent Stark coming near. "I'm still working on it, but I think we're finally on the right track. I have another meeting this afternoon, which could be very interesting. Hey, my team's back, and I've gotta get to work. Congratulations again, Jimmy."

"Come on, Emmy," Stark interrupted, speaking loudly enough for Jimmy to hear. "Say good-bye to your little boyfriend, and let's get going."

Emily turned bright red, but she calmly ended the call. "Jimmy, I'll talk to you later. Bye."

Hanging up the phone, Jimmy grinned, his heart fluttering as he envisioned the beautiful full lips that accompanied Emily's kind voice. With both hands behind his head, Jimmy set the phone at his side and rolled back onto his stomach, returning to his assigned scripture reading. He widened his eyes and stretched his jaw as he began to read, determined to stay awake long enough to finish this time.

* * * * *

Paul's limp neck straightened with a jerk when the bus lurched suddenly. Sitting straight in his seat, Paul kept his eyes closed, and he wished the tedious ride would end, but it was far from over. Stopping abruptly, the bus became still once again, but only after Paul's weary body was hurled forward in his seat. His determination to rest disappeared when his cell phone rang. Glancing at the display, he recognized Emily's phone number and answered.

"Emily, hi. I'm glad you called. Any developments in your case?" Paul asked.

"No, not a lot. Cross and I went to Prodigy this morning. Interesting place. I'll have to tell you all about this amazing model of Kansas City sometime. But the interesting thing is who runs the company," Emily said.

"That would be Alexander Nicas. He has a bit of a colorful past and is rumored to be a part of Kansas City organized crime and the next in line to take over Royal Flush Holdings after the suicide of Gordon Harrison this past Saturday," he rattled off in one breath.

"Well, yeah. How did you—?"

"Google," Paul responded.

"Of course," she said, shaking her head. "Maybe you could introduce Stark to some of your wildly creative investigative techniques," she said sarcastically. "He was supposed to research Prodigy for us, but he's totally useless. Now, I knew some of the rumors about organized crime, but I didn't realize the rest of it. Royal Flush is the parent company of Prodigy, right? And the top dog killed himself?"

"Yeah, just this weekend," Paul replied.

"I remember hearing something about that on the news. And you say Nicas is next in line to take over Royal Flush?" Emily asked with interest.

"Yeah. This is fresh news, within the last couple of hours anyway. Did you speak with Nicas? What's he like?" Paul asked.

"Don't know. Cross and I are heading back over there in a few minutes to meet with him. He wasn't available this morning. I'm getting excited to speak with this guy."

"You know, Cross still makes me nervous. Be careful," Paul cautioned. "If he really is crooked, he could turn on you in an instant, so watch out."

Emily frowned slightly at Paul's insistence. "I'll keep my eyes open. Hey, what's that sound? It sounds like you're at a football game or something."

"I wish. I'm actually on a bus right now, and I think everyone around me had a few too many drinks before getting on. It's crazy, like a party driving down the interstate. Have I ever told you how much I hate road trips?" Paul asked.

"Why in the world are you on the bus? And where are you going?" Emily asked.

"I'm on my way back to Kansas City right now. I finished my other case this morning and kind of had to leave abruptly, hence the bus. I'm hoping to get back around nine tonight, that is if things start going my way. We've already had to change buses because of mechanical problems, and then we've had horrible traffic."

"I'm so glad you're coming back, but I don't envy the bus trip. I'm impressed you already finished your case. You'll have everyone talking."

"Yeah, I'm sure I will," Paul agreed. "Hey, would you be willing to pick me up at the station at nine? I could use a ride home."

"I'd love to. Oh, call Jimmy when you have some time. He's got some news for you."

"Will do," Paul said.

"I'm excited to see you. I've got to get going. Bye," Emily said before abruptly hanging up the phone.

Paul sat in the noisy bus, the phone still to his ear. "Okay, then, nine it is."

TWENTY-TWO

THE AFTERNOON SUNSHINE WAS A welcome change to the previous weekend's rain and gloom. Walking to the Prodigy building alongside Cross, there was a bounce to Emily's step. The dreariness and stress of the past few days had worn Emily down, but the sunshine brought the smile back to her face and a quiet hum from her lips.

"Agent Mathews, you win the lottery or something?" Detective Cross chuckled, looking at her cheerful face.

"What do you mean?" she asked, grinning broadly.

"I just couldn't help but notice your incredibly good mood. An hour ago you looked like you wanted to rip Agent Stark's head off, and now you look like you're the queen of the world."

Emily laughed lightly. "What can I say? Sometimes I *do* want to rip Stark's head off, usually because he deserves it, but I just remind myself to keep the proper perspective. And you want to know something?"

"What's that?"

"I feel good because life is good, and things will work out," Emily said.

"That's very Pollyanna of you," Cross commented.

"I suppose it is," she admitted happily, undaunted by the playful jab. Arriving at the building entrance, Emily swung the door open and held it as she ushered Cross in. "Besides, I'm looking forward to meeting this Nicas guy. This ought to be interesting."

"You're certainly right about that."

Moments later, the duo entered the Prodigy office suite on the sixth floor, the large mahogany French doors closing gently behind them. Andie sat behind the reception desk, speaking rapidly into her mouthpiece. She waved Emily closer. Touching her earpiece, she ended the call and then slumped deep in her chair with an exaggerated motion of weariness.

"Is it six o'clock yet?" she asked hopefully. "I'm really ready for this day to end. The phones have never been this busy."

"Sorry, but it's only 4:30," Emily answered with an amused expression.

Andie blew a strand of hair out of her eyes and replastered a professional smile onto her face. "I'll let Mr. Nicas know you're here, but it may be a few minutes."

Emily smiled as she waited for Andie to notify Mr. Nicas of the agents' arrival. "Thanks, Andie. I wanted to talk to you anyway."

"Why?"

"The men you recognized from the pictures, you mentioned they were here last week and they were angry. Could you please tell me more about that?" Emily asked.

"I'm sorry, I don't really know anything. They were here, and they were mad when they left. That's all I know."

"Andie, you need to tell me. I'm not your friend. I'm a federal officer, and you don't want to be seen as a person who withholds information from the FBI. Trust me. Did someone tell you not to talk to me?"

Andie shook her head and lowered it but then quickly looked up with widened eyes, locking onto Emily's. "I will tell you this," she whispered, glancing subtly over her shoulder. "The other two guys from the pictures, you know, the ones I didn't recognize . . ."

"Yeah, sure," Emily responded.

"They're here."

Emily's mouth opened slightly, and her eyes bulged. She looked hard into Andie's eyes. "What? Andie, are you sure?"

"Yes. They arrived about thirty minutes ago, but I don't know where they are now. I just know I haven't seen them leave." Andie's eyes narrowed and her eyebrows rose. "Agent Mathews, if it's possible, can you please leave me out of this? I kind of want to keep my job."

Emily furrowed her brow and looked gravely at Andie. "Please excuse me." Approaching her partner, Emily called out in a forceful whisper. "Hey, Cross."

Rising from his seat, Cross quickly joined Emily. From her desk, Andie kept a watchful eye on the partners while they conversed, as if her intense gaze would somehow amplify the urgently whispered tones. It didn't.

Returning to the reception desk, Emily withdrew the pictures of the hospital assassins from her file and showed them to Andie once again while Detective Cross pulled a cell phone from his jacket pocket and pushed through the double doors, exiting the office suite.

"Andie, you're sure these two men are in the building?" Emily asked, holding the photos of the two assassins. "Why are they here? Who are they here to see?"

"They came to see Mr. Nicas. He told me to let them in," Andie responded.

Emily caught Detective Cross's attention from outside the suite doors and motioned for him to return. "Good. Andie, would you buzz Mr. Nicas and let him know we're on our way in?" Andie complied.

Cross rejoined Emily in the reception area. "Mathews, we're set. Backup will be here in ten to fifteen minutes."

Nodding her approval, Emily placed her hand casually on the firearm underneath her jacket, verifying its presence. "Good. Now, Andie, would you please show us the way to Mr. Nicas's office?"

Andie led Emily and Cross toward the office. Cross slowed his pace, pausing in front of the large model of the Kansas City Business District. Emily matched his pace, again impressed by the detailed scene.

"You see this city block right here?" Cross asked Emily as he outlined an area near Bartle Hall with the forefinger on both hands.

"Yeah, what about it?" she asked. Andie moved further down the hall.

"That's all going to be mine someday. What a great area of the city," Cross admired, gazing upon the model with satisfaction.

"Good luck with that," Emily said dismissively.

Cross chuckled. "Right—luck."

Emily considered the odd statement.

"Maybe one of us should stay out near the reception area in case our assassins try to leave the building. We don't want to lose these guys, and backup will be here soon," Cross suggested.

"Good idea," Emily said. "You wait out front. Keep your eyes open."

Cross turned toward the entrance as Emily quickened her pace to catch up with Andie, who was standing patiently at the end of the wide hallway near an open door.

"Agent Mathews," Nicas greeted, standing behind a sleek glass desk. He motioned with one hand to the chair opposite and then sat comfortably in the padded, high-back leather chair, which appeared to be raised considerably. Emily sunk low in the offered seat and wondered if the small, well-dressed man could even touch the floor with his expensive black Moreschi shoes.

"This is a lovely office, Mr. Nicas. And your model of Kansas City is quite impressive. May I call you Alex?" Emily asked pleasantly.

"I thought there were two of you," Nicas said, ignoring her question. "I know the FBI has dramatically lowered its standards for hiring young agents in recent years, but please tell me you haven't lost your partner. That would be quite embarrassing. Surely even an agent like yourself can keep track of one little partner."

Emily stared at Nicas, who sat slightly reclined with legs crossed and a smug but puckered look on his face. "Well, Mr. Nicas, thank you for meeting with me. In fact, I do have a partner, and you'll be happy to know I'm keeping close tabs on him. Right now he's waiting in your reception area in case anyone of interest attempts to leave the building."

"Well, I'm glad to hear you're on top of things. You've already exceeded my expectations. Please tell me, Agent Mathews, who are you expecting to find here? Despite what you may think, this is a reputable business and whatever I may personally lack in social grace, I make up for with perseverance, determination, and business savvy. Surely these qualities are not illegal, are they? If you would like, you may check your FBI manual before answering."

"Of course not. In many people, they are quite admirable," she said.

"So you're here to ask me questions. The FBI sends you? You're the best they can do?"

Emily forced a congenial smile.

"It's pretty pathetic, if you ask me. I'm an important man. The least they could do is send someone with a little experience," Nicas said, his eyes narrowing. "Agent Mathews, sometimes I'm too honest. I apologize. I suppose I should just be thankful I have such a pleasant view during my interrogation. But don't expect many answers. I know my rights."

Emily considered how best to approach the boorish man sitting in front of her, and then she attacked. "Mr. Nicas, you are well within your rights to be a rude little man," Emily said with a smirk.

Nicas said nothing.

Raising up slightly out of her chair and looking toward Nicas's side of the desk, Emily continued to rouse her subject. "I'm curious, are your little toes able to touch the ground over there? That chair seems awfully high for such a little guy. Do you have a box you could set them on? I'd hate for you to lose circulation in those tiny little feet." Emily sat back and watched her subject.

The amused expression on Nicas's face turned cold as his eyes became angry. "You never answered my question, Agent Mathews. Who are you expecting to find here at Prodigy?"

Opening her file, Emily removed the surveillance stills of the men responsible for the deaths of her prisoners at the hospital. She slid them across the desk.

Picking up the photos, Nicas examined them briefly and then dropped them loosely in front of him.

"Well?" Emily asked.

" 'Well?' Is that your entire question? Surely you can speak in complete sentences," Nicas mocked.

"Mr. Nicas, do you know these men? And if so, would you mind telling me who they are and what their business is with Prodigy Industrial?" Emily said clearly.

"Yes, I know these men, and yes, I would mind elaborating. I'm not sure they would want me to explain further."

"Oh, so you're afraid of them?" Emily suggested, pretending to scribble on her notepad.

Nicas rolled his head back and laughed forcefully for a moment before returning to his cold, angry glare. "Agent Mathews, I'm not afraid of anyone—not them, and especially not you."

"Really? You see, if I were to guess, I would say these two are free-lance security for you, or maybe Prodigy in general. You have a big mouth and a generally unpleasant disposition, so I imagine you have more than a few enemies, which leads me to believe you might need additional security. I'm just thinking out loud here, but maybe there are some people who would like to hurt you, present company excluded, of course. Am I right? It's okay to admit it. In any case, I'm glad you're not afraid," Emily commented, returning his stare.

Emily wasn't sure what she hated more, Nicas's puckered smile or his seething glare.

"Mr. Nicas, I agreed to interview you here as a courtesy, but I could just as easily require you to come to our field office under an armed transport. I doubt the board members of Royal Flush Holdings would mind seeing the CEO heir-apparent trotted into FBI headquarters in cuffs. It wouldn't be the first time, but wouldn't it just be easier to answer my simple questions?"

Tapping the tips of his fingers together, Nicas replaced his hostile glare with a look of amusement. He leaned forward. "You want to know about my two associates? Why don't you ask them your questions directly?" Nicas asked, motioning with his hand toward the doorway. The two men from the photos stood shoulder to shoulder, blocking the exit. "I'm getting a little tired of this game. Agent Mathews, these men are on my personal security team, and you're right, I do have more than a few enemies. You know, maybe you're smarter than you look."

Emily hopped up from her seat and in one motion unsnapped her holstered weapon.

"Okay, whoa. Think, Agent Mathews. You don't really want to do that. Can you take the three of us? Look, I understand you're a little distressed, but you should remain calm and take your seat. Think this through," Nicas said.

Emily continued to stand, assessing the size of the men, their dress, and the bulge of weapons beneath their jackets. Emily knew she wouldn't stand a chance taking them on, but she held her ground.

"Agent Mathews, I said, *sit down*."

Turning her head to glare at the men standing behind her, Emily spoke directly to them, ignoring Nicas's command. "You should know that my partner is nearby and backup will be here in five minutes. Do you really want to start this?"

The men's faces showed no reaction.

"I'm going to walk out that door. Get out of my way!" she demanded, stepping to the center of the men blocking the door.

Nicas motioned with his hand and the two men separated, allowing a narrow exit, which was promptly obstructed by a third man who stepped up from behind. Emily's head lifted, and she gasped as she looked up at her partner. Her head shook gently with displeasure. "Cross," she mumbled. Emily had hoped her suspicions would prove unwarranted. No such luck.

"Agent Mathews, I don't think we're going to allow you to leave. Now please, take your seat. We have some things to discuss. Oh, but I almost forgot, your backup will be arriving soon. Detective Cross, how long until the full force of the FBI arrives at our office?" Nicas asked sarcastically.

"I'm sorry, sir. When I called the office to advise them that Agent Mathews and I were finished here, I failed to request backup. No one else is coming. It's just us," Cross said, staring straight ahead, refusing to make eye contact with Emily.

Emily reached for her weapon and lunged at Detective Cross but was stopped instantly by the large man standing next to her. The man held Emily's arms tight at her side.

Nicas smiled with amusement. "It looks like you were wrong, Agent Mathews. You did lose your partner. How embarrassing. It appears I gave you too much credit after all. Detective Cross, would you please close the door and have a seat so we can get down to business?"

At the other end of the hallway, Andie watched sadly as the office door gently closed.

TWENTY-THREE

THE OFFICE SWIRLED AROUND EMILY and became instantly smaller as the heavy wood door closed like a jail cell on a newly captured prisoner. Nodding to his men, Nicas watched his men frisk Emily thoroughly, removing the holstered weapon from underneath the arm of her jacket and the cell phone from her pocket. The hospital assassin released his grip on Emily and backed up while the other locked down the room from any unwanted distractions or curious eyes. Emily was alone in a room of enemies.

"Thank you, gentlemen," Nicas said. The men receded to their position against the wall.

Emily's eyes darted from wall to wall, staring at the desk and the bookshelf, and then to the window and every corner of the room as she made a quick inventory of paperweights and bookends, a putter sitting in the corner, a letter opener on the desk, and any other object that could be used as a defensive weapon. With three large men and one scrawny psychotic overlord, her offensive chances were slim, but defensively, the array of items could prove useful.

Frowning, Emily closed her eyes momentarily to calm her frantic mind and then took a deep breath, exhaling as her eyes reopened. Returning her focus to Detective Cross, who was sitting next to her, Emily's eyes tightened as she allowed every ounce of anger and resentment to pour from her soul. Detective Cross looked straight ahead, expressionless, refusing to give his former partner even a sliver of satisfaction. Emily stared at the bare side of her partner's face, and Nicas looked on in amusement and adjusted his seat to a slight recline.

Turning away from Cross, Emily looked directly into the narrow face of Alex Nicas. "You know, Cross, I guess I should have kept better tabs on you, and I have to admit, I'm a bit surprised. I suspected a connection with Judge Craven, but Nicas? You got me. I assume your thuggish little friend knows about your work with the Judge." She returned her stare to Cross, watching for any hint of emotion. "I hope I'm not making you uncomfortable by pointing out your other business relationships," Emily said.

Cross blinked his eyes and flared his nostrils, preparing to respond to Emily's vitriol. He locked his gaze on Emily but said nothing as they continued in what appeared to be a third-grade staring contest. Despite their will and determination, the contest was not a spectator sport, and the amused look on Nicas's face turned to boredom.

"Now, let's talk, Agent Mathews," Nicas said. "Detective Cross, don't you think your partner deserves a little bit of an explanation? I mean, really, it's the least you can do."

"Yeah, Cross, how about a little common courtesy. I can't imagine you could be afraid of little ol' me. Spill it, buddy," Emily taunted, to Nicas's renewed amusement.

Looking to his boss and then to Emily, Cross stretched his face uncomfortably before beginning to speak. "It's nothing to get worked up about, Mathews. Nicas simply made me an offer I couldn't refuse. It's that simple. There's not much to it really, so don't take it so personally," he chided.

"So it's *simple* to hire yourself out to the highest bidder? I suppose it makes no difference to you whether it's a corrupt judge or a mob boss. By the way, since your moral intellect seems to be a bit challenged, let me explain this to you. When you involve me and put me at risk, I take it personally. I *will* hold you accountable," Emily promised.

Cross shook his head, releasing an exasperated sigh.

Emily continued, "You're not going to get away with it, you know. When you betray as many people as you have, someone's going to end up getting you. You know it's true, and if I were you, I'd be hoping it was me. Sure, I may send you to prison, but I'm not going to brutally kill you—at least, it's not likely."

Cross chuckled casually. "Actually, I'm betting on Agent Stark's continued incompetence, and the Judge? By the time he understands what's happening I'll be cashing in, and he'll be permanently out of the picture."

"It's true, Agent Mathews," Nicas began. "Cross has simply chosen to align with what will ultimately be the winning side of an internal power struggle. That's all."

"That's all? You're right, no big deal," Emily spat before turning back to Cross. "Cross, it doesn't matter that you're breaking the law and getting neck deep with organized crime? You've kidnapped a federal officer. Do you get that? That may not be a big deal to these other creeps, but it should matter to you. Now, because I like you, I'm going to give you another chance. Would you like to surrender? What do you say?"

"You sure are mouthy, Agent Mathews," Nicas interrupted. Leaning forward in his chair, his jaw tightened, and his mouth narrowed. "You can moan all you want, but you should know that Detective Cross is still your best ally here. Without him, you wouldn't be conscious enough to have this conversation. It would be a lot easier for me to get rid of you, and trust me, it would be easy, but the detective has convinced me that you may be a benefit to me. If you think he's wrong, I suppose we could proceed differently."

Emily glowered at Cross's stone face and softly shook her head. "What?" she mumbled quietly. "What . . . what do you want? I don't understand. What do you want from me? Why do you think I can help you?"

Nicas's expression softened as he watched his beautiful young prisoner. "Judge Craven actually has a pretty good plan. I'm simply co-opting his idea and using it for my own benefit. And since he's counting on you and thinks you're working for his interests, his failure will be even more splendid."

"Great, everything's clear now," Emily muttered. "Could you try to make a little sense?"

"I'm sorry, dear, I forgot who I was speaking to. Let me explain it to you with small, simple words. I'm going to crush Craven, and you are going to help me. Just think, Agent Mathews—you'll help bring down a corrupt judge who has aims at being the head boss of the Kansas City crime syndicate. Now that sounds like good law enforcement to me.

All you have to do is stay out of my way, while I continue operating as usual. You know me—I'm a nice guy. I'm not threatening your loved ones like Craven is, and I'll even throw a few arrests your way from time to time."

With tapered eyes, Alex Nicas watched, hoping for an acceptable reaction, some kind of recognition or agreement of his proposal, but Emily did not respond. Her mouth opened narrowly and her eyebrows rose casually, but despite her success in calming her appearance, Emily's heart felt like it would explode from her chest. Determined not to show any sign of fear or worry, she faked a small yawn, covering her mouth with a closed hand.

"Do you hear what I'm saying?" Nicas asked. His voice raised with irritation, but then it softened after a brief pause. "I'll help you catch your criminals. Really, if you look at it, I'm working *for* you. I'm your inside man, and like any informant, it's only natural you would want to protect your source. It's the same deal I have with Cross here. You allow me to do my job, and I help you do yours. It's easy."

"It's easy if you don't mind selling your soul. Right, Cross?" Emily said. She felt a hand angrily slap the back of her head. Turning in her seat, Emily stared down the large men standing behind her but was unable to identify the offending hand.

"I apologize, Agent Mathews. My men are sometimes overtly hostile, but they're only anxious to protect me and look out for my interests. I can protect you if you let me," Nicas said. "Would you like my protection?"

"I think you're trying to get me cheap. Detective Cross showed me an entire city block that would be under his control. That's got to be worth a pretty penny. Are you offering me the same? Do you have anything else to sweeten the deal? I mean, come on, if I'm going to sell out, it seems like I should have something to show for it."

Nicas watched her expression closely, unable to determine from her cool demeanor whether she was coming around to his thinking or mocking him. "Listen, Agent Mathews," he began softly, "perhaps I've given you the wrong idea. This isn't a negotiation. You are going to help me, and frankly, it would benefit you a great deal if you get used to the idea, quickly. Otherwise, I have no use for you. You do want to be useful, don't you, Agent Mathews?"

Emily's lips quivered with anger as she prepared to respond, but instead of uttering another sarcastic remark, she remained silent.

Nicas clasped his hands in front of him and frowned with his head lowered. His eyes focused on a speck of dirt sullying his desktop. Inhaling deeply, he glared menacingly at Emily. "Take a lesson from your friend, and choose your side wisely. The deal will only get worse from here."

Emily stayed silent as she weighed her options: bravery that would result in death—or at the very least, significant pain—or appear to sell out like Cross, living to fight another day. If she went along with Nicas's plan and appeared to work with him, would she have the courage and strength to follow through with her intentions to fight back? She clenched her fist with frustration. She had more personal doubt and questions than she had answers.

"Come on, lady," Nicas said wearily with a guttural chuckle deep in his throat. "I don't know why I'm letting you try me like this. There's something different about you, something I like, but don't push it. My good will is fading quickly. Make your decision."

Detective Cross looked at Emily with concern, but Emily ignored his stare.

"Well, gentlemen, I accept your offer to join your merry band of criminals. Thank you for the sweet invitation," she said sardonically, slipping into her mild southern accent.

Her mockery was clear, but a wry smile crossed Nicas's lips. "Good. Now that's settled—finally. Agent Mathews, although I accept your answer, I don't trust it. My men and I will be watching you closely, and to ensure your cooperation, you will be staying here tonight. Tomorrow will be a big day, and I'd hate for you to do anything foolish." Nicas nodded again to his men. They moved forward as one, standing directly behind Emily.

"Do you mind?" Emily asked, glancing at the men behind her, all playfulness absent from her voice. "Do they really have to do that? I agreed to cooperate, completely out of a sense of self-preservation, as I'm sure you're aware, but I don't intend to be your hostage."

"Of course not. You're not a hostage—you're my guest, and I've had special accommodations prepared for you. You'll be staying in my private guest quarters on the seventh floor. I think you'll be quite comfortable.

I'll have a nice meal brought in for you. Some new clothes and personal items are already waiting for you. We'll meet again tomorrow for an early lunch, and I'll explain your role more precisely."

"I'm supposed to hang around here until lunch tomorrow? Are you crazy?"

"I'm sure you can keep yourself entertained," Nicas responded with an ugly smirk.

"Aren't you the funny little man? Look, in case you've forgotten, I'm an FBI agent. I *will* be missed if I'm absent from work. Tomorrow's a big day there too. We're setting up for my meeting with Judge Craven. I can't miss it."

"You won't miss a thing. Cross has already told your people you were feeling ill this afternoon, and he'll cover for you in the morning. After our lunch, you'll return to work to prepare for your meeting with Craven. Do you have any plans for this evening?"

"Aside from playing a hostage and watching bad TV? No. I have no plans, which I guess is a good thing, isn't it?" Her eyes shifted between Nicas and Cross. "Since I'm your guest, I assume I'll be getting my cell phone and weapon back, right?"

Nicas sneered but said nothing. With a slight nod of his head, the meeting ended.

"Well, Cross, Mr. Nicas, I guess this is good night. Until tomorrow . . ." Emily said, standing and pushing her chair firmly into the man standing behind her.

"Shannon, please show Agent Mathews to her room. Help her feel at home," Nicas said in dismissal.

"Yes, sir," the man grunted, wincing at the sharp pain in his knee caused by Emily's chair. Holding softly onto Emily's elbow, Shannon walked behind Emily as they exited the room. Down the long hallway, they passed the impressive city model and approached the reception desk when Emily felt the man's grip tighten, suggesting that she keep her mouth shut.

"Good night, Andie," Emily said politely when they passed the reception area. Smiling, she made a gentle motion to shake the man's grip from her arm but his fingers clamped tighter. Andie averted her eyes. Pretending she saw nothing unusual, Andie kept silent while the unhappy couple pushed through the doors of the office suite.

Going into the empty elevator, the large man maintained his position behind Emily and pushed the button for the seventh floor.

Emily noted the man's stern face, thick neck, and muscular build. "So, Shannon, huh? What a pretty name."

TWENTY-FOUR

THE SEVENTH FLOOR OF THE Prodigy building was everything the office suite on the sixth floor was not. Instead of luxury and opulence, functional simplicity defined the space. Emily stepped from the elevator, surprised and disappointed in the incongruity of the two areas. The walls were something between a muted gray-tone and beige, and instead of beautiful marble, simple, bluish-gray industrial carpeting covered the floor. There were no names listed beside the bare metal doors, and the hallway was deserted, lit only by the occasional fluorescent security lighting outside the offices.

"Wow, Nicas was right. This place really *is* nice," Emily said to the large man walking beside her, his rough hand still gripping her elbow. "Kind of an institutional chic, don't you think, Shannon?" The man said nothing in response, but Emily thought she detected a slight upturn at the corner of his lips.

Stopping in front of one of the many indistinguishable metal doors near the middle of the hallway, Shannon unlocked his grip from Emily's arm. Reaching into the chest pocket of his jacket, he removed a plain white card with a magnetic strip on one side. Without warning, Emily stomped the heal of her shoe onto her captor's left instep and quickly spun behind him, kicking into the back of his knee with all the force she could muster. Shannon's knee buckled, and he slumped to the floor momentarily, but his right arm swung backwards, striking Emily in the stomach as she attempted to race past him. The reflexive force of Shannon's flailing arm knocked Emily off stride and into a heap on the corridor floor. Before she could even break away from Shannon's long reach, Emily's attempted escape was quelled.

Standing over Emily, Shannon reached down and reacquired his firm grip, this time on her wrist. With her other hand, Emily held her stomach, wheezing for breath.

"That was stupid," Shannon said calmly. "Next time I won't be so gentle with you." Twisting Emily's arm painfully behind her back, Shannon returned to his position in front of the door, holding his electronic key card.

Emily looked quizzically at the door, unable to locate a card reader or other electronic device and wondered how the card would be used. Like all the others she had passed, the door was bare. There was no number, no name, nothing that would distinguish it from any other. Holding the card between his index finger and thumb, Shannon inserted it directly between the metal door and the door jamb about a foot above the handle. He slid the card downward a few inches and then returned it to his pocket. After a short delay, an electronic hum emitted from the door. Reaching forward, Shannon turned the knob and opened the door dramatically, as if to impress Emily with the spectacle.

Emily transfixed on the view beyond the drab doorway. Despite her best effort to suppress her awe, Emily could not conceal the amazement on her face. Like Dorothy stepping from the black and white house into the vibrant land of Oz, the sharp contrast of beauty, color, and richness of the apartment from the dreary dungeon hallway took Emily's breath away.

Shannon motioned Emily with his thick hand to enter the room. Orange light cascaded from the opulent new-age chandelier onto the dark leather tile flooring and vibrant yellow walls, which were covered with unusually flamboyant, but certainly expensive modern art. Despite the splendor of her new surroundings, Emily knew the suite was merely a glorified prison cell. The amazement and awe that showed in her eyes just moments before was now replaced with steely determination and thought. Shannon couldn't help but notice the sudden change on his prisoner's face.

Shannon pointed around the room to highlight benefits of the apartment and then reiterated her schedule, or lack of schedule, for the next twenty hours. Although he spoke loudly, to Emily's non-listening ears, his words sounded more like clumsy grunts, but she really didn't care what he had to say. She didn't care where the toothpaste was kept or what was in the fridge, or what she might find in the media room. She was deep in thought, and his grumbling was merely a distraction to the formulation of her escape plan.

Despite her inattention, Emily occasionally nodded her head as though she was listening. But then, suddenly, she'd had enough and abruptly dismissed her captor. "I got it, buddy. You can leave now," she said.

"I'll be right outside the door, so don't be stupid. Watch some TV or go to bed. I don't care. Just don't be stupid. I'm not in the mood. Any questions?" he asked.

"I said I got it. Now go," she said, waving him away.

Shannon grabbed a slender, high-backed leather chair from beside the entrance and pulled it into the hallway. Emily could hear the gentle hum as he ran the electronic keycard back through the door. She tested the handle and examined her only obvious exit. It was indeed locked, and there was no visible locking mechanism she could tinker with, no keyhole, and no dead bolt. Whatever the method of locking, it seemed sturdy and far beyond any basic mechanical ability she could feign to possess. It appeared her only escape was tucked safely away, behind a locked door in the chest pocket of her captor.

The room was clean, museum-like. Emily scanned her surroundings, wandering from a rounded wall to the expansive wall-length exterior windows, which reached from ceiling to floor and from the hundreds of recessed and track lights on the ceiling to the unique leather tile beneath her feet. Kneeling, she felt the speckled texture of the leather. It was velvety but firm. *Was it ostrich?* she wondered. It didn't matter. She quickly regained her focus and began touring the suite to better understand her captivity.

Surprisingly, there were no visible security cameras. Either they were well hidden, or Alex Nicas refused to allow them in his private retreat. Checking the phone lines, Emily found no connection. She peeked through doorways and thoroughly rummaged through kitchen drawers and under the sink cabinets, making mental note of the items she found. She chuckled as she recognized the lack of knives in the kitchen—presumably the result of her burly captor's attempt to remove any possible weapons.

As Emily moved throughout the suite, she found only one locked door. One eyebrow rose. With a screwdriver she found in a bathroom drawer, she proceeded to remove the simple doorknob and lock, allowing the door to swing open freely. Emily expected to find a luxurious room full of private amenities, but what she found was much more useful.

Stepping over a bucket of drywall mud and loose trowels strewn across the floor, Emily entered the spacious but incomplete room. Though the room was mostly clear of tools that could be useful to a captive seeking liberation, there were remnants of building materials that might be sufficient.

Despite the expected lack of phone connection and the absence of knives, Emily was satisfied with the sundry items the suite provided. Emily's eyes brightened as she exulted in the joy of being underestimated.

* * * * *

Jimmy sat alone at the round table in Paul's dimly lit apartment, casually picking out the shrimp from his fettuccine and popping it into his mouth. Looking at the clock yet again, Jimmy reached out with his wet fingertips and extinguished the candle sitting atop the plain white tablecloth. Emily wasn't coming. Whether she had simply forgotten their dinner date or had a work emergency, he wasn't sure, but she was well over an hour late, and he was hungry. Digging into his cold pasta, Jimmy took an occasional sip from his lukewarm water, haphazardly leaning on the back legs of his chair. Being forgotten was something he had become accustomed to.

After setting his empty plate in the sink, Jimmy covered Emily's untouched meal with plastic wrap and placed it in the refrigerator.

"Another night of TV it is." He plopped into his favorite stuffed leather chair and began a channel surfing marathon. As he watched the images flashing on the screen, his mind was more focused on his silly disappointment. It was only a simple, unofficial date after all, but his discouragement was palpable. Carried away in his thoughts of pity and loneliness, time passed quickly as his finger pushed buttons aimlessly on the remote control.

* * * * *

"Hey Jimmy! Jimmy! Hey, can you help me for a second?" Paul shouted from the doorway, multiple bags dangling from each arm and a suitcase at his side.

Jimmy swiveled in the chair, turning toward the door. "Paul? Hey, how you doing? I didn't expect to see you," he said, hopping up from the chair and attempting to remove the bags from Paul's tired arms. "What are you doing back already?"

"Thanks," Paul said with relief as he finished unloading his arms. "I finished my investigation early, and well, it's kind of a long story, but let's just say, it was time to come on back. So, uh, what's up with this?" Paul asked, pointing to the tablecloth, the half spent candle, and flowers still decorating the kitchen table.

"Oh, I was going to have dinner with Emily tonight."

"Really? You two been seeing a lot of each other the last couple of days?" Paul asked with a twinge of jealousy.

"No, not really. Not like that, Paul. This is kind of fancy and stuff because we were going to celebrate my new job. By the way, I got hired today, and I start tomorrow morning. Surprise!" Jimmy exclaimed in a singsong tone.

"That's great, Jimmy! Congratulations," Paul offered graciously but with less enthusiasm than Jimmy would have expected.

"Is something wrong? You seem a little, I don't know, distracted."

"Well, yeah, actually. You said you were going to have dinner with Emily tonight. Did it not work out?"

"No. She didn't make it. But it's not a big deal," Jimmy said, suppressing his disappointment.

"Actually, I think it might be," Paul corrected. "She was supposed to pick me up at the bus station at nine, and she didn't make it there either. I tried calling her cell, but she's not answering. When's the last time you spoke with her?"

"Um, early this afternoon, I think. We didn't talk long. She had to get back to work."

The wrinkles on Paul's forehead deepened. "Yeah, when I spoke to her, she was heading over to a meeting I was a little nervous about. I think something's wrong. It's not like her to blow me off without calling or at least returning my messages." Paul couldn't shake the sinking feeling in the pit of his stomach.

"Yeah, me neither," Jimmy responded as a slight scowl covered Paul's face. "Can't you call someone at the FBI and see if she's working?"

"Calling in isn't really a great idea right now, but wait a minute . . ." Paul picked up his bag from the floor, set it on the table, and thumbed through multiple loose pages. "I've got a number here somewhere. . . . Okay, here we go. I've got the cell number for Agent Thrasher. He's on Emily's team, and I think he may be the only one we can really trust right now. Honestly, I'm not even one hundred percent sure of that," Paul said with disappointment.

"You can't trust the FBI? Seriously? Aren't you being a little paranoid?"

"No. I'm not," Paul responded with a glare. "Jimmy, call Agent Thrasher and see if you can find out anything about . . . uh, never mind," Paul said irritably, quickly dialing the numbers. He listened impatiently as the phone rang. "Come on, Thrasher. Pick up your phone."

* * * * *

Agents Thrasher and Stark sat in a black, full-size van on the opposite side of the street, two blocks down from the nightclub. The facial recognition software Thrasher had been using to identify the two hospital assassins had yielded some late but interesting results.

Although Thrasher was able to identify both men, it was difficult to determine for whose benefit they were working in their recent assassination efforts. Not only did the larger of the two men, Shannon Moore, appear to work for Alexander Nicas at Prodigy Industrial, but he was also a second cousin of Judge Craven's wife. His partner in crime, who was also identified by the software, was Nicas's nephew and, according to tax records, was officially an employee of The Wall.

Despite the complexity of the developing relationship web, it was clear these two men were connected to both Nicas and Craven in one way or another. After some late afternoon digging into The Wall, Agent Stark had also identified Susan Craven as the sole owner of the nightclub. Based on this new information, Stark and Thrasher camped outside the one place through which all parties seemed to be connected.

"So what do you think, Thrasher?" Stark asked, mostly out of boredom.

"About?"

"About whether we're just wasting our time sitting out here," Stark said. "Do you think any of these guys are going to show up here tonight? Honestly, I don't quite have my head wrapped around how this all connects. I mean it's interesting that Craven's wife may be in as deep as he is, but I'm not quite sure how this Nicas guy plays into it. What did Mathews and Cross find out from their meeting at Prodigy Industrial?"

"Not much. Cross said Nicas was a real jerk, but there didn't seem to be anything more than strange coincidence connecting our dead guys at the hospital to Prodigy or to Nicas."

"Really? I'd say the connections between our dead guys, the assassins, Craven, Nicas, and Prodigy are a little more than coincidence. What did Mathews say? Did she agree?"

"Don't know. I only spoke to Cross. Mathews is sick. She went home after their meeting," Thrasher responded quietly.

"Did you call her at home? Sick people can talk on the phone, can't they?"

"I left a message. Haven't heard back."

"Call her again. I'm not going to let her screw this up because she's sick. I want her take on Nicas," Stark said. Thrasher dialed her number. "Man, we're wasting our time out here," Stark mumbled, watching Thrasher impatiently.

"No answer . . . just voice mail."

"You've got to be kidding me," Stark huffed, crossing his arms and looking out the window toward the club.

Looking at the display on his phone, Thrasher scrolled through his missed calls but didn't recognize the repeated number. "You're the boss, Stark. Want to call it a night?"

"Do you know where Mathews lives?"

"It's after 11:00. She's not feeling well, and I'd like to go home. It'll wait. I'll talk to Mathews first thing in the morning," Thrasher offered preemptively. Thrasher frowned as he saw a sly grin cross Stark's face.

"Come on, Thrasher. You're driving. I've been wanting to see her place anyway."

Grimacing, Thrasher turned toward Stark. "You're a jerk. I do not support going to her home and will state that in my report."

Stark was undaunted by Thrasher's threat.

"Shut up and drive."

TWENTY-FIVE

Agents Thrasher and Stark strode quickly through the dim apartment complex courtyard. Thrasher's annoyance with Agent Stark was palpable, and he didn't mind showing it. As usual, he walked in silence, but he didn't even acknowledge Stark's occasional attempt at conversation. Thrasher followed his orders with a harsh scowl and clenched jaw as he headed toward Emily's apartment.

The small complex consisted of four separate buildings, each three stories high and eighty feet long, connected at the corners by stairwells and breezeways. The courtyard at the center of the buildings was adorned with well-shaped evergreen shrubs and a white bridge spanning a small fishpond with oversized carp. Next to the pond was a traditional black lamppost casting a yellow hue.

Entering from the street through a breezeway at the southwest corner, the duo moved to the stairwell at the opposite end of the yard and began ascending the stairs to the second floor. Atop the stairs, they pushed through an unlocked door and turned left. Emily's apartment was only three doors down.

Agent Thrasher's pace slackened as he turned toward the apartment. Something wasn't right. Mimicking Stark, Thrasher placed a hand on the weapon at his side and cautiously approached the partially opened door. Light gushed from inside, and the sound of muffled voices wafted into the hallway. Male voices.

Inching closer, Thrasher attempted a quick peek through the door but saw nothing. The voices were coming from deeper inside the apartment. Agent Stark moved to the front of the door and gently pushed it with the fingertips on his left hand, his weapon raised in his right. The door opened inward, slow and silent. Agent Stark turned sideways and slithered his way through the opening. Inside the apartment, his eyes were sharp and darting. He moved in further, carefully choosing each step as though he could see potential creeks in the floorboards. Behind him Agent Thrasher was still outside the door, adjusting awkwardly in a sideways position, unable to enter through the crack Agent Stark had created.

Thrasher placed his hand on the door and pushed it in further, carefully widening the opening. He was still unable to fit so he pushed some more, nudging his belly softly against the door and his back against the frame. It appeared he would make it, but then, the inexcusable happened.

Thrasher's belt buckle hit the door with a metallic thud. He started at the sound and turned slightly, but the holster at his side knocked even harder. The normally dull sounds were amplified by the harsh silence. The faint voices from inside stopped, and shadows raced quickly. Hurriedly, Thrasher completed his entrance, both hands holding his 9-millimeter upright at chest level.

Stark was positioned near the entrance to the next room. Thrasher was thankful to miss one of his usual looks of disdain. One would come later, he was sure, but for now, Stark focused on the intruders in the next room. With guns raised, both agents were prepared for the worst.

* * * * *

Although Jimmy hadn't heard a thing, Paul appeared confident there was someone else in the apartment. Paul placed one finger to his lips, commanding Jimmy to be quiet, and Jimmy obeyed without delay. Then, following Paul's hand motion, Jimmy hunched nervously on the floor near the backside of the bed. Holding his gun down, Paul aimed directly at the floor as he stood just inside the bedroom door.

Mouthing silent words with exaggerated clarity, Paul pointed to the closet near Jimmy, who watched carefully but was unsure what Paul was trying to tell him. Paul mouthed the words again and pointed at his own weapon. Jimmy understood. Standing, he pushed the folding closet doors open. He searched quickly, rifling through some boxes atop the high shelf but found nothing useful. He looked to the side of the closet and again found nothing. No golf club. No bat. Not even a tennis racquet. Jimmy grunted quietly, disappointed in Emily's apparent lack of a sports hobby. Abandoning the closet, Jimmy lay on the floor and lifted the bed skirt, peering underneath. Perfect! Jimmy arose and joined Paul near the door, his new weapon in hand. Jimmy and Paul stood ready.

* * * * *

Agent Stark motioned with his left hand, pointing Thrasher through the entrance to the next room. Stark stayed low, holding his weapon tight, with his arms nearly locked straight ahead. Thrasher moved quietly, but he felt exposed. It seemed every light in the apartment was on, making him an easy target for anyone who may emerge from a hiding place.

The agents made their way to the kitchen and carefully opened the pantry door. Nothing. They looked in the half bathroom and the spare bedroom. Nothing. They moved deliberately to the only remaining door. Standing to the side, Thrasher opened it abruptly. The door swung inward but bounced back slightly after hitting hard against the doorstop. Agent Stark crouched just outside the open doorway. Unlike the other rooms, the lights were off. Toward the back of the bedroom, the wind blew gently through heavy curtains in front of a partially opened window. Agent Stark stood and motioned to Thrasher. With one foot slowly in front of the other, Agent Stark entered, but his caution was not rewarded.

The lights flashed on as Jimmy jumped out from behind a dresser, slashing down on Agent Stark's outstretched arms with a hockey stick. The gun dropped helplessly to the carpeted floor as a precursor to its owner. Stark fell to his knees, holding his injured arms away from his body, and looked to the man holding the large stick. Jimmy stood over the agent with his stick raised for another beating when Agent Thrasher burst through the door, aiming his gun at Jimmy's head. Jimmy held his position waiting for Paul, who quickly emerged from inside the master bath, his gun aimed at Thrasher. The men stood still, guns pointed and stick raised when recognition flashed in Agent Thrasher's eyes.

"Hey, you're Agent Mathew's boyfriend," Thrasher said.

"Yes," Paul said.

"That's right," Jimmy said simultaneously.

Paul hurriedly glanced at Jimmy.

"Who are you?" Paul asked harshly, noticing that Jimmy lowered his hockey stick.

"Paul, let me introduce Agents Thrasher and Stark," Jimmy said. "I met them at the hospital the other day." Jimmy sighed in relief.

"Which one's Stark?" Paul asked angrily.

"I am," Agent Stark said. He stood, his arms still held gingerly at his sides.

"Your arms hurt?" Paul asked.

"Yeah, they do."

"Good work, Jimmy," Paul complimented.

Jimmy grinned and nodded with satisfaction.

"You won't think it's funny when I bring you up on assault charges," he threatened. "Thrasher, take their weapons."

Thrasher didn't move. "Assault charges? I don't think so. I didn't see anything," Thrasher mumbled.

Agent Stark scoffed.

Paul gave an appreciative nod to Agent Thrasher and holstered his weapon. "What are you two doing here?"

Thrasher looked to Stark, who was still red with anger. Stark began to speak, but Thrasher cut him off. "We have no legitimate business here tonight," Thrasher confessed.

"Come on, guys. What's going on?" Paul asked.

"We're checking on Agent Mathews," Stark said quickly, cutting in before Thrasher could answer. "She had a meeting today that could be critical to our current assignment, and she hasn't bothered to report. We need her report. We knew she wasn't feeling well, so we thought we'd stop in to see how she was doing."

"She's not sick," Jimmy said, glancing at Paul. "She would have called if she was sick, or she would have at least answered her phone." Jimmy retreated to the background because he felt like he was intruding on a classified briefing.

Looking at Agent Stark and then Thrasher, Paul rubbed the creases in his forehead. "And you just thought you'd stop by and check in? It's almost midnight," Paul noted skeptically.

"I don't have to justify myself to you. I've explained why we're here. Now, what about you two schlubs? I hope you have a good reason for being here and almost getting yourselves shot," Stark said, reasserting himself with his usual charm.

Paul eyed Agent Stark. His compassion for Emily's predicament increased with every moment he spent talking to her team leader. "With all due respect, Agent Stark, we're her friends. We don't need a good reason to be here."

"Of course. You're right," Stark said. "Then I suppose you used a key to get in, right?"

"Ah, well, actually . . ." Paul began.

"And I'm sure you always bring a weapon on your social visits, don't you?" Stark argued.

"Yeah, well, carrying a weapon is actually kind of new for me," Paul admitted sheepishly.

"We're lucky you didn't accidentally shoot us," Stark chided. "Now, tell me what you're really doing here."

Jimmy was still standing quietly in the background, his eyebrows raised, wincing at the painful conversation.

"Here's the deal," Paul started. "Emily is . . . we don't know where she is, and we're worried. She missed dinner with Jimmy, and she missed meeting me tonight as well. She's not answering her phone. It isn't like her."

"You're saying she stood both of you guys up in one night. That's pretty good," Agent Stark said with a chuckle. "Maybe she's got more gumption than I gave her credit for."

"Hey! Try to concentrate here," Paul growled. "She was fine when both Jimmy and I spoke with her this afternoon. She wasn't sick. Last I knew, she had a meeting at Prodigy with Alex Nicas, and nobody's heard from her since. We're just here checking up on her, and then you guys showed up."

Stark's eyes narrowed. "What do you know about Prodigy and Alex Nicas?"

"I know you've got a real problem with your case," Paul said, but then paused briefly. "I believe Detective Cross may be working against you, and Emily's stuck in the middle. Look, I know it's not my case, and maybe you're upset that I'm involved, but I don't really care."

"*Maybe*? You're accusing my team member of subterfuge, and you think *maybe* I'm upset with you? Who are you to make accusations like that? Unacceptable."

"Stark, maybe we should consider it. Why not Cross?" Thrasher asked.

"Forget it. He was part of the team that brought the whole Craven case to our attention. He's been working on it since day one, and his service record is impeccable. Why should I consider him as the mole?" Stark retorted.

"This isn't the time for boundary wars or power struggles. You may not want me in this, but you've got problems," Paul said.

"Obviously," Jimmy muttered.

"Here's what I know," Paul continued. "Detective Cross moonlights as a security consultant with a company called Affinity Pecuniary. Guess who the parent company is."

"I'm putting my money on Royal Flush Holdings," Thrasher said.

"Exactly. The same company that heads Prodigy Industrial. I don't suppose Cross told you about his little conflict of interest, did he?" Paul challenged.

Stark didn't respond.

"Look, Stark, I admit that my motivation is completely centered on helping Emily, but we're on the same team here. I help Emily, and you solve your case. Everyone's happy."

"We," Jimmy said, piping up from the back of the small cluster of men. "You said 'I,' but *we* will help Emily. I'm in this too. This stuff may not be my forte, but I can find ways to help. Whatever I have to do, I will."

Paul grinned at Jimmy's assertiveness. "I'll keep Jimmy with me. I can use him."

"The way I see it, we still have a missing agent. I mean friend, girlfriend—whatever," Thrasher said uncomfortably. "First thing we need to do is find Agent Mathews."

"That's right," Paul agreed. "And we'll start by looking at Prodigy."

"Listen up, buddy. Mathews may be your friend, but this is still my case. I'm calling the shots," Stark blustered.

"Okay, Agent Stark. Where do *you* suggest we should look for Agent Mathews?"

"Well . . . um, Prodigy would be a good place to start," he conceded.

They all nodded in agreement. "Good. Prodigy it is."

* * * * *

Emily sat quietly in the extravagant prison suite on the seventh floor of the Prodigy building. Like a large stationary disco ball, the new-age chandelier emitted a soothing array of colors in an otherwise darkened room. Emily had verified her jailer's continued presence in the hall by raising a ruckus earlier in the evening. As expected, the large man had entered the suite with a disapproving scowl. He rubbed his eyes, grunted, and then returned to his seat outside the locked door. He was tired and bored. *Perfect.*

In a cleaning pail on the floor next to her seat, sundry items were gathered from her scavenger hunt earlier in the evening. Emily offered a silent prayer and then allowed her mind to review the escape plan one last time. Now it was just a matter of timing and luck.

TWENTY-SIX

EMILY SAT UPRIGHT WITH A start. The Stevie Wonder CD continued to play soothingly throughout the room from built-in, overhead speakers. She shook her head vigorously to restore clarity to her thinking. Recognizing the song, Emily knew she had only dozed for a moment. She stretched and looked at her watch. It was nearly 2:30 a.m. She hoped Shannon was having the same difficulty staying awake. He was sure to be seated in his uncomfortable chair outside the door, and his grogginess would translate into a slower response. Emily's mind raced with nervous enthusiasm.

Reaching inside the bucket near her chair, Emily pulled out a six-inch Phillips screwdriver and placed it in her pocket, the handle sticking out. She also pulled out an acrylic oven mitt, a quart of vegetable oil, a flashlight, a cloth hand towel, two partial bottles of Liquid Nails, a thirty-foot length of rope, a hair dryer, and a five-pound dumbbell. Emily set the items neatly in a row on the couch in front of the baby grand piano. She grabbed a metal barstool from the kitchen and set it in front of the full-length window. The pieces of her puzzle were gathered. It was time to put the pieces together and hope for the best.

Standing on a chair next to the door, Emily squeezed the first bottle of Liquid Nails in between the top of the thick metal door and the doorjamb. She repeated the process down the sides with the second bottle. She had seen this trick work well on TV with superglue, but she lacked confidence it would hold like she needed it to. Her glue plan needed some reinforcement.

Emily pulled the heavy leather sofa near the door and uncapped the vegetable oil from the pantry. Then she poured it onto the leather floor tiles, rubbing it in directly in front of the doorway. As the three-by-three foot area became saturated with oil, she continued pouring, leaving a light but slick sheen. She pushed the sofa snug against the door and plugged the hair dryer into the nearest socket, laying it back on the couch. Phase one of her preparation was complete.

Next, Emily moved toward the baby grand and set the screwdriver on top of the piano bench. She tied thick knots in the rope every four feet and then attached the five-pound dumbbell at one end. Emily tied the other end of the rope to the top of the piano leg furthest from the window. Phase two was complete.

Taking the remaining items, Emily turned on the flashlight and placed it atop the piano. She then placed the oven mitt on her right hand and picked up the bucket. In the bathroom she quickly filled the container full of cold water and returned to the sofa, which was blocking the front door.

Placing the bucket of water on the floor, Emily stood on the soft cushions of the couch and turned on the hair dryer. Starting on the lowest setting, just beneath the tone of the music, Emily slowly graduated the dryer to a medium setting while tracing the glue enforced door jamb, speeding up the glue's dry time. After a few minutes, she climbed down from the sofa and placed the bucket on the seat cushion. She stood above the water, the hair dryer in hand. Emily carefully dropped it into the bucket. Although she had imagined sparks and ensuing darkness, nothing happened. Dropping the dryer into the water failed to bring the darkness she wanted. The dryer had only popped lightly when it connected with the water, but the interior lighting was still functional. "Stupid safety settings," she said.

Returning to a box beneath the kitchen sink, Emily retrieved a stubby flathead screwdriver. She flicked down the light switch near the door and quickly unscrewed the faceplate. With the faceplate removed, she continued to unscrew the switch and eventually loosened and separated the wires. The front of the room was now dark with no way of turning on the light. Emily repeated the process at three more light switches in the front room, which turned off all the lights in the suite. The room was dark except for the beam from the flashlight facing the window.

Approaching the piano, Emily picked up the Phillips screwdriver and practiced gripping it in her mitted hand. "Here goes nothing."

She raised the screwdriver and stabbed harshly at the tempered glass. Although the thick mitt made it difficult to grasp the screwdriver, it provided a small measure of comfort as she assaulted the window. As expected, the heavy glass didn't shatter; it merely fractured, although it did make a loud crack. She stabbed at the window again with greater force, successfully puncturing the window. She continued stabbing until she had four puncture holes in the shape of a cross.

Picking up the bar stool, Emily threw it violently into the window. She hit the window again with greater strength and volume, but the window only fractured into more spider web patterns. Preparing to swing again, she heard Shannon pounding and screaming at the door. Emily appreciated the force the glued door was able to withstand. With one final blow of fury, she slammed the stool through the weakened glass and inadvertently dropped it through the shattered hole onto the street below.

Shannon's pounding became more intense. The harsh sound of metal on metal rang in Emily's ears in stark contrast to the gentle music, which was still playing. Grabbing the rope with dumbbell attached, Emily tossed it out the window. The weight of the dumbbell pulled the rope taut.

Shannon's efforts became more powerful. Emily glanced at the door, which was giving way. Grabbing the flashlight from the piano, she clicked it off. The room turned completely dark. The door crashed again with a metal concussion, and then a sliver of light appeared.

Emily crouched behind a small table against the wall, watching the sliver grow to a larger beam and then finally blow open. Shannon pushed through the door, practically throwing the couch from its place and dumping the bucket of water onto the floor. Emily remained still in her hiding place. Shannon stood in the doorway, looking around the room as he adjusted to the darkness. He reached to turn on the light, but there was no switch.

"Big mistake, lady," Shannon said angrily, still scanning the room. He took his first step into the darkened suite. His right leg flew upward as it slipped on the mixture of oil and water. He reached for the wall and steadied himself acrobatically but lost balance again when his foot contacted again the slick leather tiles. His large frame came crashing down.

Emily observed cautiously from her position behind the table, pleased with the large man's tumble, even though no hint of a grin crossed her lips. Emily remained focused.

Shannon did his best to stand, but he looked like a hog slopping in the mud as he rolled onto his hands and knees. Slowly, he pulled himself away from the wet floor and tried again to stand. The remnants of oil and water on his shoes caused him to lose traction once again, and he fell forward. His muscular arms braced his fall, and his angry fists pounded the floor. "Lady, when I get my hands on you!" he screamed into the darkness. Emily watched in silence.

Shannon grabbed a throw pillow from the overturned couch that lay on the floor nearby and scrubbed it against the soles of his shoes, trying his best to remove the oil and water. After a few minutes, he stood easily and quickly focused on the broken window near the piano.

He approached the window, noting the tethered rope hanging through the shattered glass. With a hand gripping tightly to the wall, Shannon leaned out as far as he dared, peering to the street below. He looked to see if Emily had climbed down the rope but determined it was improbable.

Shannon's back was to Emily and the door. Taking advantage, Emily moved from her hiding place. Holding her shoes in hand, Emily made her way to the door. Glancing back at Shannon, she could see him peering again through the broken glass. Climbing carefully across the overturned sofa, Emily slithered through the doorway, prudently avoiding the slime that had caused Shannon so much trouble.

Once outside the door, Emily felt exposed by the bright light. She glanced again at Shannon who was pulling the rope back through the window while speaking on his cell phone. He hadn't noticed her. Racing silently down the hallway, she entered the stairwell to hide.

Behind the closed door, Emily leaned against the wall on the landing. A relieved grin crossed her face as she gloried in her relative freedom. There was still much to do, but now her confinement was increased to the entire building.

Far beneath her, on the first floor, a door opened and closed harshly.

The echo rang through the stairwell, and Emily could hear footsteps racing up the stairs. If Shannon's reinforcements were coming from below, she had only one option left—up. Without hesitation, Emily ascended the stairs silently in bare feet.

* * * * *

Paul stared out the window of his SUV at the Prodigy Building across the street.

"What could be taking them so long?" Jimmy asked.

"Who knows? It's Stark. This guy's gotta be one of the worst— Whoa! What was that?" Paul exclaimed, peering out the window. Throwing the driver's side door open, Paul bounded from the vehicle to the sidewalk across the street. Jimmy was close behind. Kneeling down, Paul examined the mangled rubbish in front of him.

"A bar stool?" Jimmy asked. He looked up but was unable to see anything but darkened windows.

"Yeah," Paul answered, trying to determine where it came from. "Jimmy, grab the emergency kit in the back of the SUV."

Jimmy ran to the vehicle, rummaged in the back for a moment, and quickly returned to the sidewalk with a large toolbox in hand. "This it?"

Paul didn't answer. He immediately opened the kit and plucked a high-powered flashlight from inside. Aiming the light high on the building, he methodically moved from the roof downward in a grid pattern. "This is weird, Jimmy. I don't like it." Paul continued to survey the exterior of the building with his light.

"Hey. You see that?" Jimmy asked excitedly.

"No. What'd you see?"

"Scroll the light down a couple more floors. I think I saw someone," Jimmy replied.

Paul scrolled the light down. "It looks like something's hanging from the window. Is that the place, Jimmy?"

"Yeah, I think so. I don't see anyone, but it looks like the window's busted."

"Yes, it does," Paul said, clicking off the light, although he continued to peer at the broken window.

"What are you doing?" Jimmy asked.

"Shhh. Hold on a second." Paul waited patiently, staring at the dark window.

"Ha! Sucker!" Jimmy exclaimed when a head peeked from the window. "You see him?"

"Yeah, I got him. I'm not sure if this is good or bad, but that's got to be Emily's doing. I'm done waiting for Stark. I'm going in," Paul said.

"It's about time. You have an extra gun?" Jimmy asked. Paul was not amused, but Jimmy wasn't joking.

Ignoring the question, Paul walked briskly to the front entrance of the building. "So, you coming, or what?"

TWENTY-SEVEN

"I'M TELLING YOU, PAUL, YOU should let me do it. I want to do it," Jimmy pleaded. They both stood next to the glass double-door entrance.

Paul studied his friend. "You're saying you *want* to break and enter into the building? We don't have a warrant yet, and you're not law enforcement anyway. You'll be breaking the law. You'll be responsible. You know that, right?" Paul asked.

Jimmy held a piece of metal from the fallen stool in his hand, ready to poke and pry at the door. "Look, I told you I'd do whatever I need to. I want to help, and it's got to be better for me to break in than for an FBI agent. I kind of owe you one."

"Jimmy, that's big of you. But I'm just going to call it 'probable cause' and hope for the best. Just back up my story, and we'll be good." With no further warning, Paul pulled his gun from the holster and shot one round into the door near the handle. He turned his head away and slammed the butt of the gun hard into the glass near the hole. The door shattered, and a deafening alarm reverberated throughout the building.

"Real stealthy there, bud. That ought to get some attention," Jimmy commented.

Looking at the gun hilt still in his grip, Paul felt a trickle of blood run down his palm and drip from his hand. He holstered his weapon and then pulled a piece of glass from his hand near the wrist. He wiped the blood on his T-shirt and reached through the door with his other hand to unlock the dead bolt. "Okay, Jimmy. Let's find Emily," he said, starting to enter. Paul paused and turned back to Jimmy. "Stay close."

The granite lobby seemed empty, but despite his eagerness to find Emily, Paul moved slowly and cautiously. His ears were sharp and his eyes wandered purposely around the building, searching for open doors, alcoves, or any other quiet place that could provide cover for an enemy.

Jimmy followed Paul into the lobby and around a corner toward a bank of elevators. Between the elevators was a three-by-five-feet LCD monitor with an interactive menu, including a register of tenants. Paul efficiently navigated the system and then stopped to read. Pointing at the tenant directory, Paul scrolled down quickly. "Prodigy Industrial Group, sixth floor. Hey, Jimmy, when we were outside how many floors did it look like this building had?"

"I don't know. Ten or eleven," he answered in a tone that sounded more like a question than an answer.

"Yeah. Ten. That's what I thought. But there's no seventh or tenth floor on the register. Does that seem strange to you?" Paul asked Jimmy.

"No, not really. Maybe they have some space that's not leased out," Jimmy responded.

"But why not lease it out? It seems like a waste—especially the top floor. That is, unless they're using the space for something else," Paul thought aloud.

"That's true. Prodigy owns the building, right?"

"Yeah, they own it," Paul said, flipping open his cell phone and speed dialing Agent Thrasher. The phone went directly to voice mail. Paul hung up.

Leaving the elevators, Paul approached the stairwell door with Jimmy in tow. "Okay, Jimmy, multiple choice question: Where should we go first? A—the sixth floor where we know Prodigy has offices. B—the seventh floor, which we know has a broken exterior window that's suspicious. Or C—the tenth floor, which we think exists but don't know anything about."

"B. Definitely B. If Emily really caused that broken window, she's going to need our help, and fast," Jimmy answered, glancing impatiently at his watch.

"I agree," Paul said, and he opened the door leading to the stairwell. He peeked inside.

"Paul. Did you hear me? I said *fast*. Honestly, can you speed this up a little?" Jimmy challenged with a harsh whisper.

"Yes, I probably could, but that might get us killed. Then what help would we be?"

"Maybe we could take the elevator. That'd be faster. Do you have a problem with taking the elevator?" Jimmy asked.

"Yes, I do. I don't know who's up there. Do you? Do you really want to announce your arrival? You get a bad guy waiting for the door to open, and we're both dead. That would be bad," Paul said dramatically. "Now, be quiet. Don't make me regret letting you tag along. We're taking the stairs."

Both men entered the dimly lit stairwell. Paul held up his hand, and they both stopped. An echo of a door closing high above fell on their ears. Paul motioned with his hand, gazing upward, and slowly began to ascend the stairs.

"This is killing me," Jimmy whispered.

"Shut up, or I'll be killing you. Seriously."

Jimmy nearly responded but bit his lip instead. He crept up the stairs behind Paul. He wanted to rush ahead to find Emily but resisted the urge. But Jimmy questioned the prudence of their sluggish approach. *What if Emily is hurt or in danger? Paul's taking too long.*

Jimmy skulked closely behind Paul, however, because one thing was absolutely clear to Jimmy—he needed Paul much more than Paul needed him.

* * * * *

Standing on the ninth floor landing, Emily kept the heavy door cracked slightly with her fingers. She listened, but with the alarm screaming wildly throughout the building, it was difficult to hear the activity on the stairs. Before the alarm was tripped, she had heard men enter the stairwell, but moments later it sounded as though they exited on a lower floor. As she continued to strain her ears, filtering out the unwanted clutter of the noisy alarm, the echoed sound of whispered voices rose to meet her.

After another moment of waiting and listening, Emily allowed the door to shut gently. With the exception of the florescent green exit sign and one bulb from a security light overhead, the hallway was dark.

Emily leaned heavily against the wall, allowing herself to rest. Her chin hit her chest as her eyes closed.

Putting her shoes back on, Emily started walking down the corridor, testing every door she passed. As expected, the doors were locked, and the ubiquitous key card entries denied access. Although she was heartened that the suites on the ninth floor seemed to be occupied by legitimate businesses, she knew she needed to gain access without drawing attention to her location. She needed a phone to call for help.

* * * * *

Agent Thrasher turned off the flashing lights when he pulled to the front of the building.

Climbing from the passenger side, Stark slammed the door shut. "What is that racket?" he asked, looking around the street.

"That's our boys," Thrasher replied, pointing toward Paul's SUV.

"And what about this?" Stark asked, walking toward the broken stool scattered on the sidewalk. Approaching the shattered glass entrance, Stark asked, "How am I going to justify that?" He shook his head.

"I've got the warrant. We knocked, no one answered, and we entered. It's not complicated," Thrasher grunted in response. Stark scowled at his chubby black colleague. With his weapon raised, Thrasher pushed through the door and heard the crackling sound of broken glass underfoot.

"Hold up, Thrasher. Let's wait for backup."

"How long? And how many are coming?" Thrasher asked.

"A couple of minutes, tops. In fact, here we go," Stark answered, watching a large pickup truck pull to the front of the building.

"You're kidding, right? Detective Cross? Did you listen to anything Paul said? Why would you call him? You were supposed to call reinforcements for us, not the bad guys." Thrasher holstered the weapon and rubbed his head vigorously, waiting for Detective Cross to join them in the lobby.

"Listen, Paul knew nothing. He had circumstantial evidence on Cross and nothing more. I'm not going to throw my guy under the bus with evidence that thin," Stark said defensively.

"You would if it was Agent Mathews," Thrasher corrected.

"But it's not Agent Mathews, is it?" Stark snapped. Glancing quickly over his shoulder toward the approaching detective, Stark lowered his voice. "Just play it cool. Trust me."

Thrasher looked at Stark askance. "I don't think so."

"What don't you think?" Cross said, stopping next to the two agents.

"Nothing," Thrasher mumbled.

"Okay, then, let's go. Stark, you were a bit vague on the phone. We have a warrant for what exactly?" Cross questioned.

"It's a broad warrant. We can search the building."

"Well, good, but what are we searching for?" Detective Cross pressed.

"I'm sorry. I thought I was clear. We're looking for Agent Mathews. No one has seen or heard from her since you two left Prodigy this afternoon. We went to her home, and she wasn't there. She's not answering her phone. You know I'm not a fan of Mathews, but this is strange for her. We think something's wrong," Stark said.

Thrasher remained quiet as he intently watched the tall detective. He watched Cross's eyes bulge with an exaggerated surprise that seemed to linger too long.

"And you think she's here?" Cross swallowed hard, his thumbs nervously searching for the corners of his front pants pockets. "She wasn't feeling well when we left. Have you checked the hospitals?"

"Nothing at the hospitals, and maybe we won't find her here," Stark conceded. "But hopefully we can find some kind of clue to point us in the right direction. She's a member of our team, and we look after one another. Now, it's only the three of us, so let's be careful."

With his lips curled up slightly, Thrasher glanced knowingly at his team leader. Not only had Stark not mentioned Paul's and Jimmy's presence in the building, he had also been vague enough with Detective Cross on the phone that it would have been impossible for Cross to warn anyone at Prodigy with any specifics.

"Thrasher, see if you can find the security control room and access the surveillance feed. Cross, you come with me," Stark said. "Let's check out the Prodigy Suites upstairs. Oh, and guys, keep the radio volume down. Channel three."

Thrasher nodded and pulled his weapon as he walked around a

corner into a long corridor. The other men headed in the opposite direction toward a short row of elevators.

Thrasher had been in many buildings like this. They were predictable. As expected, off the main corridor was a small hallway leading to rest rooms and a bar-locked emergency exit. Before reaching the rest rooms, there was a nondescript white door. Thrasher attempted to turn the handle, but it was locked.

Thrasher thumped the door three times with his closed fist, his weapon ready. "Come on, guys! Open up! I forgot my keys," he bellowed through the door. He pounded again, but there was no response. All the better.

Thrasher knew that the security room in most buildings is ironically insecure. The truth is, a basic lock usually suffices in keeping wanderers and lost building patrons out. With no one inside to greet him, entrance to this room would be even easier than Thrasher had hoped.

Backing away from the door, Thrasher raised his thick leg and kicked near the knob but was unable to reach high enough. There was a minor crack and a loud thud of his heavy shoe against the metal. He lunged again at the door sideways, this time with greater momentum and a surprisingly powerful karate kick. The door jolted harshly, and he heard an intense crack of the cylinder lock breaking against the sturdiness of the doorjamb. The door separated and slowly creaked open. Thrasher pursed his lips with satisfaction at his tremendous physical feat. But getting in was easy. Keeping returning security officers out would be more difficult.

Thrasher closed the door behind him and locked the dead bolt. Placing his gun on the desk in front of a myriad of monitors imbedded in the wall, he pulled up the uncomfortable steel chair and sat. Playing with the controls, he split the screens into four quadrants and then used the rollerball joystick to zoom in and out with his chosen camera. On one monitor Thrasher kept focused on Detective Cross and Agent Stark as they rode in the elevator to the Prodigy Suite, while on another he scanned the sixth floor to be sure it would be clear of danger when they stepped off the elevator.

On the other monitors, Thrasher scanned the other floors looking for Agent Mathews, Paul, or Jimmy. Although he had yet to find his intended targets, he could see a tall muscular man in a turtleneck moving on the seventh floor, methodically searching door to door while being trailed by two sidekicks in navy sports coats. One of the guards was tall and wiry; the other was pudgy, with a grotesquely misshapen head. Thrasher found comfort in their comical appearance, figuring he could ward them off when they returned to claim their not so secured room.

With excited eyes, Thrasher continued scanning various locations in the building with the rollerball, while keeping watch on Cross, Stark, and the building security men. With the other hand, he pulled his cell phone from his pocket and dialed Paul's number. Nothing. The small LCD on his phone was blank. Heavy usage throughout the day had killed it.

"Not good," he mumbled, tossing the phone onto the desk next to his weapon. Picking up the workstation's phone handset, Thrasher dialed Paul's number. The phone rang three times, and then Paul answered with a whisper.

TWENTY-EIGHT

EMILY PERKED UP AT THE gentle sound of a door opening at the end of the hallway. She scurried around the corner and waited with her back to the wall. Breathing heavily, she resisted the urge to peek. The soft murmur of unidentified male voices edged closer as the door clicked shut. Stealing further away from the voices, Emily passed the elevators, turned the corner into another narrow hallway, and then ducked into a men's restroom. With an ear to the door, Emily's eyes darted around the small restroom, noting two stalls and the open space underneath the sink. Neither location would adequately conceal her if the visitors down the hall came looking inside.

The clear and familiar jiggling of door handles was getting closer. Emily labored to keep her breathing steady as the voices drew near. She listened carefully, but suddenly the voices quieted. Waiting at the side of the door, she held her breath while her mind raced.

Without warning, the door flung open, nearly smashing Emily's petite body into the wall. Intuitively, Emily clasped the door handle with her hand and held the door in a concealing position, pressed tightly against her nose. Through the space between the hinges, Emily could see a man step into the restroom. Emily pleaded urgently but silently for safety.

The stall doors slammed as they were inspected, and then an abrupt tug at the opened door ripped the handle from Emily's light grip. The door closed as the man strode back into the hallway. Emily remained still, relief going through her. Once again, she was alone in the restroom. She exhaled quietly through her mouth, inhaled deeply, and then rubbed her nose, which was sore from its contact with the door. Recapture could not have been any closer. She mouthed the words, "Thank you."

* * * * *

"Hey, where'd those guys come from?" Thrasher wondered aloud as his eyes were drawn to the monitor with two burly men entering onto the ninth floor.

"What?" Paul replied abrasively.

"Sorry, Paul. This is Thrasher," he said. "I'm in the security room watching the surveillance. What's your location?"

"Stairwell, approaching the seventh floor. Nice of you to join us," Paul said sarcastically. "When we were outside, we saw a broken window. We're going to check it out."

"Negative. Hold your location. You have building security and a possible unfriendly moving on seven."

"How many men? And can you tell what they're doing?" Paul asked.

"Three men. They're moving from room to room. Don't know why."

Paul smiled. "Our girl got away from them. They're looking for her," he theorized. Paul looked at Jimmy and gave a simple thumbs-up at the encouraging news. "You're watching the surveillance? Have you seen Emily, uh, Agent Mathews?"

"No location yet. I'm still searching. Oh, and I can't see you either."

"Why not? What's the problem?"

"I don't have a view of the stairwells, and I really don't have this system figured out completely. The feeds on the monitors are rotating, which is making it difficult to control. I can isolate the cameras and maintain my watch, but I don't have a view of every location at once."

Paul didn't respond. Listening to the ambient noise in the stairwell, he motioned for Jimmy to follow him up the stairs past the seventh floor landing. Both men waited as Paul peered down over the railing. "Thrasher, let me know the instant you see her," Paul directed with a whisper and then hung up. Facing Jimmy, he pressed a finger against his lips.

The door from the seventh floor opened abruptly and two men, whom Paul assumed were the security guards, began jogging down the stairs two at a time. " 'Look there. Come here. Hurry up.' Man, get me away from that guy," one of the men complained as the duo rapidly receded from earshot.

Paul remained quiet for a moment and then dialed the number from his last incoming call. "Thrasher, heads up. Our two security guys left the seventh floor and are headed down in a hurry. Be ready in case they come your direction."

With his shoulder holding the phone in place, Thrasher instinctively picked up his weapon and checked it, moving around into the chamber. "I'll be ready. And Paul, Stark is here with Detective Cross. They're rummaging through the Prodigy Suite on the sixth floor."

Paul ran his fingers through his hair, gently shaking his head. "Unbelievable," was all he could utter.

"If it makes you feel better, I think Stark is dealing with Cross in his own way. Cross just doesn't know it yet."

"Whatever he's doing, he'd better keep Cross on a short leash and away from me and Emily." For a moment Paul listened to the silence on the phone and then hung up.

"Jimmy, there's only one guy left on the seventh floor. He may know something about Emily. You up for a little excitement?" Paul asked with a sly grin.

"Are you kidding? Just point the way, buddy."

* * * * *

Although it had been a few minutes since she'd heard a sound, Emily peeked warily through a thin opening in the restroom door. Once she was satisfied with her isolation on the ninth floor, she moved cautiously into the hallway and concluded her initial work of looking for entry into one of the many offices. Her failure to gain access was discouraging and complete. With the exception of the restroom where she had hidden briefly, not a single office, closet, or room of any kind was open.

Emily considered the men who had searched the floor unsuccessfully. The probability of their return seemed low.

A few yards away, on the other side of the hallway, was a red metal box with a glass front. Emily approached the case and picked up the small mallet attached to a chain at its side. The glass shattered with one easy blow. Clearing the jagged glass edges of the case with the mallet, Emily pulled the fire extinguisher from its metal clasp. Moving back across the hallway, she raised the metal canister and slammed it into the full-length window next to a cherry wood doorway. Reaching through the broken glass, Emily unlocked the door and gained entry.

Emily walked to the back of the room, bypassing many desks and cubicles, and entered an office with a wooden door similar to the entrance she had just come through. Sitting at the desk, she reached for the phone but recoiled at the sound of the startlingly loud ring. Her hand hovered above the receiver as Emily considered what she should do. She finally withdrew her hand and let it ring. The phone soon became quiet. Emily reached again, but the phone rang before she was able to grab it. She rested her hand, and the ringing stopped. Emily stared quizzically at the phone. Then, once again, it began to ring.

Emily gently picked up the receiver and held it to her ear but didn't speak.

"Agent Mathews, can you hear me?"

"Agent Thrasher? Is that you? How in the world . . . ?" Emily asked.

"I've been looking for you on the surveillance feed, and I found you just as you were smashing into the office. Can you tell me what's going on here?"

"Are you here in the building?" Emily asked hopefully.

"Yes. I'm here with Stark, Cross, Paul, and Jimmy. And the next ten minutes, we'll have more agents here as well," he responded.

"I've heard that one before," Emily muttered. "Listen to me—Cross is no good. He's with Nicas. Don't trust him. He's a traitor."

"I know. Well, I suspected, but I believe you. We've got to get you out of the building. Then we can take care of Cross and Nicas," Thrasher suggested.

"You're right. Where's my best exit?" Emily asked.

"I need to guide you, but without continual communication I can't do that. Wait where you are, and I'll send someone to get you."

"You said Paul's here? And Jimmy? I don't know what they're

doing here, but send them. I'd better not see Detective Cross," Emily warned.

Thrasher didn't respond. Over the phone Emily could hear loud but muffled screaming and banging. Finally, she heard Thrasher return as he cleared his throat.

"Thrasher?"

"I'm here," he said in his low textured voice. "I'll send the good guys. I've got to go and deal with some company. Stay put." Thrasher hung up.

Sitting on the floor, Emily pulled her knees up to her chest and wrapped her arms around. She blew a strand of hair from her eyes as she thought about Paul and Jimmy. They were close. Emily breathed deeply and rested her eyes.

* * * * *

Thrasher remained seated in the uncomfortable steel chair to the side of the bolted door. He rested his gripped weapon on his lap while he glanced at the monitors behind him. The two security guards screamed through the door, beating against the metal with their fists.

"You boys forget something?" Thrasher hollered through the door, looking pleasingly at a ring of keys hanging from a hook near the door. "I'll say this one more time. I am with the FBI, and I have a search warrant in my possession. Unless you would like me to arrest you, or possibly shoot you, you need to stand down."

The men outside the door continued pounding, but intermittently and with less enthusiasm. "Prove it!" one of the men yelled.

Thrasher considered the request but denied it.

"If you can prove you're FBI, we can help you," the other guard offered.

Thrasher turned toward the monitor, considering the counteroffer. His eyes widened with alarm when he saw his own face in one of the monitors. He looked quickly around the room but saw no camera. Nevertheless, his face grew larger on the screen.

"Someone is watching me. Why is the security room under surveillance?" Agent Thrasher asked anxiously. "If you show me, I can trust you, and I'll prove that I'm FBI. Deal?"

"Deal," came the guard's response through the door.

"So answer my question. How am I being monitored in here?" With his hand maneuvering across the roller-ball control, Thrasher searched urgently for a way to impede the surveillance of the unknown watcher. Suddenly all but three monitors went blank. The only pictures remaining were those of Agent Stark and Detective Cross on the sixth floor, Agent Mathews on the ninth floor, and Agent Thrasher in the control room. "Come on, guys! I'm waiting," Thrasher shouted.

"The tenth floor. It's got to be the tenth floor," came the response.

"What about the tenth floor? I didn't even know there was a tenth floor," Thrasher confessed.

"We're only night guards, but the tenth floor is off-limits. We're security for the building, but the tenth floor is security for Prodigy Industrial. Don't ask me why 'cause I don't know. That's just what I've heard," one of the security guards shouted back.

The pudgy guard tapped his foot impatiently while he and his partner waited outside the door. The deadbolt released with a clap, and the door swung open. Thrasher stood at the door with his badge extended. "Get in here, guys. This is your system." Pointing to the monitors, Thrasher asked, "Are you telling me someone on the tenth floor is seeing what we're seeing?"

The wiry guard raised his hands defensively. "I don't know. I've never seen anything like that before. But if I had to guess, I would say yes."

"Stop them. I don't care how, but I want all surveillance cut off. I don't want them to seeing anything. Can you do that?" Thrasher asked anxiously.

"I don't know. Let me think," the pudgy guard said.

Immediately, Thrasher picked up the phone and redialed the office where Emily was waiting. "Mathews, you've got to get out of there, now. Make your way down the stairs toward the seventh floor. You should run in to Paul and Jimmy along the way. Go now."

* * * * *

Bolting from the chair, Emily raced to the main entrance and over the shattered glass. She quickly peeked outside the door, and finding the hallway empty, proceeded quickly to the stairwell. As she descended the stairs, she heard the familiar sound of an opening door coming from above. She moved silently downward, hoping with each turn she would find her friends.

When she reached the seventh floor landing, the sound of descending footsteps clattered near, and her friends were nowhere to be seen. Although she cringed at the thought of returning to her seventh floor prison, the footsteps were close, and she needed to avoid detection. Emily softly opened the door and returned to the harsh, institutionally gray interior of the seventh floor.

* * * * *

"They're watching us. Get out of there," Agent Thrasher warned Agent Stark across the radio before tossing it aside.

Picking up the control room phone, Thrasher dialed Paul's number. Agent Thrasher remained on the line as Paul's phone rang sluggishly.

The surveillance from the tenth floor remained focused on Thrasher and Stark, though Emily was no longer pictured. Paul wasn't answering his phone. Everything seemed to be unraveling. The team was in danger, and there was nothing Thrasher could do to help.

TWENTY-NINE

Agent Stark, I can see you on the security monitor. What's your status?" Thrasher asked urgently into the hand radio.

The radio at Stark's side buzzed with activity, drawing Detective Cross's attention. "Still at the sixth floor Prodigy Suites," Stark answered, glancing at his colleague.

"Why are you still there? Didn't you hear me? You need to get out of there. We've got additional movement on the upper floors, and someone else has access to the surveillance feed. Come down until reinforcements arrive."

"I heard you but decided to ignore you. We're fine here," Stark said, giving a sly smile and quick wink to Detective Cross. Then, holding up one finger to his partner, Stark moved to a more private location in a nearby office. "I found something interesting in Nicas's office. Thrasher, is Agent Mathews secure?" Stark asked.

"Not yet. She's on the move. We've got additional bogeys moving around the building. I think they're coming from the tenth floor. We should have reinforcements here any minute."

"Good."

"She said Cross is the mole."

Stark paused, looking at the radio in his hand. "I want incontrovertible proof. I don't want him wiggling out of this in court. I want to see this with my own eyes. Time to put Cross to the test," Stark said, glancing over his shoulder.

"How?"

"Simple. I'll lure him with some bait. When he bites, I'll yank back hard to make sure the hook is set so he can't escape. Then I'll reel him in. Here's what I need you to do . . ."

* * * * *

Jimmy stumbled around the hallway corner with a crumpled, bloodied shirt held tightly against the back of his head. Raising his other hand directly in front of him, Jimmy called out loudly, bumping repeatedly against the wall as he labored forward.

"I got her," Jimmy called out again, after which he groaned loudly. He scanned the area nervously, worried about his overacting. From down the hallway, a thick-necked man emerged from an open door, obvious confusion registering on his face. Jimmy took another step forward and then stumbled backwards into the wall before falling to one knee. The muscular man approached slowly, his damp shirt clinging tightly to his chest and his jacket disheveled.

"Who are you?" the man demanded. "What are you doing here?"

Jimmy looked as though he would answer but then fell back again, this time hard onto his hip. "Ouch!" he grumbled, wincing at the pain. "The girl we've been looking for. She put up a surprisingly robust fight, but I got her," Jimmy said with a large toothy grin.

"Looks like she got you," Shannon commented.

"Hey, I said the fight was *robust*. All that matters is who won. That's me," Jimmy said with exaggerated swagger. "I was bringing her down to you and somehow she got a hold of my gun and knocked me on the head." Jimmy attempted to stand, but his legs buckled beneath him, and he collapsed back to the floor. "Hey, do you mind?" he asked, reaching toward Shannon.

Shannon grabbed Jimmy's hand and pulled him easily to his feet. Looking Jimmy over, Shannon scoffed at his white tank undershirt, blue jeans, and inexpensive sneakers. "New guy, huh?"

Jimmy nodded sheepishly. Under Jimmy's arm was an empty holster, a prop provided compliments of Paul. "Where's your weapon now, you idiot?" Shannon asked in disgust.

Jimmy patted his chest and holster nervously. "I don't know. I just had it. The girl—the girl must have taken it . . . again!"

"Where is she?" Shannon asked angrily.

Jimmy moaned for effect. "The stairwell. She's in the stairwell."

Satisfaction covered Jimmy's face as Shannon lumbered heavily around the corner toward the stairwell. Shannon stopped suddenly, staring down the barrel of Paul's Glock 9-millimeter.

"Well, hello there," Paul greeted. "Hands where I can see them," Paul warned when Shannon's large hand moved shrewdly toward a bulge under his jacket. Shannon complied, placing his hands directly in front of him, palms down. "That's better."

Despite the large man's effort, Paul was not intimidated by Shannon's seething glare. As Jimmy emerged from around the corner, no longer wobbling or holding the fake wound on his head, Shannon's gaze turned away from Paul briefly.

"How was I, Paul?" Jimmy asked playfully. "A little over the top I think, but I captured the essence of my character. What do you think, muscle man? Gotcha, didn't I?" Jimmy taunted, flexing his upper body in mockery.

"That was the best performance ever," Paul said, exaggerating his praise while grinning at Shannon. "Nice work, Jimmy."

Shannon shifted his stance subtly as though preparing to lunge. Recognizing the move, Paul emphasized his weapons readiness with a light jab in Shannon's direction. All playfulness left instantly from Paul's face, and he nodded to Jimmy. "Pat him down, Jimmy," Paul requested. With some fumbling, Jimmy removed the weapon and replaced it in the holster he was still wearing. He frisked the man quickly and backed away.

"So who are you, and what are you doing here?" Paul asked.

Shannon didn't answer.

From behind, a familiar voice called out. "I'll answer that," Emily said, eliciting two tremendous grins and one large frown. Emily sauntered from the far end of the hallway, surprising her two friends and her former captor.

* * * * *

"Agent Stark, I found Agent Mathews. She's on the ninth floor in an office down the west hallway," Agent Thrasher said into his hand radio. "I had her on surveillance but lost the feed. I no longer have visual."

"Okay. We're on our way. Where is she exactly?" Stark asked. He and Cross started walking quickly toward the suite exit.

"There's broken glass at the door where she gained entrance. You'll know it when you see it,' Thrasher said. "And one other thing, it looks like there's a hostile on the seventh floor. I didn't see what happened, but he's lying on the ground, and it looks like he's beginning to stir. I recommend you pick him up. Elevator's clear on seven, but use the stairwell going to nine."

"Got it," Stark said and then reattached the radio to his belt. "Cross, let's split up. We need to secure Mathews, but I don't want this other guy to get away. He may have valuable info."

"I agree. I'll get Agent Mathews, and you get the hostile," Cross suggested. Stark cocked his head and looked at Cross questioningly. "What? She likes me better," Cross said.

"You're right about that," Stark agreed. "Be careful. We don't know what other surprises may be roaming the building. I'll go to the seventh floor." Agent Stark radioed to Thrasher, "Cross and I are splitting up. Cross will get Mathews. I'll get the hostile. Contact Cross on his cell with any updates."

Separating, Detective Cross moved down the hallway to the stairwell, and Agent Stark to the elevator.

* * * * *

"Emily!" Jimmy exclaimed, racing toward her and being careful to remain out of Shannon's reach. Paul glanced back at Emily but maintained his focus, his weapon on the prisoner. Jimmy grabbed Emily around the waist and pulled her close. "We were so worried about you."

"That's an understatement," Paul said coolly, his back to Emily and Jimmy. His chest heaved and his heart pounded with relief. In his mind, he pictured racing to Emily, burying his face in her neck, and smothering her with kisses, but Paul stifled his emotion. Now wasn't the time. "Emily, are you okay? Did this guy hurt you?" Paul asked, staring angrily at his captive.

"I'm doing great now that you're here. You're an answer to my prayers," she said, her eyes glistening. "But it's still not safe here. We need to get moving."

Paul pulled his cell phone from a front pocket and held it out, extended near his side. "Emily, redial the last call. Ask Thrasher about our exit."

Emily grabbed the phone and dialed. She spoke briefly and then turned off the phone. "Easy. We'll take the elevator to the main floor. Backup is arriving now. Shannon, you know the way. Let's move."

Jimmy was incapable of suppressing his goofy chuckle. "Shannon. How pretty." Emily grinned at the familiar joke.

With Shannon handcuffed and positioned a safe distance to the front, the three friends approached and entered the elevator. Emily looked up at Paul and smiled wearily. His face was stern with concentration, and he continued fixing his weapon on Shannon. Emily moved closer and leaned her shoulder lightly against Paul. She longed for his touch, but for now, this was the best she was going to get.

Emily's gaze moved to Jimmy, and her eyes widened as she noticed the sticky substance matting his hair. "Jimmy, what happened to your head? Let me take a look."

Hunching over, Jimmy enjoyed Emily's soft touch as she gently picked through his hair. Paul looked on bitterly, considering Jimmy's flirtatious ruse.

"I don't see a wound. What is this stuff?" Emily asked with a bewildered expression.

"Oh, that. Did I mention I'm not really hurt? Not really," he said nervously.

"Not yet," Paul muttered.

Jimmy pointed to his head. "This was for muscle man's benefit. Just a little liquid soap in my hair." Emily's look of disapproval was unmistakable. "But the blood on the shirt is real," Jimmy offered, as if justifying his short-lived deception.

"So you were bleeding for real?" Emily asked suspiciously.

"Well, it's actually Paul's blood. He cut his hand earlier. But I think it made my character more believable. Muscle man bought it anyway," Jimmy said, pleading his case.

Glancing at Paul's hands, Emily couldn't see any obvious wound and was relieved the damage was minor. "Jimmy, I can't believe you," she said harshly.

With a pained look on his face, Jimmy lowered his head with

embarrassment. Paul's and Emily's eyes met momentarily. Slow grins overtook them, and then Emily let out a light chortle. Jimmy looked up to his smiling friends. A broad smile enveloped his face, and he joined in the fun.

"I'm sorry, Jimmy. I guess you're not the only one who can play a part convincingly. You're a good sport," Emily said, reaching over and gave him a sideways hug.

"You can mess with me any time you want, as long as I get a hug at the end of it," Jimmy said with his most endearing smile.

The elevator door dinged and then opened. The group exited onto the first floor where numerous armed agents stood ready.

* * * * *

Emily, Paul, and Jimmy hovered around Agent Thrasher as they watched Detective Cross on the security monitors. They watched Cross exit the stairwell and make his way quickly down the hall. He pulled the cell phone from his belt and dialed. Seconds later the security room phone rang. Thrasher picked up.

"Thrasher?" Cross asked.

"Yes."

"I'm on nine. Have you reacquired video yet?"

"No. Someone else has control of the system. They're messing up my feed. I'll keep trying," Thrasher replied, hoping his lie sounded more believable than it felt.

"Let me know the instant you have something," Cross said and then hung up.

The short, chubby security guard standing at the back of the room gave a high-five to the other guard and let out a "Booyah!" as he reveled in their sneaky success. Jimmy joined in, giving high-fives to the men and then let out a "Booyah!" of his own, although he didn't fully understand why. Despite successfully deceiving Detective Cross, irritation covered Thrasher's face as he listened to the gloating men standing behind him.

"Good work regaining control of the system. You can leave now," Thrasher mumbled politely, as much as he could muster. The two guards looked at each other and shook their heads, muttering when they exited the room.

Jimmy looked at Paul with a question in his eyes as he pointed to himself. "You can stay, Jimmy," Paul said. Jimmy bobbed his head with satisfaction.

As the team continued to watch from the security room, Detective Cross progressed down the ninth floor hallway and made another call. Cross spoke briefly and then reattached the phone to his belt. He approached what appeared to be the entrance he was looking for. Next to a broken glass window by the door lay a red fire extinguisher. Stepping over the extinguisher, Cross drew his weapon and slid the action, moving a round into the chamber with one fluid motion. Cross entered the office space and disappeared from view of the hallway camera. The watchful group of agents and Jimmy remained fixed on the monitor as they stared intently at the empty hallway.

Stark waited patiently, hunched in the darkness behind a heavy fireproof cabinet in the ninth floor office. His keen ears listened carefully as the waft of nearly imperceptible breathing drew closer. Then he heard the whisper.

"Agent Mathews, I'm here to get you out. Agent Mathews?" Detective Cross held his gun ready. He peered into the shadowy cubicles and through dim office doorways.

"Who's there?" a quiet voice inquired.

"It's me, Cross. I'm here to help you. Where are you?" Cross asked. There was silence. "I'm sorry I had to pretend to betray you earlier. I know it's hard to understand but I can explain. I'm on your side. You can trust me." The silence persisted.

Emitted from a speakerphone Stark had placed on the floor behind the desk, Agent Mathews voice was nearly a whisper. "I don't trust you. But if you want to convince me I can, lay your weapon on a desk and return to the hallway." Stark listened for the sound of metal contacting the hard surface of a desk. There was no sound.

Moving briskly past the remaining cubicles, Cross gave scant attention to the nearby offices until he approached the furthermost office door. "Agent Mathews, I know you're in there. Please come out. I'm here to help you." Cross waited outside the opened door, listening for a response but none came.

Detective Cross shook his head, displeased with the decisions that had spiraled out of control that brought him to this end. Agent

Mathews knew too much, but still, he didn't enjoy the inevitable action before him. "Mathews, you know I can't put my weapon down," he said sadly. "I really am sorry things have to turn out this way. I like you, but I can't have you talking. I just can't. Please, let's make this as painless as possible."

"Fine. But answer a question for me first," Emily requested quietly, the sound from the speakerphone muffled behind the desk. "You worked for both Nicas and Craven. They're competitors. How did you pull that off?"

Detective Cross chuckled under his breath before answering. Despite his better judgment, he said, as if in a confessional, "You'd be surprised how easy it was. All I had to do was make them think I was their inside guy with both the police and their opponent. I just stroked their egos. I made them think I was loyal only to them and that they were in control. Not much to it, really."

"One last thing. You're not going to shoot me with your own gun and pretend you found me dead, are you? There's a little thing called ballistics. I'm sure you've heard of it," Emily said into the phone, watching the empty hallway on the monitors.

"No. I wish it was that simple." Cross holstered his weapon and removed a large serrated hunting knife from a sheath on his calf. "I wish I could shoot you, but this will be more convincing. I'm sorry, but time's up." Cross pushed through the door, his knife held menacingly in front of him.

Emerging from behind the cabinet Stark stood firm, his gun aimed at the silhouette of Cross illuminated against the dimly lit doorway. "I'm sorry to hear all of that, Detective," Stark said, wishing he could see Cross's face when he realized the con. Cross expressed no noticeable reaction, continuing to walk toward Stark, his knife extended. "Cross, stop. You can't win this. If you take another step, I'll have to shoot you," Stark warned.

"Good," was Cross's only response as he took another slow step.

The agents in the security room listened breathlessly, and then flinched with dread as the harsh ring of a gunshot echoed over the phone.

THIRTY

AGENT STARK HOVERED OVER DETECTIVE Cross, the dim light from the doorway casting a shadow over his disgraced colleague. Kicking the knife that had fallen from Cross's grip to a safe distance, Stark immobilized the reaching hand with a heavy foot on the wrist. The injured man lay on the floor holding his bleeding shoulder while Stark's weapon lingered over his chest.

Detective Cross knew he was beat. He lifted his head briefly as if preparing to sit up but then let it flop back to the floor with a thud of surrender.

"Agent Stark, can you hear me? What's your status?" Thrasher called across the speakerphone. Stark continued to stare down his traitorous opponent and failed to respond. "Agent Stark," the call came through again, more forcefully.

"Hold your horses. I'm fine, but you might want to send up some paramedics for the other guy," Stark suggested.

"They're already on the way. And Cross? Is he . . . ?"

"The schlub will be just fine. But I don't think the guy will be shooting baskets any time soon. That shoulder has gotta hurt, but then, bullets tend to do that," Stark said with a grin.

The team listened over the open phone line and watched the monitors as personnel raced down the ninth floor hallways toward Agent Stark's location. Emily sighed in relief. Though she was pleased Stark was uninjured and that Cross would recover, Emily was taken aback by her concern. After all Stark had put her through during the investigation and after Cross's betrayal, she was surprised she cared about either of them at all.

"Thrasher, what's the status of the tactical team?" Stark asked.

"They're moving into position now. ETA one minute."

"Good. Send them as soon as they're ready. Oh, and Thrasher, advise them I'm in plain clothes and I'll be arriving shortly. I don't want any misunderstandings. I'm on my way."

"Got it." Thrasher radioed the lead agent with the assault team and then leaned in his chair, holding the back of his head with intertwined hands. Spinning in his chair, he looked into the eyes of each person in the security room. Despite emoting only a sliver of a grin, his gentle head nod adequately expressed his satisfaction.

Emily stood between Paul and Jimmy. Recognizing that their portion of the operation was completed, the trio relaxed. Their bodies became less rigid and their faces brightened. Paul had waited long enough. Turning toward Emily, Paul held her face in his hands, staring into her eyes. Emily could see the deepness of his relief. His thumbs traced the soft skin below her cheekbones and then he pulled her close, his lips resting comfortably on the top of her head. Emily wrapped her arms around Paul and leaned her face against his chest. *Much better,* Paul thought. Jimmy looked on, eagerly awaiting another squeeze of his own.

As the embrace ended, Paul placed his arm over Emily's shoulder, and they walked from the security room. They stood briefly amongst other agents in the grand lobby, talking and answering questions, when finally Paul indicated it was time to leave.

"I know we're all tired, but we're not done quite yet. We still need to debrief at the field office," Emily told Paul as they walked out of the building and toward a waiting FBI cruiser. Jimmy watched Emily and Paul with their arms around each other and followed them, moping a few steps behind.

Looking at his watch, Jimmy's eyebrows lifted as he noted the time. 4:00 a.m. Weariness washed over him, and he slowly climbed into the back seat of the cruiser next to Paul. Jimmy rested his head against the back of the seat and closed his eyes.

* * * * *

The assault team leader stood in the tenth floor corridor with one man at his side while team members moved briskly down the hallway two by two with their weapons raised. Although the team dressed alike with helmet, goggles, black fatigue style clothing, gear, and Kevlar vests with "FBI" displayed prominently across their backs and chests, team leader Mancuso simply wore blue jeans, a navy blue windbreaker, and a dark ball cap with yellow FBI lettering. He spoke briefly into his radio and received updates while watching his men move further down the hallway, opening doors and then moving on once the area was secure.

Agent Stark stepped carefully across the stairwell door, which had been forced from its hinges. Striding quickly to the team leader, Stark positioned himself directly between Mancuso and the assault team. "I'm Agent Stark," he introduced with confidence.

"Fantastic. I'm Mancuso. I'll be with you in a moment," Mancuso said, stepping around Stark. He continued barking orders into the radio. Though not tall in stature, Mancuso had a wrestler's build and appeared annoyed.

Irritated by the brush off, Stark stepped back into Mancuso's line of sight. "I am leading this investigation under authority of the ASAC," Stark said clearly. "I would like a full briefing . . ." he started, but Mancuso ignored him.

Receiving another report from his radio, Mancuso muttered a few words to his assistant and then reattached the radio to a Velcro patch near his collarbone. He adjusted the cap on his head and then locked on to Agent Stark.

"If you ever interrupt me in the middle of an assault again, I will drop you. Are we clear?" he asked stepping closer, his mouth mere inches from Stark's chin.

With jaw clenched, Agent Stark considered his response. Putting the man in his place would be enjoyable, but Stark wasn't in the mood. He took a step back, allowing for a more comfortable distance.

Stark allowed a phony smile through gritted teeth. "Okay, tell me what's going on."

Mancuso remained stern. "So far, the place is empty."

"I know men were coming from this floor. I'm sure of it. There must be another exit. Have you found anything?" Stark asked.

"My men have not completed the search. As soon as we have

something, I will let you know," Mancuso said. His radio suddenly came alive.

"West end . . . south hallway . . . room with a secure door at the back. Three men entered. We'll have it open in moments," the voice from the radio said in short bursts.

"I'm on my way," Mancuso said, and he started jogging down the hall. Stark ran to keep up, turning down one hallway and then another.

Outside an average looking office door, four men stood in full gear, their backs against the wall. "Clear," a voice hollered. A mild concussion and wafting smoke exited the room into the hallway. Three members of the assault team raced into the room with Mancuso directly behind them and Agent Stark a few steps back.

Through the smoke Stark spied a narrow set of stairs. Ascending behind the team, he stepped into the cool breeze on the roof of the Prodigy building. The scream of an engine and beating air dominated the rooftop. Turning in place, Stark searched for the deafening rotors.

Twenty yards behind were more steps. Stark clamored up two at a time and then stood at the edge of a large white circle with a massive X in the middle as a black helicopter swooped below the concrete ledge. Stark ran to the building's rim, drew his weapon, and watched the blinking red lights from the helicopter's tail disappear from view.

* * * * *

With the back legs of his chair anchored to the floor, Jimmy leaned heavily against the textured interrogation room wall, waiting impatiently for Emily and Paul to be debriefed with ASAC Murphy. Despite being offered a more comfortable chair in the conference room, Jimmy had requested the unique experience of sweating out his time in the interrogation room. After all, when else would he get the chance to stare down a two-way mirror? Hopefully never. Paul was happy to oblige his friend.

For the first hour Jimmy had entertained himself with some basic role-playing. He put himself in Shannon's place and imagined how the obstinate thug would withstand his interrogation. Jimmy practiced a steely stare into the observation mirror, and when he became bored with being the villain, he morphed into a hard-core FBI agent who refused to play by the rules. He practiced his methodical pacing and casual sitting on the corner of the table while he spoke sincerely to an invisible interrogation subject. Despite his games, time passed slowly, and he soon abandoned the futile habit of looking at his watch.

Deciding that the only cure for his boredom was sleep, Jimmy positioned himself as comfortably as he could and within moments fell into a restless sleep.

* * * * *

Emily brightened the lights and then crept toward the interrogation room table. She smiled down at Jimmy, who had not only sacrificed an evening of sleep but had also put himself in serious jeopardy. He had proven himself to be a true friend. Emily's eyes glistened as she watched Jimmy sleep.

She knelt down and rested her chin on her hands, staring at her friend's amusing position. Jimmy was always good for a laugh, even when he was unconscious.

With one leg draped over the corner of the table and both arms hanging haplessly at his side, his head flopped backward with his mouth agape. Emily marveled that he could rest in such a position. She watched tenderly, not wanting to disrupt his rest but knowing she had to.

Rising from her knees, Emily enjoyed one last moment of humorous tranquility and then slapped the table as hard and as loudly as she could with both hands. Jimmy's eyes opened wide with shock, and his arms flailed at his side. Trying to sit up, he lifted his leg from the table and fell backwards in the chair, crashing to the floor. Jimmy hopped to his feet and looked bewilderedly around the room, trying to pretend he had been alert the entire time. He blinked repeatedly and crinkled his nose, sustaining a more believable state of awareness.

Emily covered her mouth with her hands, watching in horror at the ruckus she had caused. She had merely wanted to see Jimmy's expression as she startled him awake but did not expect him crash to the floor in a fit of grogginess. She glanced back at the two-way mirror as if she could see through it, hoping no one was watching, and then quickly returned her gaze to Jimmy.

"Jimmy, I'm so sorry. I didn't mean to . . . ," she said with an awkward laugh.

"That's okay. I knew you were there. I just wanted to give you a show and see you squirm a little," he said nonchalantly. His effort at cool and casual was not convincing.

"Uh-huh. Sure," she said with a broad smile, approaching him with open arms. "I thought it would be funny to see you jump, but I didn't want you to crash and burn," Emily said, wrapping her arms around Jimmy.

Jimmy held her tight. "Like I said before, you can mess with me anytime you want, as long as I get a hug at the end of it." Jimmy held Emily's hands, taking a step back in order to gaze more easily into her eyes.

"I really owe you one, Jimmy. You saved me this week. Your friendship has made a huge difference to me. Thank you," she said earnestly.

"Emily, it has been my absolute pleasure," he said with charming sincerity. "Really it has. This has been one of the best weeks of my life. Kind of weird, I know. But I care about stuff again. That's all because of you."

Emily lowered her head and blushed at Jimmy's kind words. Meeting his eyes, she pulled him close. "All right, buddy. You ready to get out of here?"

"Absolutely. Where's Paul?" he asked, savoring the embrace.

"Well, we finished our debrief a while ago, but he has a meeting with his supervisor about his assignment in Oklahoma City. Apparently it couldn't wait, so he's going to stick around for a while. Why don't we go grab some early breakfast?" Emily suggested. "I'm starving."

Jimmy hadn't thought much about food, but he quickly realized how hungry he was. "Breakfast sounds good. I'll cook, and we can save some for Paul."

Emily nodded.

From the other side of the glass, Paul watched jealously as Jimmy wrapped his arm around Emily's waist and exited the interrogation room, smiling.

THIRTY-ONE

T HE FINANCIAL ANALYSIS AND CYBER crimes unit of the Kansas City Field Office filled with half-conscious agents arriving for work in their dark suits, carrying coffee and attaché cases. They wandered to their desks and made small talk as they settled in for a fresh day of work.

Paul did not feel fresh or even alert, but he sat up straight, facing his scowling supervisor. Both men sat silently as supervisor Jerome Dallas organized a heap of paper and then read an interoffice email. Dallas was turned sideways at his desk, facing his monitor. With jaw clenched, he glanced quickly at Paul and then continued reading.

"Agent Stephens, it appears you've made quite an impression in Oklahoma City," Dallas commented stoically, still facing his computer. Reaching with his right hand, he turned off the power to the monitor and then swiveled in his chair to face Paul. "Is there anything you'd like to tell me about your recent assignment in Oklahoma?"

"Yes, sir. My investigation was efficient, and I turned in my final analysis long before I was required. I believe my investigation exceeded their expectations," Paul stated formally.

"Right." Dallas stared directly into Paul's eyes. "I've been reading all about it. There are a couple of notes about the success of your formal investigation, but then I have pages of complaint about your informal inquiries." Dallas arose from his seat and leaned forward with his fingertips pressed firmly against the surface of his desk, his knuckles lightening.

With eyes straight ahead and his posture holding firm, Paul attempted to deflect the criticism that was bearing down on him. "Sir, let me explain."

The large black man looked incredulous. "Let you explain? Yes, sir, I'll let you explain," he said, his voice growling with intensity. "I'll let you explain why you broke the law and stole a password from the ASAC of the Oklahoma City Field Office and hacked into private personnel files. I'll let you explain why you interfered with an ongoing investigation from another department. I'd love to hear this," he said, flopping back into his seat and leaning back as though preparing to be entertained.

Dread enveloped Paul's mind. His future was in Dallas's hands. "Sir, I know I skirted propriety, and I'm sorry about that. I will accept any and all consequences of my actions. However, I will point out I was instrumental in solving an important investigation for the Kansas City office. Had I not taken it upon myself to investigate this other case, a federal agent would still be held hostage, and a mole from the Kansas City Police Department, who was working with our office, would remain unidentified. Sir, a major player in Kansas City organized crime has been brought down," Paul said, fatigue and frustration creeping into his voice.

"Well, to listen to you, it sounds like we ought to give you a commendation. Would you like a commendation, Agent Stephens?" Dallas asked sarcastically.

"No, sir."

"Then what should we do with you? Oklahoma City wants us to fire you yesterday and pursue legal charges for your hacking activities." Dallas stared down his agent.

Paul looked at his supervisor. Nothing smart came to mind so he remained silent.

"Why don't you start from the beginning and tell me everything that happened, ending with your activities last night. Then I'll decide what to do with you."

Paul's eyes roamed upward as he considered how to properly explain. He took a deep breath and began a slow, methodical recitation of the events of the past few days, interweaving his actions related to both investigations.

Dallas listened with an amused smirk.

* * * * *

The tortilla was folded expertly around the gooey, cheese-infused scrambled eggs, hash browns, and sausage, and placed next to a bright orange slice of cantaloupe. "Voilà! Two delightful breakfast burritos for the lady," Jimmy said, topping the breakfast with a dollop of sour cream and a spoonful of salsa. He handed the plate to Emily.

"Mmm. Thank you," Emily said. She set the plate in front of her glass of orange juice and waited for Jimmy to finish assembling his food. Once he was seated, Emily blessed the food and commenced feasting on the Americanized Mexican breakfast.

Jimmy listened intently while Emily related the events of Detective Cross's betrayal and her ultimate capture. A chunk of egg fell from his mouth when she described her escape. He couldn't help but laugh as she gestured how Shannon flopped on the ground in the mess of oil and water. His mind lingered on the image, but his eyes lingered on Emily.

"That is *incredible*," Jimmy noted in a high-pitched, singsong tone. "Now it's all behind you, and you can relax a little bit. I bet a boring day at the office sounds pretty good."

"Yeah. I could handle boring right now, but I'm not quite finished with this case. I'll catch a quick catnap, and then I've got to get back to work," Emily said.

Jimmy's brow furrowed. "You got Cross and Shannon, and it's just a matter of finding Nicas, right? You can charge him with a ton of stuff, including your kidnapping."

"Abduction," she corrected with a wink. "That's true, but Nicas isn't actually the original subject of the investigation. Unraveling his criminal activity and involvement in organized crime was just kind of a bonus. The syndicate is still operational, and there's one more major player I need to deal with before easing off. I've got a meeting tonight that should be interesting. If it goes the way I hope, I may get to think about normalcy again."

Although he didn't fully understand the implications of what she was saying, Jimmy nodded anyway. "All right then. Let's finish up, so you can get some rest before you have to get back to work."

Emily finished eating while Jimmy grabbed a comforter and pillow from Paul's room and placed them on the couch for her to use. Emily curled up eagerly on the sofa and became lost in the pillow's softness. She was breathing deeply and sleeping soundly before Jimmy finished clearing the table.

As Jimmy continued to clean the messy kitchen, one innocuous phrase stuck in his mind. "Get to work," he whispered to himself. Why would he be focusing on such a phrase? Thinking required too much effort, so he pushed the thought from his mind and quickly finished the dishes.

Walking into his room, Jimmy closed the door and stood at the foot of his bed. With arms outstretched, he fell face-first onto the mattress, his face buried in his pillow. Rolling onto his back, he stared at the white ceiling. His exhaustion kept the sleep from conquering him. Then, with a start, his eyes widened, and he sat up. In one motion his legs flew off the side of the bed as he looked at his watch—8:55 a.m.

Jimmy was already three hours late for his first day of work. Hitting the palm of his hand to his forehead, Jimmy wondered how he could possibly explain his tardiness to Brother Jenkins. Why would anyone believe the story of his heroic night? Jimmy barely believed it himself.

With a groan, Jimmy stood, grabbed his wallet and some loose change from his dresser, and walked quietly to the exterior door of Paul's apartment. He closed it gently behind him, careful not to wake Emily. He descended the stairs rapidly and then ran to a bus stop down the street to wait. No matter how late for work he was, Jimmy had to try to make things right.

* * * * *

Jerome Dallas nodded thoughtfully. "What you did was wrong. Based on the gravity of the offense, I have come to a decision about your formal discipline."

Paul nodded like a guilty child. His mind raced as he considered the possible penalties he could face, from legal prosecution to unemployment and blacklisting from all future law enforcement positions. The options were grim. All he could do was hope for the best and take his punishment like a man.

Powering on his monitor, Dallas clicked his mouse twice and began typing. He pulled department letterhead from his desk drawer, fed it into the printer, and waited for the completed page to emerge. Lifting the page from the printer, Dallas examined it closely, scribbled his signature, and then set it on the desk facing Paul.

"This letter of reprimand will be placed in your permanent file, and if you ever pull any shenanigans like this again, I will be forced to take harsher action. Do you have any questions?"

Picking up the page laid in front of him, Paul read the reprimand:

> *Agent Paul Stephens is hereby formally reprimanded for his unapproved actions and investigation, which resulted in the capture of members of the Kansas City organized crime syndicate and the safe rescue of Agent Emily Mathews. While his actions were outside the approved parameters of FBI protocol, he acted in the best interest of the Bureau.*
>
> *As a consequence of his initiative and premeditated actions, Agent Paul Stephens' promotion to Special Agent will be postponed six months.*
>
> *Jerome Dallas*
> *Supervising Agent, Financial Analysis Unit*

Paul looked at his supervisor with disbelief. "Promotion?" he asked.

"Only if you keep your nose clean for the next six months." Dallas's bright white smile lit up the room. "Any questions?"

"No, sir. No questions," Paul said, reaching across the desk and shaking Dallas's hand vigorously. "Thank you, sir." He had been given a second chance. Paul hesitated. "Well, actually, sir, there is something. Would you be willing to do me a favor?" Paul asked.

"A favor? Did you read that reprimand?" Jerome Dallas laughed, looking at Paul suspiciously. "Stephens, you've got guts. Lucky for you I'm in a giving mood today. Tell me, what favor could I possibly do for you that I haven't already done?"

"Well, two favors actually. Here's what I need . . ."

* * * * *

Slowing to a fast walk, Jimmy entered the loading bay and looked around at the bustling action around him. Tractor-trailers were pulling out, and forklifts were in constant motion, moving large loads of parts on wooden pallets. Workers swirled around, moving boxes throughout the spacious parts warehouse. Walking across the depot floor, Jimmy made his way to the back wall and through a swinging door, which lead to a short hallway of offices.

Jimmy waited nervously outside the office of Brad Jenkins, his hand poised to knock. Peeking inside sheepishly, Jimmy knocked softly. Brad looked up from his paperwork and eyed Jimmy and then turned his gaze to the clock on his wall. Jimmy stepped inside slowly and trained his eyes on the same clock. 9:30 a.m.

"Not exactly on time, are you, Jimmy?" Brad said gruffly.

"No, Mr. Jenkins. I'm sorry. I questioned whether I should even bother coming in this morning after I realized how late I was. But I at least wanted to come in and tell you I'm sorry. I was really excited about the job, but I know it's not fair asking you to overlook me being three hours late on my first day." Jimmy looked down at the floor.

Brad sat in silence, looking Jimmy over carefully. "I'm impressed you made the effort to come in and talk to me. I must admit I was disappointed when you didn't show this morning. Like we discussed yesterday, I expect my employees to be men and women of character— reliable, loyal, and hardworking. Is this asking too much of you?"

"No, Mr. Jenkins. It's fair. I would like another chance to prove myself," Jimmy said, raising his head to make eye contact.

"Well then, I was willing to give you a chance the other day, and I still am."

Jimmy's jaw dropped, and his eyes brightened as some of his usual confidence returned.

"Just like that?" he asked doubtingly. "I'm three hours late on my first day, and you're willing to overlook that?"

"Three and a half hours, actually. Are you trying to talk me out of it?" Brad asked. Jimmy shook his head and lifted his hands as if protecting himself.

"And yes. I'm willing to overlook your late arrival. I think the fact that you came at all says a lot about you. Your circumstance is unique, and I'd be happy to have you work for me."

Jimmy was in shock. "My circumstance is unique?"

"Don't you think I should give consideration to a man who is late because he was helping the FBI save the life of an agent?"

Grinning broadly, Jimmy nodded his head vigorously. "Yes, I do. Thank you, Mr. Jenkins. How did you know?"

"Paul Stephens came by a few minutes ago and explained what happened last night. No details really, just the basics. He said your service was invaluable. He asked me to consider going easy on you. Oh, and he gave me this," Brad said, handing Jimmy a piece of paper.

Jimmy held up the FBI letterhead. The note of appreciation was extraordinarily brief but was signed by Supervising Agent Jerome Dallas. Jimmy smiled.

"I don't know exactly what you did last night, but I do know you've got a good friend there. Paul seems to be looking out for you," Jenkins said.

Jimmy nodded in agreement. Just a few days ago, Paul had driven Jimmy to alcohol, but now, with the exception of Emily, there was no one Jimmy admired more. He smiled. "Yeah, he really *is* the best."

"He seems to have a lot of faith in you. If he can believe in you, well, so can I. Look, you've already missed half the day. Why don't you go home and get some rest and start fresh tomorrow morning," Jenkins suggested.

Jimmy considered the kind offer. "Mr. Jenkins, if it's all right with you, since I'm already here, could I stay and work to the end of my shift?"

Brad was impressed, and his broad smile proved it. "I'm glad to have you on board, Jimmy. I'm expecting good things from you. Let me make a call and have someone come show you around the facility. I'm glad to see you're so eager to work."

"I'm just not eager for another thirty minute bus ride," Jimmy corrected with a smirk.

Brad laughed and shook Jimmy's hand. "Well done, Jimmy."

THIRTY-TWO

WITH HIS CUFFED HANDS SET on the tabletop, the burly captive sat stoically in his chair. Despite the long wait, he didn't fidget. His muscles didn't even twitch. He didn't glance around the room nor did a single sound escape his mouth. He breathed imperceptibly and seldom blinked, looking nearly catatonic. Shannon patiently awaited his interrogator.

Although they had never come face to face, Agent Stark knew Shannon from his dossier. He had memorized every detail of the man's official file photo and the still frame image from the hospital assassination. He had read everything they knew about the man, which wasn't much. Setting the closed file atop his desk, Agent Stark placed a Styrofoam plate with a sandwich, a bag of chips, and a cookie on top. He grabbed a can of soda and shimmied it into his large front pants pocket. Picking up the file with the plate of food balanced on top, Stark carefully opened the door to the interrogation room.

Stark walked to a chair that was opposite his prisoner and set the file on the table. Sliding the dossier to one side, Stark sat with his food directly in front of him. Reaching into his pocket, he attempted to retrieve his soda but was unable to free it, so he stood quickly to get it out. With an unnatural grin and raised eyebrows, he held the soda can in one hand and pointed to it with the other, like a silly soda pop commercial. He popped the top and set it near the plate of food as he reclaimed his seat. Opening the bag of chips, Stark tossed a couple into his mouth, chomped loudly, and then slurped the soda.

Shannon stared through Agent Stark with no acknowledgement of his presence. Stark ate his meaty sandwich and chips sloppily with his mouth open and washed them down with deep gulps of soda. He occasionally glanced at the prisoner seated across from him but didn't speak. He was too busy eating. Tossing one last bite of chocolate cookie into his mouth, Stark pushed his chair back and stood, gathering his file and the trash from his lunch. He walked to the interrogation room door and left—not a word spoken.

* * * * *

With the team gathered in the third floor conference room in preparation for Emily's scheduled meeting with Judge Craven, and Shannon still awaiting his next interrogation, Stark sat at the head of the long table eager for updates. "Mathews, what did you find out from the receptionist at Prodigy?"

"I spent about an hour with Andie looking at mug shots and photos of individuals we suspect of participation in the syndicate. She didn't recognize Judge Craven or his wife, but she did recognize a couple of mid-level guys. I think she'll be most useful corroborating information we gather from other sources. She's willing to help. I just don't think she's likely to understand what she really knows without some help," Emily said.

Stark looked across the wide table at Agent Thrasher, who continued typing on his laptop. "Any updates?"

"Cross is on painkillers. He wants to make a deal," Thrasher said.

"Good."

"Also, because of the early morning timing of the raid at Prodigy, I believe we were able to keep it quiet for now. The switchboard has reported no media requests today asking about Prodigy, so it's not public knowledge yet," Emily said.

"Perfect. What are the chances Judge Craven knows what happened?" Stark asked.

"Don't know. But he's at work this morning. Whoever escaped from Prodigy in the helicopter could tip him off, but I doubt it. Chances are slim that he's aware of the raid. If the Judge doesn't show at the meeting tonight, we'll know I was wrong," Thrasher added.

"Cross was Craven's inside man. Could we use Cross to find out if

Craven is wise to the takedown at Prodigy?" Emily asked.

"I'll see what I can do," Thrasher replied.

"And what about Shannon?" Emily asked, facing Agent Stark. "Did you learn anything from the interrogation?

Stark bit his lip. "He was less than forthcoming. I'll take another shot at him in a while, but he's a cool customer. I need something to really rattle him. Mathews, from what you've told us, he doesn't seem to be worried about his role in the murder at the hospital, and so far, I'm not hearing anything else that's going to help motivate him."

"What deal can we offer Cross?" Thrasher asked.

Stark rubbed his head as he contemplated the question.

"Why don't we tell him we're open to a deal based on his coopera-tion in implicating Judge Craven and Alex Nicas? Nothing crazy, but maybe we can drop some of the conspiracy charges. He wouldn't be completely off the hook, but he'd be looking at less jail time. We tell him we'll need a goodwill gesture before we make any deals, and we push him to confirm my meeting with Craven tonight and see what he knows about Shannon," Emily offered.

Thrasher and Stark nodded in agreement.

"Excellent. Thrasher, I need Cross to give us something actionable on Shannon," Stark said forcefully. "Tell him we need a goodwill offer-ing before we make a deal."

"Yeah, I heard her the first time," Thrasher muttered.

"We're on a deadline here, folks. Mathews is meeting with Craven in a little over three hours. I really want this guy to crash hard, and I want it to happen before he gets spooked and flees the area. We can make it happen," Stark said enthusiastically.

The door to the conference room burst open as Paul walked in. "Stark, you were right," he said, smiling and holding up a manila folder. "Hi, guys," he said to the others around the table.

Grabbing the file from his hand, Stark leafed through a few pages and then closed the file. "I love it," he said with a big grin. "You spoke with her?"

"Yes. She's here. I had her picked up an hour ago," Paul said.

Stark rubbed his hands together with giddy anticipation.

"What are you talking about?" Thrasher asked gruffly.

Paul stepped up to the table, pulled out a chair, and sat next to

Thrasher. "Susan Craven," Paul said.

Stark stood. "I found some documents in Nicas's office detailing how Craven had been doing all of his business in his wife's name, and I asked Agent Stephens to follow up."

"You mean like how the nightclub is titled under her name so it wouldn't appear he was involved directly," Emily confirmed.

"That's right, but there's quite a bit more. For years, the judge has been using his wife as a straw man for his illegal business activities. Nicas must have known and has been keeping the information, probably for future blackmail," Stark suggested.

"Oh, she's mad. Seriously. *Mad*," Paul emphasized. "When I showed how her husband had been using her to shield himself, she became very talkative. I actually feel bad for the lady. I think she had an inkling that something wasn't right, but the level of her husband's betrayal floored her. I'll hold her here until after Emily's meeting with Judge Craven, but I think we can count on her for some juicy information," Paul said.

The conference room was abuzz with energy.

"Paul, that's great news, but what are you doing here?" Emily asked.

"Oh, I forgot to tell you all. Agent Stephens has officially been assigned to our team for the remainder of the investigation," Stark explained.

"Excellent," Emily said happily. "How did you pull that off?"

Paul shrugged casually. "Based on my unofficial involvement, my supervisor put in a formal request to have me reassigned temporarily. Since your team is now a man short, the SAC signed off, Agent Stark agreed, and here I am."

"According to this," Stark said, holding up the file, "your time here may be short lived. We're going to take down Craven tonight. We've got his wife on board, but now we need to pull some information out of Cross and Shannon. Guys, this is coming together," Stark said, clapping his hands. "Let's get this done."

The team stood and began gathering their things. "Thrasher, I need some dirt on Shannon, and I need it now. Let's get it!"

* * * * *

Emily and Paul lingered in the conference room as the other men exited through the heavy wood door. The room was empty and quiet. For a moment the two friends enjoyed more privacy than had been afforded in days.

With the image fresh in his mind of Emily and Jimmy embracing in the interrogation room, Paul took a tentative step toward Emily. He knew she cared for him and valued his friendship, but it was clear she also cared for Jimmy.

Just a week ago Paul had been thrilled to simply eat lunch and spend time with her, but now he wanted more. He had invested too much emotionally and risked too much to be content with simple friendship, as sweet as that was. Although his relationship with Emily was young, it had been tested intensely, but so had Jimmy's. Paul's heart leapt nervously as he gazed into Emily's smiling eyes.

Emily was not timid. She moved confidently toward Paul and held his hands softly. Guiding his fingers to her face, Emily placed Paul's hand gently across her cheek, the other over her ear combing through her soft blonde hair. Although they had never kissed, she longed for the feel of his lips on hers.

Paul's face moved closer, their noses nearly touching. Emily closed her eyes in anticipation. Then, removing his hands from her hair and face, Paul slipped into a friendly embrace and held Emily gently. Her eyes shot open with disappointment.

"Paul, is everything all right?" Emily asked, moving lightly away from him to better examine his puzzling expression.

Paul trained his eyes on the floor and wondered how honest he should be in answering. It felt like he was falling in love, but he was wary of her relationship with Jimmy. His pulse quickened, and his lips became dry. What if he was overreacting? What if he said the wrong thing? There was so much to say, but it wasn't the right time.

"I'm fine. But we probably ought to get to work. There's lots to do before your meeting with Craven," Paul said.

Emily's brow furrowed as she considered the brush off. "I don't think so. I think we should talk about this now," she said. "If you're not interested, that's fine, but I want to know why. And I'd rather not be distracted from the investigation as I wonder about it. Really, let's get it out in the open. Frankly, I find your sudden lack of interest a bit confusing."

"Emily, there's no lack of interest, but I think we ought to focus on preparing for your meeting tonight. You don't really want to have this discussion right now," Paul stated.

Emily smiled gracefully. "I do. We've got a few minutes. Let's sit and talk," Emily suggested, motioning to a couple of chairs.

"Look, Emily, I asked to join this team because I want to be a help to you, not be a distraction." Emily watched him patiently but didn't speak.

"Okay, here it is," Paul said. "I find myself thinking about you all the time. I want to spend every minute I can with you. When I can't be with you, I want to hear your voice on the phone. I know exactly how I feel about you. I am very clear about what my feelings are. I'm not confused in the slightest."

Emily's face would have been covered with a smile had she not been so confused. "So what's the problem? Why are you pushing me away now?"

Once again Paul considered how much he should say. "Let me ask you this. Why do you think I risked my job trying to investigate your teammates? And why did I come to help rescue you from Prodigy last night?"

"You did it because you were worried about me, and you care about what happens to me," she said softly.

"That's right. Here's another question. Why do you think Jimmy risked himself coming to Prodigy last night?" Paul asked.

Emily didn't want to think about it, but she knew the answer. "Same reason, I guess."

"That's right. Are these things casual friends do for each other?" Paul asked. He waited a moment, but she didn't respond. "The answer is no. Casual friends don't take these kinds of risks for each other."

"Then why did you do it?" Emily asked, her expression earnest.

"You don't know? Emily, I'm crazy about you and would do just about anything for you. I think I've proven that. And judging from what I've seen of Jimmy, I'd say he's smitten as well. I think we're both fairly obvious about our desire for a relationship beyond friendship." Paul watched Emily mulling his words.

"I'm not sure what I can say, Paul. You and Jimmy are both special to me. Are you asking me to decide between the two of you?"

"Absolutely," Paul said firmly. "It may not be easy, but you have to choose. Otherwise, it's not fair to me or Jimmy. Don't get me wrong, I'll still be your friend, but I don't kiss my friends."

Emily's lower lip quivered as the dread of having to decide between Paul and Jimmy set upon her. Paul's words made sense, but the sting of rejection hurt. She wasn't trying to lead them on. How could Paul think that? Silently, she considered her own question. Then, the light of recognition flashed in her eyes and her cheeks flushed with embarrassment.

"Emily, I don't expect you to decide this instant. I understand it may be difficult for you. Give it some time, and let me know when you're ready." Paul looked at Emily sweetly, but his insides churned, hoping he hadn't ruined his chances with the girl of his dreams. "Now, really, we've got a lot of work to do."

Offering his hand, Paul helped Emily from her seat. They exited the room and turned opposite directions to accomplish their individual assignments.

THIRTY-THREE

WITH TWO ARMED GUARDS WAITING outside the room, Agent Thrasher stood next to the hospital bed, a cell phone in his hand. Detective Cross looked at him dismissively, unwavering in his determination to get a reduction in charges before offering any assistance.

"Do it, Cross," Thrasher growled, pushing the phone toward him. "Make the call."

"Look, Thrasher, I'd be happy to help you, but I need to get something out of this. I can't give you something for nothing. You know how it works," Cross rebutted. Studying Thrasher, Cross chuckled quietly, surprised Thrasher was tasked with making a deal. Big mistake.

"If you call Judge Craven to tell him Agent Mathews is still on board for their meeting and that she has been following his rules, I'll make a call for you in return," Thrasher offered.

"What kind of call will you make for me?" Cross asked suspiciously.

"You don't think I have authority to make a deal, do you? I don't have any pull, but the ASAC does. You do this simple thing for me, and I'll see what we can do. But if you're unwilling to make a simple phone call, why would we trust you to uphold your part of any deal?"

Cross laid his head deep into his pillow and jiggled the cuffs attaching his wrists to the bed. "Fine. I'll make the call, but you need to uncuff me first. I can't even dial like this."

"Tell me the number, and I'll dial," Thrasher suggested.

"I don't think so. I'm sure you'd like to have Craven's private number, but I'll hold onto that until later," Cross insisted.

"Fair enough." Thrasher removed a small key from his pocket. "I'll uncuff you long enough to make the call." Thrasher unshackled each wrist and extended the phone once again. "You say exactly what we talked about. Nothing more. Don't get creative. If he asks you any questions we haven't discussed, tell him someone is coming and get off the phone. Try to tip him off in any way, I guarantee you will be sorry," Thrasher warned.

Cross grabbed his phone from Thrasher's hand, but Thrasher held it tight as he gave one last look of warning. Cross yanked again, and Thrasher released his grip.

Holding the phone out of Thrasher's view while he dialed, Cross then pulled it close to his ear and waited. "It's me. Yeah. We're still on. . . . Mathews has done what you asked. She seems a little nervous about meeting with you again but hasn't told anyone why. If she had trusted anyone, it would have been me. Yes. Seven," Cross said, and then hung up.

"There I did what you asked. He bought it. Now make your call," Cross demanded, handing the phone back to Thrasher. Thrasher smiled at Cross's feeble attempt to keep Craven's phone number a secret. Had he never heard of redial or caller displays?

"I will, but first I want to ask you a question," Thrasher said as Cross ardently shook his head in denial. "Don't shake your head at me. I haven't even asked the question yet."

"We had a deal," Cross reminded.

"And I'll keep the deal. My question has nothing to do with Craven or Nicas. I'm just curious about the other guy we picked up from Prodigy last night. I think his name is Shannon—something or other. Is that right?" Thrasher asked through a thin grin.

Cross nodded.

"Don't worry. I'm not asking you to give up your bargaining chip or anything. This Shannon guy doesn't really matter. I'm just curious because he seems so nervous. It's like he's afraid of something. I mean, really afraid." Thrasher watched his former colleague for a sign of recognition or any desire to respond favorably to the bluff.

Cross looked at Thrasher suspiciously but didn't speak.

Thrasher continued, "I don't know the guy, but as big and strong as he is, I thought he'd be a little tougher, that's all." The round black man shook his head and chuckled. "Forget I mentioned it," he said, pulling another phone from his pocket. He held it up for Cross to see and headed to the door. "I'll make that call now."

Thrasher waited outside the door for a few minutes while he pretended to make the promised call to the ASAC. Moments later, he returned to the bedside and nodded at Cross, who knowingly held his hands near the bed railings for Thrasher to recuff.

"Well, what did he say? Do we have a deal?" Cross asked, trying hard to sound casual.

"Nope," Thrasher said, shaking his head. "ASAC Murphy wasn't impressed with your level of cooperation. For some reason, he doesn't trust you." Thrasher paused as he casually turned to look out the window. "Besides, we have other sources that are being much more helpful than you are. We'll get our information. If not from you, then someone else."

Thrasher held up two fingers, waving good-bye as he left the bedside and strolled to the hospital room door. He opened it slowly. As he took one deliberate step out the door, he heard the groveling voice he hoped for.

"Wait," Cross pleaded. "I have information. I know things others won't tell you." Thrasher counted to three silently and then turned to face Cross.

"What do you know? I don't have time for games. There's a meeting with Craven I need to prepare for," Thrasher said.

"You said Shannon seemed really scared, right?" Cross asked anxiously. Thrasher nodded. "He has good reason to be. You get me a deal, and I'll tell you what he doesn't want anyone to know," Cross offered eagerly.

"I told you, this Shannon guy doesn't really matter. We'll get him on a dozen or so charges. He's a nobody. He'll go away," Thrasher said.

"But it will prove I have other valuable information."

Thrasher considered the offer. "If you tell me something meaningful, something I don't already know, then I'll ask the ASAC to reconsider. If you impress me, I'll push hard to get some of your charges reduced."

Cross bit his lip and scowled. He thought for a moment and then described Shannon's brutal role in the ominous Saturday morning meeting at the Missouri River bottoms. The police and the media had reported Gordon Harrison's death as a suicide, but Cross knew it was really a murder, and Shannon pulled the trigger.

Thrasher cocked his head and flashed a bright white smile.

* * * * *

Once again, Agent Stark sat in the chair across the interrogation room table from Shannon. This time, through the two-way mirror, the video was recording everything that was happening. As he did before, Shannon looked right through him, expressionless.

The two men had spent a good deal of time together throughout the day, but Shannon had frustrated Stark with his refusal to speak. But this time, armed with new information, Stark was hopeful he would finally break the man's steely will.

Stark's eyes narrowed as he stared into Shannon's vacant eyes. "Tell me about Gordon Harrison. He was murdered this past Saturday morning." Stark paused briefly, watching his opponent. "I know you were there, and I know you pulled the trigger."

Shannon licked his lips and then pressed them tightly. Still he remained silent.

"Hmm. I think we're getting somewhere," Stark muttered quietly. "Not only will we prosecute you for the murders of our surveillance suspects at the hospital, but we'll also get you for the murder of Gordon Harrison, leader of the Kansas City crime syndicate."

Shannon eyed his interrogator spitefully.

"I wonder what the rest of your crime buddies will think when they find out you murdered old Gordy," Stark said. "But I wouldn't worry. I'm sure they're a forgiving bunch."

Shannon's shoulders rose sharply with a loud breath. His mouth relaxed. For the first time all day, the prisoner spoke. "I want to deal."

Stark nodded, and a gigantic grin engulfed his face. "I thought you might."

* * * * *

Sitting alone in the rear of the black Ford E-series van, Agent Thrasher adjusted his earphones and focused on the video feed from the nightclub security cameras. "Give me a sound check," Thrasher requested.

"Is everyone in position?" Emily asked. "And what about Stark? Does he have any new information I can use to rile Judge Craven?"

"We're in position," Paul said.

"Sound is good," Thrasher acknowledged. "Stark's still talking with the prisoner. I'll let you know if we hear anything from him." Thrasher typed briefly into his computer and then reviewed the security cameras one last time before glancing at his watch. "I think we're ready. We've waited as long as we can. Mathews, don't let Craven spill anything on your microphone tonight," Thrasher quipped in his low monotone.

"Only because you asked nicely," Emily bantered. "Here I go."

Bounding from her rental car parked at the side of The Wall, Emily walked to the club's entrance. She prepared to pay and have her hand stamped when the club's assistant manager recognized her.

"Miss Emily, it's good to see you again," he greeted. "The Judge is already here and waiting for you. If you will follow me, I'll show you to your table."

"Thank you, Marcus," Emily said and followed her escort to the same table where she and the Judge had met previously.

Judge Craven stood graciously and softly grabbed Emily's hand, kissing her knuckles. "Emily, it is wonderful to see you again. I trust you have had an enjoyable weekend," he said casually, motioning for her to sit.

Emily repressed a shudder from the feel of Craven's moist lips. "Yes, the weekend was eventful. I apologize for my tardiness," Emily said. From behind, Marcus pushed in her chair as she sat. Emily nodded to the man with gratitude. "Marcus, would you please bring me a virgin strawberry daiquiri?"

"Of course. I'll have it brought out right away. I took the liberty of having a glass of white wine ready for you," he commented, motioning to the drink in front of her.

"You can take it away, but thank you for the gesture," she said gracefully. Marcus looked at the Judge, who nodded. Marcus removed the glass and walked away.

"You look beautiful as always," Judge Craven commented. "However, I must admit I am somewhat disappointed you did not dress up for our date. Maybe next time," Craven said with a wry smile. "The other night your hair was so lustrous and your silk dress was truly flattering."

"Yes, well I was a little rushed tonight, so I didn't have time to primp for you like I had hoped. I see you're wearing the exact same clothes as the other night. I hope you at least had them laundered," Emily said, eyeing Craven with a smirk.

Dressed in a similar sports blazer and khakis, the Judge did not appreciate the humor in her comment. "You are certainly more playful tonight. It is nice when one can leave the stresses of work at the office. I often have difficulty with that myself," he admitted.

"You mentioned that before," Emily recalled, continuing to play along with Craven's ruse. "Being a judge is a great responsibility. There is tremendous trust placed in you. It must be a real burden," she said with a wink.

Emily looked up as a server reappeared and set her drink on the table. Emily began to thank the server but was suddenly distracted as Thrasher started talking to her through the earpiece. She tried to listen but was unable to concentrate on both the Judge and Thrasher.

Taking a sip from her drink, she set the glass down near the edge of the table and politely made small talk with Craven. Then with a wild arm gesture, she knocked her daiquiri into the Judge's lap. Craven stood defensively, wiping the thick red drink from his pants with a black cloth napkin from the table.

"I'm so sorry," Emily said, feigning embarrassment. "You spilled a drink on me last time, and I spilled on you tonight. We're just a couple of klutzes," she said, handing him another napkin.

Scowling at his date, Craven grabbed the napkin from her hand and dabbed at his pants. With a look of disgust he excused himself and headed toward the restroom to clean up more properly.

While another server rushed over to help clean the mess, Emily stood up and could hear the mild chuckles of her teammates in her ear. "This is painful. Please tell me Stark has something good," she mumbled quietly, turning her head to block the words from the server's ears. Emily's head bobbed with satisfaction as Thrasher recounted the specifics of Stark's interrogation with Shannon.

"That's all we needed. Everyone is in position and ready for your signal," Thrasher said.

"Good. Let's end this farce." Emily sat back in her seat and waited for the Judge.

After a short delay, Judge Craven rejoined Emily at the table but sat directly across from her. His khakis were still clearly stained from the red drink. "It appears you owe me one," Craven said, referring to his ruined pants. "I will collect from you later."

"No, you won't," Emily said, relieved to be rid of the polite pretense.

She watched with pleasure at the astonishment that appeared on Judge Craven's face quickly turned to anger.

"I have a confession to make, Judge. I did not follow your rules this weekend," she said with mock apology. "The FBI knows your plan. It seems I trusted the right people, which is more than you can say." Emily watched Craven's eyes flutter. "Your plan may have actually worked, except your partner, Alex Nicas, didn't seem to share your goals. It was an unreliable partnership. Pity."

Craven stammered, attempting to speak.

"Oh, and I've been talking to one of your friends, Shannon Nigh," Emily said coolly.

"I do not know any person by that name."

"Really? He knows you, and that's all that really matters. He told us an interesting story. Stop me if you've heard this," Emily said. "It turns out Gordon Harrison, Kansas City philanthropist and mob boss, was called to a special meeting with his partner, Alex Nicas. Unfortunately, Mr. Harrison didn't survive the meeting. His death was officially declared a suicide, but we know now he was murdered. He died a violent death at the instructions of two men who were seeking to overthrow him: Alex Nicas and you. Is any of this ringing a bell?"

Judge Craven stood with contempt and stared down the insolent agent sitting across the table. "You can't prove anything. You don't have any evidence," he said dismissively.

"Two of the men who participated in Gordon Harrison's murder have been silenced. You know, the ones who followed me but were later killed at the hospital? Personally, I think we have enough evidence. We have the testimonies of Shannon Nigh placing you at the scene, Detective Cross detailing the conspiracy and your rivalry with Alex Nicas, and Susan Craven providing some important physical evidence. Yeah, I think we'll do just fine. What do you think, Judge? Strong case?"

"My wife? You can't use my wife." Craven flushed as he sputtered.

"*You* did," Emily said, glaring at Craven. "If she wants to help, and believe me, after the way you used her, she *really* wants to help, I can use her too."

Motioning insistently with his hand, Judge Craven called over the nightclub's assistant manager. "Marcus, get this woman out of here. Now."

Marcus took a step toward Emily, but she pulled a badge from her pocket. He stopped instantly. "Good choice, Marcus," Emily said. "*Engage.*"

From the back of the van, Thrasher gave the order, "Move in, everyone."

The assault team exploded from their vehicles and took up position at the front and rear exits of the club. Paul immediately arose from his seat at a nearby table and a fashionably dressed agent near the catwalk stairs leapt into action. Paul moved aggressively toward Craven.

Craven grabbed Marcus by the shirt collar, shoved him into the table toward Emily, and bolted in the opposite direction. Emily avoided the crashing table and followed Craven while Paul and the other agent moved quickly, funneling the Judge toward the front entrance. Ricocheting off a round table like a pinball, Craven sped more hastily toward the exit with the agents pursuing him.

Pressing past the entry desk, Craven pushed through the twin glass doors and onto the sidewalk. His momentum stopped instantly. Craven stared down five black assault rifles aimed directly at his head. He swiveled back toward the door where Paul and Emily stood, cutting off his return into the club.

John Craven slowly dropped to one knee and then the other. He intertwined his hands behind his head and closed his eyes.

As another agent took Craven into custody, Emily gazed at Paul and breathed a deep sigh of relief. Paul nodded as their eyes met, smiling with satisfaction.

THIRTY-FOUR

T HE AUTUMN EVENING WAS COOL. Underneath the illumination of the nightclub's entrance, Paul stood in the background, watching as members of the assault team loaded Judge Craven into the backseat of a waiting cruiser. Behind the perimeter established by the assault team, onlookers gaped as they observed the excitement. Nearby, Emily spoke with Agent Thrasher and the stylishly dressed agent from inside the club.

Watching Emily from a distance, Paul couldn't help but smile at the relief radiating from her countenance. Paul was quite content to stand back and privately admire her.

Glancing around the scene as she spoke, Emily noticed Paul's stare. He turned away awkwardly, but after a brief hiatus returned to his gazing. He couldn't help himself. Emily caught his eye and smiled alluringly. Embarrassed that he was caught gawking, Paul raised one hand and acknowledged Emily with a childish wave.

Excusing herself from her peers, Emily walked toward Paul. During the course of the investigation, she had been tested physically, emotionally, and spiritually. At times, the darkness had seemed to drag her down with self-doubt, pity, and fear, but she had escaped. Stepping from the shadows of the street scene, Emily walked beneath the light of the club's canopied entrance. She quietly stood beside Paul and then lifted her arm to place it around his waist but stopped. Her hand fell back to her side. Emily wanted to hold him, but she couldn't. Paul had been clear, and she had not yet made her decision.

Looking away awkwardly, Paul's heart fluttered, just knowing Emily was near. He had made it clear that he was unwilling to invest in a romantic relationship if Emily was reluctant to commit, but even though he meant it, he wished he could take back those words.

Unclasping his hands behind his back, Paul raised his arm behind Emily, but then hesitated. Then, even though he knew he shouldn't, Paul rested his arm over her shoulder as they watched the activity in front of the nightclub wind down. Neither one said a word.

* * * * *

Returning to his apartment after church, Paul opened the door. The aroma of roasted potatoes, carrots, and beef roast hovered in the air. Paul breathed deeply, as did Emily, who followed in closely behind. Entering last, Jimmy clapped his hands together and let out a whoop of satisfaction.

"That, my friends, is what I'm talking about," Jimmy said, closing his eyes and inhaling. Jimmy entered the kitchen and opened the oven. Pulling a fork from the drawer, he poked the potatoes and carrots and peeled away a sliver of meat. "The food is ready whenever you are."

"You guys go change out of your church clothes, and I'll set the table," Emily offered. She opened the cupboard and pulled down dishes while Paul and Jimmy retreated to their rooms.

Jimmy returned quickly wearing a T-shirt and flannel pajama bottoms. Paul was a little slower but emerged wearing a traditional outfit—jeans and a collared golf shirt. He looked at Jimmy's sloppy attire and scoffed.

"I call this my 'giving up on life' outfit," Jimmy said, responding to Paul's playful ridicule. Jimmy noticed Emily's head snap around. "Don't worry, Emily. Now I only 'give up on life' when it's time to relax. Paul, remember my 'give up on life' outfit from a couple of weeks ago?"

"I remember I made you trash it your first night here. What was it? Bermuda shorts and a T-shirt with dogs playing pool?" Paul asked with a grin.

"Wrong. The correct answer is—dogs playing cards. It was the nicest outfit I had." Jimmy looked at Emily, who was enjoying the banter. "I gave up on life once, but those days are over."

Jimmy pulled the roast from the oven, set the pan on the stove, and transferred the contents to a medium-sized platter. "You guys ready to eat?"

The three friends sat at the table with the food at the center. They folded their arms and bowed their heads as Jimmy blessed the food. As soon as the "amen" was said, both Paul and Jimmy reached for the utensil to serve up their food. Jimmy won the skirmish but noticed Emily looking on.

He handed the oversized meat fork to Emily. "Ladies first," he said.

"Nice save, Jimmy," she responded.

Paul chuckled. "So, Jimmy, you want to tell Emily the good news?"

"I'd characterize it more as 'adequate' news myself, but sure. Drum roll please," Jimmy said with expectation. Neither Paul nor Emily moved. "Very disappointing, guys. I've got to be honest."

"Just tell her," Paul prodded.

"Okay, Emily, the big news is that Paul and I are going to officially be roommates. He asked me this morning before church, and I said yes."

Emily looked at Paul with surprise. "That must have been a very special moment for the two of you." Emily laughed. "What brought this on?"

"I don't know," Jimmy responded. "Paul?"

Paul placed a morsel of potato in his mouth and chewed slowly while he thought. Jimmy continued to shovel in his food, but Emily waited patiently for Paul's response.

Paul looked at Emily nervously. "Well, you know, I want him to stay. Despite a couple of minor disagreements, I'm kind of used to him being around, and since he doesn't really have anywhere else to go, I just thought it made sense."

"And now that I have a job, I can help out with rent. Oh, and we're definitely upgrading the TV package," Jimmy said between bites.

"That's really great. I'm so glad you'll be around. You mean a lot to me, and it looks like you mean a lot to Paul as well," she said, looking squarely at Paul.

Paul lowered his head and crammed a bite of food into his mouth, successfully avoiding eye contact. Even though it was the truth, hearing the words out loud felt weird.

Jimmy reveled in Paul's discomfort. "So, Emily, where have you been all week? I haven't seen you since breakfast Tuesday morning."

"Well, after everything that happened the last week and a half, I needed some time to decompress. After work, I've gone home and watched a little TV, read, the usual stuff. Actually, Jimmy, you've kind of inspired me."

"I inspired you to watch more TV?"

Emily laughed. "No. Frankly the change in you over the past couple of weeks is breathtaking. Even though you struggled at first and you had no idea what you wanted out of life, it looks like you figured it out. You realized there was more than just wandering aimlessly and that life could be, and should be, better. You realized what you really wanted and you went after it. You're going back to church, meeting with the bishop, reading your scriptures, and saying your prayers."

"I am rather impressive, aren't I?" Jimmy crowed.

Emily rolled her eyes. "You're certainly not perfect."

"Hey!"

"But you have your moments. Not only did you help save my life, you also have a new job and a new roommate. I'm impressed," Emily said.

As usual Jimmy basked in the adulation. "It has been my pleasure to impress and inspire you," he said with great charm, but then became more serious. "Really, Emily, that's nice, but how did that inspire you?"

"Well, it helped me realize that there are some things I want to change about me. Since I had some time, I decided to inventory my life—you know, my failures and successes, my goals, and even my relationship with you and Paul. I spent the week trying to figure out if I was the kind of woman God wanted me to be. It's basically the same thing you've been doing, Jimmy. I didn't mean to be anti-social, but even though it's only been a few days, I can see more clearly. I know what I want and I know what I expect from myself," Emily said.

Paul stared across the table at Emily. He hadn't taken a bite since she started talking. She was so beautiful, kind, and courageous. Like Emily, he knew what he wanted, but it was out of his reach.

As the conversation lulled, Paul returned to his food. "Jimmy, this is an excellent lunch. The food is delicious, and it just feels like home."

"It's my pleasure," Jimmy said graciously. "Next week—same time, same place."

"Sounds good, but we need Jell-O. You know, with fruit in it," Paul suggested.

"Next week we'll have Jell-O. I promise," Jimmy said.

As Emily finished her food, she leaned back and looked across the room toward the window, squinting at the sunlight. She turned and smiled at her friends. "Jimmy, you want to go for a walk?"

Jimmy glanced at Paul, who showed no reaction. "Sure, let's go."

"Would you like to change your pants first?" Emily asked.

"Not really. Why?"

"Never mind. Paul, we'll be back in a little while," Emily said. She and Jimmy locked arms and walked toward the door.

Paul's heart sank as his eyes followed them out of the apartment. He sighed. "I'll be here," he said, but no one was around to hear him.

* * * * *

Paul paced between the kitchen and the living room before finally lumping on the sofa. For a moment he stared at the blank TV screen but then picked up the remote and aimlessly switched channels. He watched the Chiefs game briefly but then turned it off. The team wasn't any good, as usual, but he didn't really care. Looking at his watch again, he wondered where Emily and Jimmy could be. His head shook listlessly. There was no one to blame but himself.

"Paul," a soft voice called from the doorway.

Turning to face her, Paul's eyes widened as Emily walked toward him and stood beside the coffee table with her hand outstretched. Preparing for rejection, Paul softly touched her palm with his fingers before he stood.

"Welcome back," Paul said. "Did you have a good walk?"

"We did. Very good."

"Where's Jimmy?"

"Oh, he's still walking around. I think he wanted to give us a little time alone."

"Okay."

"I told him about our conversation earlier this week, when you told me how you feel about me. I told him it wasn't fair how I was stringing you both along. I knew I liked both of you, but I didn't want to make a choice. After our talk, I knew I had to decide."

Emily released Paul's soft grasp and reached toward his face. Her touch glanced across his freckled cheek and above his ear where she held his thick hair in her fingers.

Confusion, excitement, uncertainty, and hope consumed Paul, and he looked into Emily's eyes. "What else did you tell him?"

"I told him he's a good friend, that I respect him, and that he has a lot going for him. I told him I'm proud of the changes he's making in his life, but ultimately I had to decide who was best for me."

"How did you decide that?" Paul asked.

"I figured out what I needed. I had to base my decision on the men you are now, not on what I hope you will become. The rest came easy."

With one hand on Paul's neck, Emily reached with the other and found a spot between his shoulder blades. She pulled him close, watching him and wondering if he would deny her the kiss she longed for. Emily didn't have to wonder long.

Brushing away a strand of hair that hung low across Emily's eyes, Paul slowly leaned in, kissing her forehead and then her cheek. His nose nuzzled next to hers as their lips grazed. Paul pressed his lips onto hers and lingered in the soft warmth of her touch.

Although only a few seconds long, the tenderness of the kiss sent chills scurrying up Emily's neck to the crown of her head. Smiling, she kissed him on the cheek and then buried her face against his neck.

Paul held tight. He didn't want to let the moment go. "So, you made a decision?" Paul asked, his eyes gleaming.

"Like you said," Emily replied, "friends don't kiss."

Paul's silly grin stretched from ear to ear. He tried to hold back his enthusiasm, to play it cool, but he couldn't, and Emily didn't mind. Grabbing Emily by the shoulders, Paul pulled her forcefully to him and locked his lips on hers.

After a few moments, Paul opened his eyes, hoping to see Emily's reaction. She was staring straight at him, her lips barely functioning, because she was too busy smiling. Paul reciprocated.

"You have no idea how long I've been waiting to do that," Paul said.

"Really? Probably about as long I've been waiting for you to do it," Emily replied with raised eyebrows.

The first thing that popped into Paul's mind was, *Thank you*. It really was a great kiss, but the words didn't seem quite right. *I love you*, invaded his thoughts next, but although it was true, he was afraid saying it was too soon. Paul didn't know what to say, so he remained silent, holding Emily in a tight embrace.

Motioning toward the sofa, Paul held Emily's hand as they sat. He tussled his hair and let out a sigh, as though he had just avoided a major catastrophe. Then, he remembered his friend walking alone on the city streets. "How did Jimmy take it?" Paul wondered, thinking of Jimmy's certain disappointment.

"Jimmy understood. He told me that if he was going to lose the girl, he wanted to lose to you. He said it wouldn't change anything between the two of you," Emily said.

"It won't."

"I know," Emily said, her fingers interlocking with Paul's. "You know, we never really celebrated after arresting Judge Craven the other night."

"No, but can we really celebrate?" Paul asked. "We never did catch Nicas. He's still out there, somewhere."

"We may never find him. At least not before the syndicate does. But we did well," Emily said. "I think we deserve to celebrate."

"You're so right," Paul said. He stood and placed his arm over Emily's shoulder. "Celebratory dessert sounds perfect. Let's go find Jimmy."

DISCUSSION QUESTIONS

1. Emily was required to choose between upholding her personal moral standards and performing her undercover assignment as directed. Is it ever right to temporarily set aside your personal standards to complete a job?

2. After his family tragedy, Jimmy lost his way. Are we all just a tragedy away from losing our faith? What can we do to protect our faith from the traumas of life?

3. Paul decided to help Jimmy, partly as a way to avoid feeling guilty. How can we know if we are doing the right thing for the right reason?

4. Jimmy gave up on the possibility of his family being united forever. Is it possible to have too much hope, even when family members may stray?

5. Is there ever a "point of no return" in our lives when we have no chance for redemption?

6. Jimmy pushed the limits of his contract with Paul. Is it ever appropriate to cut a friend or family member off from continued aid?

7. Was Emily unfaithful to Paul when she kissed Jimmy, even though Paul and Emily were not officially a couple?

8. Emily did not mention Agent Stark's harassing behavior to her superiors. How should you deal with workplace harassment?

9. Was Paul justified in breaking FBI rules as he sought to protect Emily? Is "breaking the rules" different than temporarily "setting aside your standards"?

10. What role should prayer play in our personal relationships and employment?

ABOUT THE AUTHOR

Steve Westover was born in California and has also lived in Ohio, Utah, and Idaho, but most of his life, he grew up in Salem, Oregon. He is a graduate of BYU and served an LDS Mission in Independence, Missouri. After school he moved back to rural Missouri where he lives with his wife and four kids on a small hobby farm with chickens, two calves, cats, and a dog. Professionally, he works in retail banking. *Defensive Tactics* is his first attempt at writing, but he has also recently finished the first book of a youth fantasy adventure set at Crater Lake in the Oregon mountains. To learn more about Steve, read his blog, westoversleftovers.blogspot.com, or visit his website, www.stevewestover.com.